SHUTTERBUG

LAURENCE GOUGH

An M&S Paperback from
McClelland & Stewart Inc.
The Canadian Publishers

An M&S Paperback from McClelland & Stewart Inc.

Canadian Cataloguing in Publication Data

Gough, Laurence
    Shutterbug

An M&S paperback.
ISBN 0-7710-3429-6

I. Title.

PS8563.08393S58 1999   C813'.54   C99-931106-9
PR9199.3.G68S58 1999

We acknowledge the financial support of the Government of Canada
through the Book Publishing Industry Development Program for our
publishing activities. Canadä

We further acknowledge the support of the Canada Council for the
Arts and the Ontario Arts Council for our publishing program.

Cover photograph: Renzo Cattoni
Typeset in Minion by M&S, Toronto
Printed and bound in Canada

McClelland & Stewart Inc.
The Canadian Publishers
481 University Avenue
Toronto, Ontario
M5G 2E9

1 2 3 4 5   03 02 01 00 99

Author's Note

Sad but true, the delicious On-On restaurant no longer exists. I should mention that the On-On was never owned by a drug dealer named Sammy Wu. Mr. Wu is a figment of my imagination.

Shutterbug is a more or less light-hearted work of fiction, neatly categorized by Graham Greene as an "entertainment."

Light demands shadow.

On July 15, 1997, more than one thousand simple, white-painted wooden crosses were sunk into the hard-packed turf of Oppenheimer Park. The park is located in Vancouver's downtown eastside, only a few blocks from the Public Safety Building at 312 Main. Each cross symbolized the death of a Vancouver heroin addict who had accidentally overdosed during the past four years.

Four years. One thousand dead.

At the moment, there are about one thousand addicts packed into the city's downtown eastside. Amazingly, this number remains constant despite the high fatality rate. One in four is HIV positive. During the past six months, more than *two hundred* have died.

But the drug problem isn't restricted to the downtown eastside. There are addicts all across the city, in every neighbourhood.

Is it time to legalize heroin? In 1994, B.C.'s Chief Coroner recommended that the Province provide a heroin maintenance program as part of a harm-reduction policy.

So far, nothing has been done.

1

By the time he graduated from diapers, Wayne was known all over the block for his exceptionally high standards.

Of cleanliness, friendship, and beauty.

Especially beauty.

Understand, we're talking about Wayne Sharpe.

Aka "Wayne the Brain" aka "The Main Wayne" aka "Main-Frame Wayne" aka "Plain Wayne" aka "The Same Wayne" aka "Larry Loam" aka "Larry The Loam Shark," etcetera.

A long time ago, and this is the stuff of legends, Wayne fell hard for a woman named Laura Lederer. Laura was an expatriate Swiss. Like most women who are unfortunate enough to spend their formative years in the cold and barren mountains of rural Switzerland, Laura was sexually naive, and sexually repressed. She might have stayed that way forever, if she hadn't emigrated to hot-blooded Canada.

She'd just started making up for lost ground when she happened to meet Wayne.

Laura was a beaut. More often than not, strangers mistook her for a gorgeous film star named Nicole Kidman. Laura was blessed with Nicole's wonderfully long legs, her taut, perfectly proportioned body, lovely face, glossy mane of chestnut hair, mischievous, sexy, sparkling green eyes, perfect nose, teeth, mouth and ears. Laura and Nicole were virtually clones; Laura was able to match the film star *perfect* for *perfect*, from her shapely head all the way down to her irresistibly cute 'n' cuddly little toes!

In fact, Laura so closely resembled Nicole Kidman that people who'd met Laura, and subsequently got to know Nicole, often asked the film star if she was really Laura Lederer, from Switzerland.

Wayne met Laura at a Vancouver cocktail lounge that is not much short of internationally famous for its tasty martinis and stunningly tall waitresses. Laura happened to be exalting one end of the bar, while Wayne was holding down the other. This was during the brief period in his life when Wayne was always accompanied by hired muscle.

This one's name was Arturo.

Wayne was telling muscular Arturo a hilarious joke about a near-sighted ostrich, but Arturo, unwisely, wasn't paying strict attention. Worse, he kept climbing up on his pointy black toes so he could see over Wayne's brawny shoulder. Arturo was gaping. But what was he looking at? Wayne got out his dentist's mirror and took a quick peek.

His dark, smouldering eyes touched down on Laura with all the subtlety of a doomed, completely out-of-control Boeing 747 plummeting vertically into the Pacific Ocean.

What a babe. Wayne fell in lust. Love at first sight. Passionately swelling violins, and body parts, galore. Hell, he'd kill for her, even if it wasn't necessary.

Putting it crudely, he had to have her.

Which he did, about an hour later, and again not long after that, and first thing the next morning, right after breakfast.

What a lovely couple they made! Pretty soon, the whole darn town was talking about them. It was considered a treat and a privilege just to catch a glimpse of that star-crossed couple dancing by, as they waltzed from posh nightclub to seedy lounge to five-star luxury hotel to rundown Kingsway hot-sheet motel to . . . well, wherever they happened to be going next.

The romance might have lasted forever, but about a month after it got rolling, Laura made a terrible mistake.

She smiled.

Due to circumstances entirely beyond her control, when Laura smiled, she flashed her upper gums in their entirety. Not that her gums weren't just as pink and healthy as the rest of her. They were, they were! But when she smiled she looked . . .

Kind of like a hysterical burro.

Just like that, Wayne dumped her.

Laura wasn't thrilled. She had never been dumped before. Like most novel experiences, it was unwelcome. Because she had no life skills in the area of being dumped, Laura committed a grievous tactical error.

She made a fuss.

Standing there in the Meridien hotel's posh lobby, she cranked it up to full volume, took full advantage of the acoustics afforded by all that marble and brass.

Laura loudly told Wayne he was a cold-hearted sonofabitch, a miserable little prick. If he thought he could drop her like a hot potato, he had another think coming. Heads turned all the way to the far distant, most intimate, recesses of the hotel bar. Staff began to gather. Passers-by loitered on the busy sidewalks.

A quick-thinking receptionist made an emergency phone call to a bulky, steroid-enhanced member of the staff, whose services were rarely required, except in the wee small hours of dawn.

Laura told Wayne that he better reconsider the situation, unless he had a secret desire to spend the rest of his miserable life in a maximum-security institution full of miserable pricks just like him!

That was more than enough for Arturo. He stepped between Laura and his boss, positioning himself so neither of the two combatants could see the other. Arturo cut quite an imposing figure. His unnaturally widely-spaced eyes, which were the colour of virgin olive oil, were so lifeless they might have been transplanted from a corpse. His russet polyester suit shone like a puddle of oil lit up by a spectacular sunset. His teeth gleamed like antique ivory. His slick-backed smile matched his slicked-back hair, and he had so liberally slapped on his cologne that he smelled like ten thousand acres of roses in full bloom.

Flopping a manicured hand on Laura's shoulder, Arturo lubricated his sausage lips with his furry, lolling tongue. By now Laura knew the signs. The Spanish Slug was about to lecture her.

She power-lifted her knee into his groin. It was as if he'd been assaulted by a forklift. Squeaking shrilly, he hit the marble floor, bounced once, and was still, except for his madly fluttering eyelashes.

Wayne realized he'd made a mistake. He hauled Arturo to his feet, brushed him off, and instructed him to empty his fat wallet into the eager hands of the assembled staff. Dozens of crisp new hundred-dollar bills vanished like grains of sand into the Mohave Desert. Wayne contritely apologized for any inconvenience his lover's spat may have caused. He voluntarily promised to never again darken the Meridien's shiny glass doors. Then he enfolded Laura in his enormous hairy arms, and got her the hell out of there.

Wayne had a weakness for feisty women.

But not that feisty.

About a week later, the first sunny day in August, he and Arturo and Laura drove out of town, for a picnic.

The unhappy trio ate on a sun-drenched, grassy slope just a hill and a dale from the site of a new mall.

They drank ice-cold champagne imported all the way from France, and dined like royalty on delicious take-out grub from Meinhardt Fine Foods Inc., on Granville. As they ate, Arturo squatted evilly in the unbalanced shade of a lightning-crippled beech tree, playing solitaire and drinking lukewarm Perrier. Wayne had borrowed Arturo's portable Sony CD player, so he could spin a little mood music, play a few tunes from a romantic disc called *Lovely Lovin'* that he'd bought by mail from a late-night TV 1-800 number. The music came faintly to Arturo and made him want to bend over and puke.

Wayne, too, believed the music was truly awful. The only reason he put up with all that racket was because, talk about sheer coincidence, the first pouring of the mall's concrete foundation was scheduled for that very day. Large-scale construction was a noisy business. Some of those union guys had mouths as foul as the back end of a diarrhetic elephant. No point in upsetting Laura. Much better to provide a little something in the way of background harmonics, to drown out all the noise. Those big tandem-barrel cement trucks, for example, made a hell of an unpleasant racket.

So, as it turned out, did Arturo's pistol, when the food and drink and poor Laura's time had finally run out. Not that there was anything wrong with the Glock. The problem was with the knuckleheaded hitman; he'd forgotten to pack his silencer.

What the Spanish Slug liked to call his *silencio de pistola*, when he was trying to impress the ladies.

2

VPD Homicide Detective Jack Matisse Willows stood close by the luminous green glass wall of the courthouse, in the scant shelter of the overhanging glass roof. His lawyer, Peter Singer, morose, bald and bearded, suffering from a recurring pelvic infection, offered a hand that was no less cold and limp than the rest of him.

"Congratulations, Jack."

Willows nodded. He could find no words that were even remotely appropriate. A courtroom appearance had been forced on him because he'd let his ex-wife, Sheila, off the child-maintenance hook. The judge had, naturally enough, wanted to be sure that the two children were going to be well taken care of. The handshake dispensed with, Singer quickly put his glove back on. He shifted his grip on a stack of file folders, thick as a telephone book, that he seemed to carry everywhere and perhaps accounted for the slight hunch in his narrow back. Retreating down the broad concrete steps, the lawyer wished his client the very best of luck, and warned him to expect a final accounting in the next few days.

Willows and Sheila had been legally separated for the better part of two years, and now, suddenly, they were divorced. Split asunder by the mighty sword of law. His chains had been snapped. He was a free man. Free as a bird. Free at last to marry his boon

6

live-in companion, gorgeous homicide detective Claire Parker. Free to marry, or suffer her wrath.

He was gleeful as a broken-stringed kite. But at the same time, he was as desperately sour and glum as man could be. He'd loved Sheila for a great many years. It wasn't so long ago that he had believed they would be together for all the rest of his days. Then Sheila had told him, in great detail, how discontent she was, and why. She'd threatened to leave him, and kept her word.

Poor Jack. But he had recovered, in time. Parker had been his partner, his cop partner, for eleven years. A damn long time. She'd been thrust upon him when his previous partner, Norm Burroughs, had died of cancer. God, but he'd resented Parker. Resented her youth and beauty, her boundless good health.

He wondered when he'd fallen in love with her. Was it before Sheila had left him, or a long time afterwards? He wished he knew, but suspected he never would. He had no memory of realizing how beautiful she was, though he certainly thought her beautiful now, and couldn't remember when he hadn't.

In Jack Matisse Willows' humble opinion, love was endlessly perplexing. It could hit you like a ten-pound sledgehammer to the heart, or bind you up in a million gossamer threads of silk. Either way, you were stricken to the point of being immobilized. And you were grateful as hell, to be so lucky.

But in the end, he supposed, love was that wonderful, wonderful thing that just might happen to you if you were willing to let it happen. You had to be ready, willing, and able.

Not everybody met those criteria.

In the line of duty, he had bumped up against plenty of guys, and women too, who were ready, willing, and completely unable to fall in love. Something was missing. He wasn't sure what it was. An important cog, something crucial to their basic humanity, that prevented them from developing lasting relationships, caring deeply for someone, falling in love. Willows didn't understand them; he only knew they existed.

He stood there on the courthouse steps, in the shelter of the glass roof, inches away from the steadily falling rain. He wore a charcoal suit, a white shirt with button-down collar, a dark blue tie, black brogues and a black trenchcoat. He wore no hat. He carried no umbrella. A gust of wind flapped the trenchcoat's lapels, and worried his tie, and lifted up a lock of his hair and laid it neatly down again. Rain ricochetting off the concrete beaded his shoes, and dampened the cuffs of his pants.

Jack Matisse Willows was cold, and tired. His face was pale, his eyes dark and shadowed. He'd cut himself shaving that morning. Well, he'd been nervous. A crooked line of dried blood lay along the underside of his jaw, and lent him a faintly disreputable look.

When he'd strode into the courthouse, not half an hour ago, he had been full of manly resolve. Now he was exhausted. All he wanted to do was go home and crawl into bed and pull the covers over his head and shut his eyes and sleep right through the weekend.

He wanted a drink. A double Cutty, on the rocks. He desperately wanted, though he hadn't smoked since his undercover years, more than twenty years ago, an unfiltered Export "A" cigarette.

He hadn't heard the first few bars of the national anthem blaring from the speakers atop the old B.C. Hydro building, but the high-noon notes must have sounded nevertheless, because suddenly the streets were crammed with a flood of humanity. A quartet of lawyers in black robes flew in tight formation down the courthouse steps. The lawyers might have been ravens; they were too large to be crows. Willows watched the self-serve restaurant across the street fill up with hungry people. The place was empty one moment, full to capacity the next. Two middle-aged women sitting at a window table stripped away the stretch 'n' cling wrap from their salads, and tucked in busily, with white plastic forks.

A man who closely resembled a two-thirds-scale Woody Allen saw Willows, waved, and called out to him in a friendly manner.

"Hey, Jack!"

The man trotted up the steps, smiling broadly. Willows turned to face him more squarely. His hands hung loosely at his sides.

The man slowed as he drew near. His smile faltered. "Jack, you don't remember me?"

Willows stood quietly.

"Christ, I don't believe it. Bryan Galt. Aggravated manslaughter, five years ago the middle of next month."

Willows said, "Got something for me, Bryan?"

"Like what?"

"You and Teddy Hayes used to pal around, didn't you?"

"Yeah, that's right."

"I hear Teddy was the genius behind that Chinatown jewellery-store robbery last week."

The last faint vestiges of great good humour fled Bryan Galt's sallow face. "Don't know what you're talking about."

"Three wounded, one fatally."

"Doesn't ring a bell, Jack."

"You're sure about that?"

Bryan Galt bent his head to light a cigarette. A filtertip Marlboro. He inhaled deeply, exhaled with a rush. Willows caught a whiff. There was something wrong about a miniature Woody Allen snorkelling away on a cigarette. In high school, there was a kid who used to sell cigarettes for a dime each, and make a good profit. George. The entrepreneur's name was George. Willow frowned, squeezing his brain. George Hetger. No, Hertger. George Hertger.

Bryan Galt flipped his yellow disposable lighter into the air and caught it, but just barely. He put the lighter away in the pocket of his suede windbreaker. Willows wondered if Galt deliberately dressed like Woody Allen. No, that was crazy. He wondered what he'd find if he reached out and frisked Galt. What was under that puffy jacket? A 9mm semiauto? A roll of fat?

Bryan Galt said, "I haven't seen Teddy in years."

"Too bad. Got the time, Bryan?"

Galt unthinkingly shot the cuff of his jacket. The gold Rolex on his wrist seemed to surprise him. Recovering, he said, "It's ten past twelve."

Willows smiled down at him.

The watch vanished. Galt turned and ran, with Willows in hot pursuit.

Galt was quicker than he looked. Quicker by far, Willows judged, than Woody could ever hope to be.

Panicked, Galt bolted blindly down the courthouse steps and across the crowded sidewalk. He hit a parking meter hard enough to bend the steel post, and spun away at an unlikely angle. Willows snatched at him and missed. Galt ran full tilt through and over the dense one-way crawl of traffic on Thurlow. He was still accelerating when he reached the sidewalk on the far side of the street, and was unlucky enough to reach his maximum speed in the same instant he crashed headlong into the self-serve restaurant's plate-glass window.

The window turned white, and then collapsed, like the last gasp of a dying waterfall. Galt had vanished. Tables were overturned, and chairs, and the people that had been sitting in them. Everybody in the restaurant had been served a three-course meal of dazed and bewildered, but nobody seemed seriously hurt. Willows pushed against the outgoing flow of the mob to get in through the door. He followed a blood trail across the soup-'n'-salad-strewn floor, past the open cash register and an open-mouthed clerk, frozen in the moment of offering change to a customer who was busily picking steamy-hot lasagna off his suit. The spoor led him over a stainless-steel counter and down a narrow hallway, where it disappeared beneath the door to the ladies' washroom.

Willows glanced behind him, down the hallway. There was a lot of yelling and screaming going on back there. No uniforms, but there were always cops hanging around the courthouse, waiting to testify in various criminal trials.

He clipped his badge to his trenchcoat lapel, and hit the door with his fist. "Bryan, it's Jack. Come on out of there, Bryan!"

He might have heard a muffled reply, but he wasn't sure, because of all the wailing and howling from the restaurant. Not to mention the sirens racing towards him from at least two directions.

He was in no hurry to kick in the door, not in his lightweight courtroom brogues, not when his Glock was locked away in the gun safe in the trunk of his car.

He got set, turned the knob. The door wasn't locked. He pushed it open, and risked a quick look inside.

There was only one cubicle. Bryan Galt sat on the toilet, tending to his wounds. His hair was sprinkled with fragments of glass. His face and left leg were swathed in layer upon layer of red-tinted toilet paper.

Willows said, "You're under arrest, Bryan."

"For what?"

"Break and enter?"

"Very goddamn funny."

Galt snuck a hand under the shredded remains of his suede jacket, and Willows tensed, but all Galt wanted was a cigarette. His hands were shaking, and he was a little careless with the lighter. Several small fires broke out in the toilet paper on his face, but died of their own accord, as Willows lurched forward to slap them silly.

Galt unclasped the Rolex. "How about you keep the watch, and I stroll outta here?"

"Forget it."

Galt spread his legs and dropped the Rolex into the toilet bowl. "Okay, how about I pull the chain on this solid gold baby, and tell you to get stuffed, 'cause suddenly you ain't got any evidence?"

Willows smiled.

Galt reached down between his legs, fished around for a moment and came up with the watch. His sleeve was wet to his elbow. He gave the Rolex a brisk shake. "Okay tough guy, let's try this one on for size. How about I roll over on Teddy, and you sweet-talk those dinks down at the prosecutor's office into making allowances for my weak and avaricious nature?"

Willows heard boots pounding down the hallway. Uniformed cops, a brace of paramedics.

"Sounds like an idea to me," said Willows. He borrowed a pair of latex gloves from the paramedics, handcuffs from one of the cops. He cuffed Galt, patted him down, and was rewarded with a 9mm Baby Desert Eagle he found tucked in the waistband of Galt's baggy, rust-coloured corduroy pants. Galt burst into tears. He swore up and down that he hadn't used the pistol in the Chinatown robbery, that he'd never shot anybody in his life. He said the only reason he was carrying the gun was because he feared for his life.

"Somebody out to get you?" said the taller of the paramedics.

Galt held out his cuffed hands. "What's it look like to you, moron?"

The paramedic smiled grimly. He said, "We're going to take the long way around to St. Paul's. You're probably going to bleed to death before we get there, but don't worry about it, because nobody's going to miss an obnoxious little twerp like you, Woody."

3

Lewis wore a black double-breasted Hugo Boss suit over a crisp white linen shirt, maroon silk tie by Leone, no overcoat. He carried a black umbrella with a hardwood handle and matching tip, capped in solid brass that had been filed to a sharp point. A shopping bag from an exclusive Robson Street boutique dangled nonchalantly from his left hand.

He'd bought the suit second-hand at a consignment store on Fourth Avenue, and it hung a little too loosely on him, but to the casual observer Lewis looked like a prosperous young executive making the very best of his hectic lunchtime schedule.

The shopping bag contained a used shirt bought for a dollar from the Salvation Army, and a red Gortex jacket Lewis had lifted from a Chinatown coatrack.

Lewis's umbrella was, like Lewis himself, extremely snugly wrapped. He intended to use the umbrella as a rapier, if he found himself in a tight corner.

Full of that special sub-species of arrogance that only youth and money can buy, Lewis angled sharply across the harried, compact flow of Granville Street pedestrians, pushed open Birks Jewellers' heavy glass door and went inside.

A lovely young woman smiled demurely at Lewis from behind her sparkling glass counter.

Lewis blessed her with a terse nod, and continued on his way to the watch department. He explained to an equally lovely and faultlessly attentive female salesperson, a honey-toned blonde in a black sheath dress, that he was in the market for a birthday present for his fiancée.

He said he was prepared to spend between five and six thousand dollars.

The blonde asked him if he had a particular brand in mind.

Lewis said no. What he wanted was . . . He fished around in his mind for a suitable catchphrase, and came up empty.

The salesperson mentioned in a casual sort of way that her name was Amanda. She suggested he do a little browsing. If something in the display cases caught his eye, she'd be happy to give him a closer look.

Fine, said Lewis, and snuck a quick peek at the ripoff TAGHuer he'd bought off the hirsute wrist of a Yonge Street sidewalk vendor, shortly before fleeing Toronto. The watch was authentic in every detail, except that neither of the stubby buttons on either side of the bezel actually did anything; you could push them all day long, and all they'd do was wear out. Aside from these minor imperfections, the watch was a flawless masterpiece.

The time was seventeen minutes past twelve. Lewis relaxed a notch or two; he still had plenty of time before the lunch-hour crowds trotted back into their skyscraper cubicles, to toil and digest.

Amanda gave him a few minutes and then drifted in for the kill. Was he thinking gold, or silver? Clasp-type metal strap, or leather?

Lewis was thinking gold, or at least gold highlight. He thought his fiancée would prefer a metal strap. But he wasn't interested in any of that bulky, twelve-button aviator-style product. Sue was a fine-boned girl, delicate as, uh . . .

Bone china? suggested Amanda, with a sly little smile. Was she flirting with him? Lewis decided yes.

She suggested a Rolex Lady Datejust in stainless steel with gold trim. The Datejust was a classic, and came in men's and ladies' models that were identical except for size. The men's being larger. Amanda coyly suggested that, when Lewis's birthday came up, it might be a nice thing if his fiancée bought *him* a Rolex.

Lewis smiled, and said he thought that was an absolutely fine idea.

A squiggly little cord, also in basic black, encircled Amanda's pale, blue-veined wrist. Dangling from the end of the cord was a small brass key. She used the key to unlock the shatterproof Lexan display case, slid aside the Lexan door and delicately plucked a Datejust from its bed of lint-free black velvet.

Amanda placed a smaller black-velvet display pad on the counter. With a quaint little flourish, she placed the watch on the velvet. Lewis stared down at it. The Rolex's crystal had a built-in magnifying bubble that allowed the owner to easily read the month and date, should she so desire. The sweep second hand proceeded around the nifty little dial in a clockwise direction and in an orderly fashion.

What more could any sane person demand of a watch?

Well, for starters, how about a cheapo Timex with twin analog and digital readouts, accurate to 1/100th of a second; a night-light powerful enough to run a freight train; alarm functions for daily, monthly, and annual use; the capability to store five hundred messages of up to fifteen alphanumeric characters each; a chronograph with a fifty-lap capacity; five appointment alarms (ideal for busy terrorists); plus the ability to download information from any IBM computer, or clone. Not to mention water resistance to twenty thousand leagues and a three-year battery life; the whole package wrapped up in a virtually indestructible graphite case, for about eighty bucks, retail.

But the Rolex was nothing less than . . . a Rolex. It was made of precious metals, in Switzerland, by conscientious human beings. The Rolex had a certain *cachet*. It said, "Here I am. I've arrived, and I'm worth noticing!"

The Datejust was priced way over Lewis's maximum. But what the hell, it wasn't as if he intended to *purchase* the damn thing.

He tested Amanda with pertinent questions regarding accuracy of time, number of jewels, eighteen-carat screw-down bezels, warranties, band adjustments, depreciation, insurance against loss, and areas of flexibility regarding the holy bottom line.

Amanda patiently explained that Birks accepted trade-ins, but that this Rolex – Lewis admired the cultured way she rolled the word "Rolex" around on her tongue, as if it was a particularly succulent oyster – would be full price.

If Lewis cared to wait until the pre-Christmas sales of early December . . .

Four months, and it was already twenty-three minutes past twelve, if the Rolex was running straight and true, which meant he was down to his last thirty-seven minutes, max.

No, he did not care to wait until December. His fiancée's birthday was next Tuesday.

Finally, with a certain studied reluctance, Lewis picked up the watch and nestled it into the palm of his hand. The precious metals were cool to the touch, and glittered seductively under the lights. Lewis observed that the watch had a certain heft, a solid weight to it, that was somehow exactly right.

Amanda demurely concurred. She leaned across the counter. Her flaxen hair fell across her peaches 'n' cream face, and she brushed it back behind her ear with a practised gesture. Lewis felt compelled to admire the way her dress clung to her body. My, but she was cute.

She caught him looking, and didn't seem to mind. Probably she was on commission. He asked if he could borrow her battery-powered calculator, so he could run through the numbers one last time.

Amanda discreetly checked Lewis's math as his longish fingers tap-danced across the calculator's buttons. Her sharp eye took note of his ruby ring, the high quality of the gold setting and the cut and weight and fine colour of the stone. She noticed also his professionally manicured fingernails, fifty-dollar haircut, and the Hugo Boss suit, his slim but muscular body.

His eyes had certainly bugged out of his head when she'd leaned across the counter, showing him a little cleavage. She wondered, in an offhand, noncommittal sort of way, what he was like in bed and whether he was truly Rolex-serious about his girlfriend, or fiancée, or whatever he called her. *Fiancée.* Such an old-fashioned, deadly ardent word.

Lewis laid the watch reverently down on the rectangle of black velvet. He said, "I'll take it."

Amanda blessed his decision with her very nicest smile. She kept smiling as he slipped his eelskin billfold from the breast pocket of his suit. He flipped open the billfold, and winkled out a gold Royal Bank Visa card.

Amanda accepted the card. Their fingers touched, bumpety-bump, and she did a little thing with the corners of her mouth that somehow contrived to indicate barely controlled lust.

In the moment that Amanda accepted Lewis's credit card, a woman pushed into the store waving a five-dollar bill and loudly demanding change for the bus.

A sales associate at the counter nearest the door broke off his conversation with a customer to reluctantly but firmly inform the woman that, if she required change, she'd find a bank just down the street and around the corner.

The woman ignored him. She caught Amanda's eye, and honed in on her, waving her five-dollar bill like a battle flag.

"Can you help me, *please*? If I miss my bus, I'm going to be late for a job interview, and . . ."

Amanda tuned her out.

The flyaway, bleached-to-death hair, the purple eyeliner, enormous false eyelashes, clown rouge, black lipstick, cheap plastic raincoat and too-short tartan skirt, the bulky Doc Martens . . . It was all too much. Too, too much by far. This creature was not a Birks customer, and she never would be. Not in a zillion years.

Lewis picked up the Rolex, turned it so he could more easily read the time. He said, "Look, I have an appointment. Do you think we could speed things up a bit . . ."

The woman said, "Could I just *please* have some quarters!"

Amanda wanted her out of there. Christ, the stupid little bitch was going to queer the fucking sale! She smiled sweetly at Lewis, snatched the soggy five-dollar bill out of the woman's hand and unlocked and popped open the cash register.

It took her only a few seconds to count out five dollars' worth of change. By then, Lewis and the Rolex Datejust were gone. But for the stolen, and useless, credit card and stolen umbrella that he'd left behind, he might never have existed.

Amanda hit the alarm. The bitch's raincoat billowed like a spinnaker as she scurried towards the exit.

Lewis strolled casually out the door, made a sharp left, and bolted. He ran as fast as he could until he heard a shout behind him. Slowing to a brisk walk, he put on his bright red Gortex jacket, and pulled up the hood. He was pumped, floating along on a riptide of adrenalin, his heart crashing against his chest, his vision slightly blurred, a certain tightness in his joints. He bobbed and weaved through the lunchtime crowd, then joined a crowd of jaywalkers cutting across Granville. He walked briskly up Granville for about a quarter of a block and crossed the street again, cutting so close behind a passing bus that the turbulence ruffled his lightly gelled hair.

He ducked into the mall, hurried down a narrow corridor, through a doorway, and down two flights of grey-painted concrete steps to the mall's vast subterranean parking lot. He was sweating. Everybody was looking at him, or so it seemed. He was dying for a cigarette.

So, why not light up?

No time, no time.

The cops would be there by now. In numbers, because the 911 call had originated from Birks, and there were always lots of cops on Granville. Liz would be surrounded by them, all of them yelling at her, knowing she was part of the scam. But what could they prove? Nothing. Frustrated, they'd drag her down to 312 Main, plunk her ass on a hard wooden chair for a couple of hours, and then let her go . . .

Lewis had lost his Econoline. Where was his van? Parked exactly where he'd left it, by that big concrete post. He got out his cigarettes and lighter, lit up. The Rolex lay snug in his pants pocket, but where were his keys? He patted himself down, found the keys, and hurried around to the driver's side of the van, unlocked and opened the door.

"Excuse me?"

Lewis spun around. The woman standing close behind him looked a little like the Birks salesgirl, Amanda. But this was an Amanda five years down all the wrong roads.

The woman said, "I know who you are."

"Yeah?" She had a great body, though she was definitely a little hard around the eyes. She was approximately his age, midtwenties, which meant, from his point of view, that she was way too old for him. He couldn't place her, but that was no major surprise, given the amount of time he spent at the clubs, the sheer number of women he met. A sudden jolt of fear zigzagged through his pounding heart. Christ, she was a store detective! Or was she?

He said, "Do I know you from somewhere?"

She smiled, but fleetingly. "My name's April. I've been watching you, the past few weeks. You and a few other guys just like you, but not so handsome."

What was that supposed to mean?

She said, "I saw you take that portable computer. Tuesday, wasn't it? The guy was sitting on a bench, drinking an Orange Julius." She saw something twitch in Lewis's eye, and laughed. "There you go, now you remember, don't you?"

Lewis's hand curled into a fist. He drew back his arm. Not that he felt very good about punching a woman. But he knew with a terrible, gut-wrenching certainty that he'd feel a lot worse if he didn't.

April hit him in the face with a protracted burst of pepper spray from a family-size can. She spun him around, shoved him towards the Econoline's open door, kicked him in his cute little Hugo Boss ass and yelled at him to keep moving, don't *mess* with her. Lewis, gagging and choking, crying so hard the tears threatened to wash his face away, unwisely offered up a feeble resistance.

April zapped him with the Taser.

Very few people acquire a taste for raw electricity, and Lewis was no exception. Yelping and screeching, he scuttled over the bucket seat and into the back of the van. Now that she finally had her quarry where she wanted him, April no longer required that he be mobile, or even conscious.

She hit him with the Taser again. Lewis's pretty blue eyes bugged out of his head. His lightly gelled hair stood on end. His mouth gaped open. His arms shot out. His legs buckled, and he dropped like a shot duck.

April put her foot down on his cigarette, rolled him over on his stomach and secured his ankles and then his wrists with nylon tie-downs. She joined the two sets of nylon cuffs together with a third pair. Now the only way that Lewis could go anywhere, in the unlikely event he regained consciousness in the next half hour or so, was to throw himself out of the speeding van and bounce along the road on his knees and chin.

April hiked up her skirt and wriggled out of her pantyhose and black silk panties. She knelt beside Lewis, and kissed him fleetingly on the mouth. Then she stuffed her panties into his mouth, and tied them in place with the pantyhose.

What did he do with the van's key? She found it in the door-lock, climbed behind the wheel, slammed shut the door and locked it, shoved the key in the ignition and started the engine.

She had him! She'd done it!

April hadn't been this excited in her whole life.

At the exit, April discovered that Lewis hadn't left his parking ticket on the dashboard or tucked it away behind the sun visor. What an idiot. She smiled at the attendant, and told him she'd been in the lot for half an hour at the most.

He told her if she didn't have a ticket she'd have to pay the maximum daily rate.

April told him to hold on a minute. She shoved the gearshift into park, unbuckled her seatbelt and scrambled into the back of the van and patted Lewis down until she found his billfold.

He had seven different credit cards in seven different names, but only one driver's licence, in the name of Lewis John Tucker. He was so incredibly handsome that even his driver's licence snapshot looked pretty good, or at least presentable. He was carrying six five-dollar bills for a total of thirty dollars in cash. He'd folded the parking ticket in half and snugged it in next to the currency.

April handed the attendant ten dollars from Lewis's billfold, and received six dollars in change. At the very last moment, just as she was about to haul ass out of there, she remembered to ask for a receipt.

Her husband, Wayne, a freelance drug dealer who was bent on controlling wholesale heroin distribution in the entire city, was big on receipts. He was always looking for ways, large, small, and miniscule, to cut down on his income tax. Four bucks. He'd be so pleased with her. Maybe cut her a little extra slack with regard to her new acquisition.

Behind her, a horn blared.

April fastened her seatbelt. She stuck her arm out the window and gave the horn-blaring dork the finger.

Driving out of the parking lot, she was shaking so hard she could hardly hold onto the steering wheel. The van's offside panel grazed a concrete wall. Sheet metal crumpled. The headlight burst.

April said, "Oops! Sorry, Lewis!"

Lewis. What a nice name. So masculine, and strong. She repeated it like a mantra, all the way home.

Lewis Lewis

Etcetera, etcetera, etcetera.

4

VPD Homicide Detective Claire Parker, aka Bank of Montreal loan application #98-112574-A, was nervous. She was sitting in the loans officer's cramped office, waiting for Willows to show up. Willows was, inexplicably, late.

The loans officer, a woman named Mary Sanderson, bore an uncanny, oddly unsettling resemblance to Mary Tyler Moore. She'd left the office ten minutes ago, without explanation, and hadn't yet returned.

Parker was nervous. The only time she'd ever applied for a bank loan was when she'd traded in her ageing Volkswagen on a new Mazda. She'd been saving for a year, and had only needed to borrow five thousand dollars. Now she was about to try to convince a perfect stranger that she was a suitable candidate for a one-half share of a two-hundred-and-forty-six-thousand-dollar mortgage.

Two hundred and forty-six grand. Just short of a quarter of a million dollars. It wasn't an unimaginable amount. Six months ago, she'd watched a middle-echelon drug dealer named Leo Pope unzip a suitcase containing a million dollars in cash, a split-second before he was shot dead at point-blank range.

But of course the financial dealings of the drug world were peanuts compared to professional sports. Jack was a basketball fan. They went to several Grizzlies games every year, sat in fifty-dollar seats, drank a six-dollar-and-fifty-cent beer, cheered for players tall and graceful as giraffes, who made millions of dollars a year and had great smiles, but couldn't seem to shoot three baskets in a row . . .

Parker checked her watch against the big clock over the row of tellers' cages. The bank clock was running three minutes fast. Worse, Willows was running twenty minutes late, and counting. She crossed and uncrossed her long legs.

Her cellphone warbled. She got the phone out of her purse and flipped it open. Jack apologized for being late. He explained that he'd run into an ex-con named Bryan Galt, and that shortly afterwards, Galt had run into a plate-glass window. Willows was down at 312 Main, climbing a mountain of paperwork. Sorry, but she was going to have to reschedule their meeting.

"Until when?" said Parker.

"Any time after four. Or tomorrow morning. No, wait a minute, we're supposed to meet your landlord some time this afternoon, aren't we? And I've got an eleven o'clock meeting tomorrow with that crown prosecutor, owns the racehorse . . ."

"Gelbardt," said Parker. Shirley Gelbardt. A three-time loser, on the hunt for victim number four. Parker had heard a rumour that she liked to tear a blank piece of paper from her notebook, hand it to her new boyfriend, and tell him it was a list of things she wouldn't do on a first date. Gelbardt openly lusted after Willows, and had made a point of letting Parker know about it.

Through the open door, Parker saw the loans officer approach a teller, say something that made the teller smile. It was amazing, how much the woman looked like Mary Tyler Moore. Parker said, "She doesn't seem terribly overworked. I'll talk to her, see what I can do. Take care, Jack."

"Love you," said Willows.

"Me too," said Parker as Mary came in through the open door. She disconnected, and launched into her tale of woe.

The loans officer consulted her daybook. She was booked solid right through to five o'clock.

"Five is just fine with me," said Parker.

"We close at five. How about early tomorrow morning, say about ten?"

Ten didn't seem very early to Parker. But it was an hour earlier than eleven, and if they hurried things along . . .

Standing, Parker apologized again for Jack's inability to be in the right place at the right time. Offering her hand, she said, "Ten o'clock tomorrow morning would be just perfect, thank you."

Willows had inherited his house from his parents. When Sheila filed for divorce, she'd demanded, as was her legal right, half the value of the house, in cash.

Willows' lawyer, Peter Singer, had convinced Sheila that Willows' cop's salary was not large enough for him to arrange financing on a house worth upwards of six hundred thousand dollars. Did she really want to force the sale of the house? Singer had tactfully pointed out to Sheila that her son, Sean, was still recovering from the long-term trauma of a gunshot wound. Her daughter, Annie, was still in high school. Moving would be extremely disruptive for both children.

Singer suggested to Sheila that Willows might be able to arrange an interim loan for as much as twenty thousand dollars, to help her get through the next year or so. He realized it wasn't a great deal of money, but, given that she was now living with her fiancé in a small coastal village in Mexico, her costs must be fairly low.

The main thing, Singer persuasively argued, was the welfare of the children. They had been made aware that their mother was legally able to force the sale of their home. They had also been told of Willows' offer.

Sheila's lawyer had been called to the bar not much more than a year earlier, but had already gained himself a reputation for sharp teeth and a large dorsal fin. He was young and preternaturally aggressive, without a compromising gene in his body. His name was William Cole, and Singer would have bet a silver dollar against a stale donut that nobody, including his mother, ever dared call him Bill. Sheila agreed that the children's emotional stability was an important factor. She and Cole huddled. Cole demanded thirty thousand dollars.

Singer flatly refused. He told the young lawyer that, from what he knew about rural Mexico, Sheila could live like a queen on twenty grand a year, unless she had a drug habit, in which case she'd be dead in six months anyway. Cole was told that, if his client didn't accept the offer by the close of business that same day, the sum on the table would be reduced by five thousand dollars.

Cole excused himself and had a brief-but-intense conversation with his client. Willows' offer was truculently accepted. Willows had already negotiated the loan with his bank. Peter Singer had couriered a certified cheque to William Cole first thing the next morning.

Sheila had picked up her cheque – less Cole's hefty fee – within the hour. She flew to Seattle that afternoon, for an overnight stay. Early the next morning, she caught a direct flight to Mexico City.

Six months later she telephoned Willows and told him, desperately, that she was flat broke.

She needed a thousand dollars in the next twenty-four hours, to cover two months' back rent and the tab she'd piled up at the local *supermercado*. If she didn't pay the money, she would be evicted from her home, and probably thrown in jail.

Willows said he'd do what he could. He talked the situation over with Parker, and wired Sheila five hundred dollars in U.S. currency.

Three weeks later, Sheila had called again.

This time, Willows sent her two hundred and fifty dollars in U.S. currency.

Sheila had phoned him eight days later, just after midnight. She was broke again. In the background, Willows heard loud music, shouting. He reluctantly promised he'd do what he could. He offered to call in the morning. Was there was a phone number where she could be reached?

Sheila told him she needed the money right away, *now*, and hung up on him.

First thing the next morning, Willows drove five blocks to his neighbourhood travel agent, and used his Visa card to buy an open, non-refundable one-way airline ticket, Alvarado to Vancouver via Mexico City and Seattle, with a brief stopover in Los Angeles. He sent it off.

The ticket was never used. He didn't hear from his ex-wife again until another five months had passed, even though he continued to write regularly, with news of the children.

When he finally did hear from Sheila, it was via Peter Singer, the unhappy recipient of a brusque telephone call from William Cole.

The year that Willows had bought his children was up in thirty days. Sheila did not expect to have to wait for her long-overdue windfall. She was prepared to force the sale of the house.

Willows had already made preliminary overtures to his bank, and discovered that, given his outstanding debt load, he had absolutely no hope of qualifying for close to three-hundred-thousand-dollar mortgage.

Parker did a little investigating of her own. Why not, since she was a trained detective? She learned that, if she and Willows *combined* their incomes, the mortgage application would be approved.

She told Willows about her brainstorm on a Monday evening. Jack had been watching football in the den. Towards the end of the game, Parker settled in at the far end of the couch with a book. Willows had bet fellow homicide detective Eddy Orwell twenty dollars that the Green Bay Packers would beat the New England Patriots by at least ten points. It was an away game for the Packers. New England was on a three-game winning streak, and the bookies had the home team winning by a field goal. So Willows was giving up thirteen points.

It was a close game, but the Packers dominated the final quarter and won going away, thanks to a pair of timely interceptions, by three touchdowns. Willows couldn't have been happier. It wasn't the twenty dollars, though he'd spend it. What rankled him was that, as he and Eddy had shaken hands, Orwell, cackling evilly, had called it a sucker bet. So what really cranked Willows up was the idea of rubbing Orwell's face in his miscalculation.

As the game ended, Parker got up from the couch and went over to the tiny bar and poured Willows a small Cutty on the rocks, and then a glass of white wine for herself.

Willows eyed her with jovial suspicion as he accepted the drink.

They clinked glasses.

"Go Packers!" said Parker.

Willows smiled, and used the remote to kill the television. Mission accomplished. Packers gone.

Parker sipped her wine. Choosing her words with caution, she told Willows she'd done a little basic math, and worked out that if they joined forces, they'd be eligible for the fat mortgage Willows needed to arrange if he hoped to avoid a forced sale of the house.

Willows leaned back against the sofa. He swallowed half his Scotch and stared contemplatively at the ceiling.

Parker waited about half a minute, until she couldn't stand the suspense any longer.

"What d'you think, Jack?"

"I don't know what to think. You've caught me by surprise. It's quite an idea. It's also a hell of a big commitment."

Now Parker didn't know what to think. What kind of commitment was he talking about, financial or emotional?

Coming out of the bank, into a light drizzle, Parker briefly considered enjoying a solitary lunch before returning to 312 Main. She was hungry, but decided to go straight in. She was going to have to talk to Inspector Homer Bradley, con him into giving her another hour off for tomorrow morning's appointment.

She hoped Willows would be able to make it.

5

Lewis was out like a cheap lightbulb one moment, wide awake and terrified the next.

He glanced wildly around. The room was dark. He was flat on his back, lying in what sure felt like a large bed.

Nothing but a dream.

His head ached. The contents of his bladder weighed heavily on him. He tried to get up to go to the bathroom and discovered he couldn't move.

Not more than an inch.

Lewis was no fan of involuntary bondage. Shouting, he demanded that he be set free, or else.

Fairly quickly, he shifted ground from stage one, murderous threats and vile imprecations, to stage two, reckless pleading and then full-bore whining. All for naught. When he had regained his wind he screamed, stage three, for the cops to come and save him.

But you know what they say about cops.

Lewis, moving right along to stage four, prayed fervently to whatever gods might take pity on him.

A familiar sound came faintly to him. Frank Sinatra, singing "My Way."

Lewis cried so hard he nearly drowned.

In the kitchen, April hummed along with Sinatra as she diced and sliced, putting together an enormous beef stew.

Wayne was a voracious meat-eater. A ravenous carnivore. His was a world of Big Macs, Christmas turkeys, juicy racks of lamb, frying pans crammed with sizzling pork sausages and slabs of bacon, massive T-bones running with blood . . .

April thought about the hundred and sixty pounds of raw meat laid out on the king-size Sealy in her bedroom. It had been quite a struggle, hauling him into the house. She'd dragged him out of the van, bounced his head off the garage's cement floor a couple of times, poked and prodded him, and finally left him lying there, breathing erratically, while she drove over to that tool-rental place on Dunbar, to rent a dolly. Even then, getting him from the garage to the bedroom hadn't exactly been a picnic.

When they were unconscious, men were so *limp*.

April finished dicing the last of the carrots and, knife in hand, went into the living room and cranked up the stereo until she could no longer hear poor Lewis's anguished screams for help.

Half an hour later, the big stew she'd made was simmering on a back burner, in an enormous stainless-steel pot.

April shucked her apron, wriggled out of her jeans and sweater and Calvin Klein panties as she headed for the bathroom. She showered, shaved her legs, put on a little makeup and a dab of perfume, and then slipped into a devastatingly simple black cocktail dress with spaghetti straps and a traffic-jam neckline. Standing in front of the mirror, she opened wide and stuck out her tongue.

The stud diamond Wayne had given her shone brightly.

In the living room, the CD changer clattered. Sinatra was shuffled off stage in favour of Holly Cole.

April stole a slim pink candle in a heavy brass candlestick from the dining-room table, lit it, and followed its romantic glow into the bedroom.

Lewis's eyes glittered almost as brightly as her diamond. April went straight over to the bed. She thumped the candle down on the night table, and then reached over and squeezed the tips of his fingers in a kind of half-assed handshake, and introduced herself.

"Hi, I'm April."

Lewis struggled to break free of the stainless-steel handcuffs that now tightly encircled his wrists and ankles and securely fastened him to the four-poster bed.

April leaned over him and kissed him chastely on his forehead. She drew back, startled. "Yuck, you're all clammy!"

"Did I do something to you?"

"No, of course not."

"Where am I? Why am I locked up like this?" Lewis was trying his hardest to sound reasonable but perplexed, but above all reasonable. The situation was too much for him. It was too scary. Too weird. He had been zapped and then kidnapped, stripped naked and cuffed to this huge bed, in this unnaturally dark room. His eyes were puffy from crying. Who was this totally crazy woman? What kind of evil did she have in mind for him? "What are you going to do with me!" His grief-clogged voice climbed the scale, shrieking into the ozone. April's hair fluttered, and was still.

She said, "Would a nice cold glass of white wine help calm you down?"

Lewis said, "Okay, I stole a watch. An expensive watch. Is that such a terrible crime? I can't get a job. What am I supposed to do, starve to death?"

April pinched a teardrop of melted wax from the candle, and squeezed it between her finger and thumb until it was flat as a coin. She peeled it away from her finger and admired her perfect fingerprint.

Lewis said, "It's a victimless crime. Birks is a huge store. They've got lots of money, and anyway, they're totally insured!"

"If you say so."

Lewis lay there for a moment, passive, catching his breath. He said, "I have to go to the bathroom."

"Oh. Okay, fine." She gave him a brief, uncertain smile. "I should have thought of that. Going potty. I mean, who doesn't?"

A silver key hung around her neck on a thin silver chain. She made as if to unlock a handcuff, had second thoughts, and pulled back.

"Oops!"

"I won't try to get away," promised Lewis.

"Yes you will, you liar!"

April flounced up off the bed and skipped out of the room. She was back in less than a minute, armed with the Taser.

"Do you know what this is?"

Lewis shuddered.

"Good." April pulled the silver chain over her head. The key twinkled merrily in the light.

She said, "I'm going to unlock your left hand, and then you can do all the rest of the unlocking yourself. But I'm warning you, if you try anything stupid, I'll zap you full of high-voltage electricity. Understand?"

"I understand," said Lewis. He noticed at last that she was wearing the Rolex Lady Datejust.

April glared down at him. "This thing's no toy. Back there in the parking lot, all you got was half-power. Right now, it's cranked up all the way. If I use it on you, it'd hurt like anything. Who knows, you might even die." April waved the Taser around, as if on the hunt for a target of opportunity. "Wayne used this thing on a family of raccoons that was always getting into the garbage. It was as if they'd been hit by lightning bolts. They burst into flames, Lewis. Into flames! It was really unforgettably awful."

Lewis nodded. He said, "I bet it was."

"I was looking at their little bandit heads sticking out of the garbage can, thinking that they were cuter than Tickle Me Elmo, and then Wayne zapped them, and all of a sudden they looked like a bunch of great big oversized Christmas puddings, all blue flame and *flambeau*."

April levelled the Taser at his heart and unlocked his left wrist. She dropped the silver chain in his hand. "I don't want to turn you into a Christmas pudding, even though I bet you'd be the tastiest pudding I ever met. But you better believe I'll do it if I have to."

Lewis concentrated on staying absolutely rock-still.

"It's okay, go ahead. Set yourself free. I don't know what kind of a person you think I am, but I'm not the least bit kinky, no matter what Wayne tells you. As far as I'm concerned, urine-soaked beds are not the least bit alluring."

Lewis wanted to be sure he didn't make any mistakes. He said, "I can unlock the cuffs?"

"Go right ahead."

It took only a moment. April retrieved the chain and key. Lewis lay there on the bed, flexing his muscles, trying to work out the kinks. His head throbbed.

"The bathroom's right over there." April pointed at a mirrored door. "It's an en suite. There's a window, but it's barred, because Wayne doesn't like the idea of some low-life creep sneaking into the house under cover of darkness, so he can take advantage of me." April smiled. "I think he was talking about my friendly nature, but I'm not sure." She rolled her eyes. "And also, to be perfectly honest, there was a time not so long ago when I was seriously thinking of splitting. Wayne didn't want me sneaking out of here any more than he wanted some unknown creep sneaking in."

Lewis swung his legs over the far side of the bed, so he had his back to her.

April scurried around the bed as he dropped lightly to the floor. She kept pace with him as he padded across the floor to the bathroom. As he neared the mirrored door she said, "You sure have a nice body."

"Is that why you brought me here?"

"Partly. Wayne likes to say that the world isn't so ugly if you fill it with pretty things."

"Wayne's your boyfriend?"

April laughed, delighted by the question. She had a sudden urge to tell Lewis all about Wayne's grandiose plans to violently wrest the city's network of organized dealers from the liver-spotted hands of ageing and therefore vulnerable crime kingpin Jake Cappalletti. But wisely, she held her diamond-studded tongue.

Lewis put his hand on the faceted, crystal doorknob. He pulled open the door, and turned so he was directly facing her. Full frontal nudity. He cocked his hip. "You coming in with me?"

"Not this time, loverboy."

Lewis nodded, went inside and shut the door. The window was high up on the wall, a rectangle of dirty grey light. It was permanently shut, protected by two sets of sturdy steel bars, one interior and one exterior. It was almost full dark outside. He'd been unconscious for hours.

He found the wall switch. There was a tub-shower combo, a toilet and a vanity with double sinks, all the enamel in a putrid, pea-green colour. Too many lights, too many mirrors. His wrists had been chafed by the handcuffs. He combed his hair with his fingers. He didn't look half-bad, considering.

He locked the door, and sat heavily down on the toilet.

April, sounding anxious, called to him through the door. "Are you okay, Lewis?"

No, he wasn't. His bladder felt as if it was full of sawdust. The way he felt right that minute, he doubted he'd have to piss again if he lived to be a hundred years old.

Which seemed increasingly unlikely, despite recent breakthroughs in the impenetrable fields of genetics and cloning. They'd cloned a sheep, or so they said. A *sheep*! Why bother? More to the point, how could they tell?

Lewis sat there on the ugly pea-green toilet, enjoying his dumb little joke, chuckling like a brain-bruised fool. Gut-twisting terror had squeezed the sweat out of him. He smelled of naked fear, and pepper spray, and he couldn't say which was worse. One thing for sure – he was in desperate need of a shower. Had anybody told him it was forbidden to shower? Nope. April had the hots for him. Hadn't she more or less come right out and said so? Women liked clean men. To hell with April. Who cared what she craved. Not him. He didn't smell bad. He stank. If he wanted a shower, he'd take a shower.

Lewis took a long hot shower. He dried himself with a purple towel, wrapped another purple towel around his waist and exited the bathroom.

April didn't look happy to see him. She said, "I don't like your hair like that."

"Like what?"

"Slicked back."

Lewis turned to look at himself in the mirrored door. He said, "It's wet, that's all."

"Dry it."

"With what?"

April playfully poked at the towel with the Taser. "With the towel, silly." She smiled. "Or there's a hair dryer in the bathroom, if you're feeling shy."

Lewis was definitely feeling shy. Uncharacteristically shy. Or at least modest. He wasn't sure why this was. Maybe he should just put it down to the unusual circumstances.

Or the Taser, and his memory of the sharp, lightning-like *crack!* the wand had made when it touched him, and the sudden feeling of intense heat, an internal searing and sizzling, the unwelcome sensation that his bones had turned to rubber, the muscles and ligaments of his joints melted into a soft and useless mush.

There was also the fact that he had a strong hunch that Wayne, whoever he turned out to be, was lurking in the middle distance, crowbar in hand, waiting for his unwelcome guest to make a wrong move, or any kind of move at all . . .

Lewis used the dryer on his hair, fluffed it up with his fingers the way he always did. Was this what she wanted? He teased his hair this way and that. Was that right? He hoped so. He turned off the dryer and slipped it back into its wall mount.

He came back out of the bathroom to find that April had turned on a massive 54-inch rear-projection Hitachi that was wedged into a corner opposite the bed. A chrome kitchen chair with bright yellow Naugahyde upholstery had been placed in front of the TV.

April told him to sit down.

He sat.

She told him to cross his right ankle over his left thigh. For some reason he got it backwards. She didn't seem to mind – not that he trusted his judgement. Following her directions exactly, he handcuffed his right wrist to his left ankle.

On the TV, a mass of water fell at least a hundred vertical feet to a glassy calm lake.

April said, "Just a minute."

She fumbled with the remote, turned up the sound until the sound of the waterfall was a steady roar.

Lewis concentrated on the waterfall as she walked slowly around him, lightly touching him, exploring his bone structure, musculature. She told him to open wide, stuck a finger up under his gums and bent to examine his teeth.

She asked him to neigh like a horse.

Lewis eyed the Taser. He hesitated just long enough to let her know that he was no wimp. Then he did what he was told.

"Louder."

Lewis whinnied like a whole corral full of stallions.

She kept circling him. She asked him increasingly personal questions about his employment history, age and education, health, family background. Did he have any brothers or sisters? No. Were his mother and father alive? He couldn't say. Was there anyone in the whole wide world who'd miss him, if he decided to take an extended holiday from his life?

Lewis knew where she was heading – straight for the intersection of Missing and Permanently. His mind raced. He almost mentioned Liz, aka Elizabeth, his partner in crime. But no, he wouldn't do it. What was the point? Liz couldn't help him. If this woman, this *Wandmeister*, wanted him badly enough, Liz's life wouldn't be worth a bag of stale donuts. He wasn't going to sacrifice her, not when there wasn't anything to be gained. Or even, he told himself, if there was. He just wouldn't.

He said, "Nobody'd miss me."

"You sure about that?"

He nodded.

April said, "I didn't think so. Know why? The Ontario plates on your van. And also, I hate to tell you this, but I saw the way your girlfriend kissed you, for luck before the big Birks caper. As if she didn't care one way or the other what happened to you."

But there was another, even simpler reason April had snatched Lewis. It was because she was running out of time, and there he was, exactly when she needed him. Hell, she was getting so desperate she'd have grabbed the Pope, given the opportunity.

The picture on the big screen shifted, the camera zooming in for a closeup of the foaming lip of the waterfall. Something moved among the trees.

"Watch," said April.

A burly man wearing jeans and a black-and-green lumberjack shirt and a black balaclava strolled out of the woods. He was carrying another man over his shoulder, carrying him as effortlessly as if he were a loaf of bread.

"That's Wayne," said April, "Cool mask, huh? He took it off an ERT or a SWAT guy, I forget which."

Wayne lifted the man high over his head, held him there for a moment, and then tossed him into the river. A few seconds later, the man's head, all eyes and mouth, rose up out of the foaming water.

Freeze frame.

Then the man was swept over the lip of the waterfall. He fell, and kept falling. The camera followed him all the way down to the lake. He made quite a splash.

Lewis waited for him to come bobbing to the surface. It never happened.

April squatted in front of him. She had papers, a plastic baggie of fine-cut marijuana.

"You smoke dope?"

"Sometimes."

"This time being sometime," said April, "I guess you're going to smoke some now." Her long white fingers made quick work of the fixin's. She lit up with a heavy table lighter, inhaled deeply, coughed, and lightly thumped her chest.

"Yummy. Your turn."

Lewis accepted the cigarette, toked up. It was a lot more fun than being zapped. Or so he thought.

"Ever chase the dragon, Lewis?"

"Excuse me?"

April smiled a smug, smug smile. The marijuana had been laced with heroin, and Lewis had unwittingly taken that crucial first small step towards addiction.

Lewis, stressed to the max, didn't need much urging to smoke the joint down to his fingernails. Soon enough, he was basking in a sensation of great serenity and contentment.

6

Inspector Homer Bradley leaned back in his burgundy leather chair. His feet hurt. Both of them. During the weekend, he'd bought a pair of expensive Italian shoes. He was wearing them for the first time since trying them on. They pinched his toes. Was that because they were Italian, and therefore somewhat licentious? Why had they felt so comfortable when he'd worn them in the store? He had no idea. Maybe he'd been wearing thinner socks. In future, he would have to remember never to shop for shoes while wearing thin socks.

Parker and Willows were standing there in front of his desk, looking serious. What was it they'd wanted?

He said, "Sorry, I must have drifted off." Should he tell them about the shoes? No way. A detective's life was too frivolous as it was. He smiled up at Parker. "Would you mind repeating that?"

"Just reminding you that we'd arranged to take some personal time, Inspector."

Bradley checked his watch. He'd missed lunch. He was starving, but he didn't want to go anywhere because of the damn shoes. He said, "Both of you, right? Didn't we already talk about this?"

Parker nodded.

Willows said, "Claire's lease is up. She has to be out of her apartment by midnight."

"You weren't evicted, I hope."

Parker smiled.

Bradley didn't ask where she was moving to. He didn't need to, because he'd find out soon enough. Departmental regulations demanded that she immediately notify him of any change of address.

Willows said, "Claire's moving in with me."

Bradley grunted. He tried to think of something appropriate to say, but his feet so nagged at him that it was hard to think clearly. He reached down and untied and loosened his shoelaces.

Was that better? Not that he noticed, no.

"No?" said Parker, startled.

Had Bradley been thinking out loud? If so, he hoped it was for the first and last time.

He said, "Your desks clear?"

"Pretty much," said Parker. The murder business had been slow, lately. Vancouver is the crime capital of Canada, and her citizens are proud of it, even if they're too bashful to say so. But demographics, the black art of numerologists, play a big part in crime rates. Vancouver's population was ageing. It's hard to work up a whole lot of enthusiasm for an eight-hour shift of breaking and entering when your arthritis is absolutely killing you. Much nicer to stay in bed.

"Have fun, kids, but don't turn off your beepers." Bradley waved them out of the office, and swung his chair around so his knees were clear of his desk. He grunted as he removed each shoe; first the left and then the right. On any level, nothing felt quite so luxurious as release from captivity.

He wriggled his toes. The shoes had cost him two hundred and eighty bucks, the pair. Maybe he could take them back. No, he couldn't. The right one was irreparably scuffed. A sour bile rose in his throat. In the department store, his old shoes tucked in the new box, he had veered away from the escalator, thinking he would take the elevator down to mall level, and buy his ex-wife a box of chocolates, a token present to mark her sixtieth birthday.

A pale woman carrying an umbrella had crowded into the elevator when it stopped at the next floor down. The woman was expensively dressed. She smelled expensive, too. She was in her late twenties, had red hair and green eyes and the sort of complexion usually encountered in a television commercial. Bradley knew the moment she stepped inside the elevator that she was one of those unfortunate women who live off their beauty, and consequently lack character.

Someone else had got on, a sopping-wet bicycle courier. The red-haired beauty had shuffled sideways to get away from him. She'd leaned the point of her umbrella onto Bradley's shoe and put her weight on it. He was certain it was an accident. Even so, the pain had been nothing short of excruciating. Tears had sprung to his eyes. He had ground his teeth, and almost cried out, as he jerked his foot away. He might have whimpered; he wasn't sure. The pain, and attendant shock, had made him suddenly feel the weight of every single day of his age. The woman had muttered a hasty apology, but in such a way as to subtly convey her disinterest. She hadn't even bothered to glance in his general direction, and had gotten off right away, at the next floor, eliminating the opportunity for a caustic, withering remark.

The damn umbrella had slashed deeply across the top of the shoe, scarring it for life.

Bradley smiled sourly down at his stockinged feet.

No wonder the damn shoes didn't fit properly. How could they, when they were so heavily freighted with unpleasant memories.

Parker wore a snug-fitting black leather jacket, black jeans, and a pair of knobbly street/hiking shoes that were extremely comfortable but made her feet look at least two sizes larger than they actually were. On the job, shoes were always a problem. Her superior officers expected her to look reasonably well-dressed when she was in plainclothes, but at the same time it was crucial that she be able to engage in a hot pursuit, should the opportunity arise. Most of the time she wore sensible flats, or running shoes. Never heels, unfortunately. Police work was anything but glamorous, so that side of her never came out, except when she was off-duty.

Willows wore a scuffed brown leather jacket that had seen better days, a pair of faded Levi's, and white Reeboks, sparsely trimmed in a coarse-grained khaki-coloured fabric. The Reeboks were almost brand new. It had taken him a few days to break them in, but now they were so comfortable he was hardly aware that he was wearing them. He did wish they weren't so startlingly, blindingly, uncompromisingly *white*. But at the same time he knew they wouldn't remain pristine as a pair of mobile snowfields for very long. Running shoes were like people; they aged imperceptibly, but inevitably, and shockingly quickly.

Willows reached for the door, but Parker got it first. They stepped into the alley behind 312 Main. It was raining. The rain fell through the tangle of electrical wires, past ranks of desolate pigeons and into the narrow space between the Public Safety Building and the towering red brick wall of the Remand Centre and City Jail. On the cracked, uneven pavement of the alley, shallow puddles showcased pretty pink-and-blue doilies of oil.

Willows and Parker walked down the alley towards the entrance to the police garage. They walked purposefully but without haste. Neither of them hunched their shoulders or otherwise indicated in any way that the rain concerned them.

Both coppers had learned early in life that looking miserable in a shower doesn't prevent you from getting wet.

Parker's Mazda 626 was parked on the third level. She unlocked the car and got in and reached across the seat to unlock Willows' door. He got into the car and fastened his seatbelt as she reversed out of the parking stall.

As they drove out of the garage and into the rain, which seemed to be coming down a little more briskly than it had only a few moments earlier, Willows said, "Want to get a bite to eat?"

Parker shook her head, no. Earlier, she'd been starving. What had happened to her appetite? Not that she was complaining. She turned on the wipers.

Willows' stomach rumbled. No problemo.

They were on their way to Parker's one-bedroom apartment on West Eighth, just off Burrard. She'd hired a couple of guys with a cube van to move her sofa and matching chair, as well as a few pieces of antique pine, to Willows' house. The other larger pieces, the kitchen table and two chairs she'd bought at Ikea, the bed and night table from The Brick, had been sold to a used-furniture store. She hadn't liked any of that furniture when she'd bought it, and she was glad to get rid of it now. Most of it was so badly worn she could easily have thrown it out without feeling wasteful or guilty. It was odd how a person's taste could change over the years. Or maybe it wasn't.

Now, all that remained was a small antique pine chair and a circa-1920s mahogany serving cart. She'd inherited the cart from her mother. She hoped to have children of her own to pass it on to, some time in the vague, distant future.

Willows said, "Pull over at the end of the block, will you?"

Parker signalled, checked her mirror. The street was metered, and there were several parking spots available.

Willows said, "Yeah, right here." He had unbuckled his seatbelt, and began to open his door before the car had fully stopped.

"What's up?"

Willows pointed at a crude hand-painted sign.

A pizza joint. Pizza by the slice. Why wasn't she surprised? Because repetition dulls the senses.

Willows paused with his hand on the door. "Want a Coke?"

"No thanks, Jack."

"Diet Coke?"

Parker shook her head. Willows shut the door and strode across the sidewalk. The business was take-out only. Parker adjusted the wipers, speeding them up. Willows stood at the white-painted counter, opposite a man in a white chef's cap. The man said something. Willows pointed. The man separated a slice of pizza from the mass, slid it onto a paper plate and put the plate down on the counter. He turned his back on Willows and swung open a refrigerator door, reached inside for a bottle of pop. Willows paid for his meal, pushed open the door with his shoulder, crossed the sidewalk. Parker opened the car door for him. Willows put the slice of pizza down on the dashboard and shut the door. The pizza was steaming up the windshield.

Parker said, "What've you got there?"

"Green pepper, mushrooms, anchovies."

"No, I mean *that*."

Willows held up the bottle of pop. It was a lovely shade of clear pink. "Cream soda."

"They still make that stuff?"

Willows fastened his seatbelt. He picked up the slice of pizza and took a big bite, chewed and swallowed. "I guess so."

Parker said, "I haven't had a cream soda in about thirty years."

"C'mon, it couldn't have been that long."

"A quarter-century, minimum," said Parker. "Can I have a sip?"

"Nope." Willows bit into his pizza. He chewed and swallowed. Parker put the car in gear and pulled away from the curb.

Willows said, "One large slice of take-out pizza requires, for purposes of balance, one bottle of cream soda. The beverage of choice doesn't really matter, because the equation remains constant. If I share my soda with you, I'm going to have to toss the last bite of pizza out the window." Willows lowered his voice so he sounded mock-ominous. "That just doesn't make sense, Claire."

"How about if you give me a sip of pop *and* a bite of pizza?"

"Now you're talking," said Willows. But the truth was, when it came to food, he wasn't a nineties, sharing kind of guy.

Parker's one-bedroom apartment, stripped of furniture and her collection of colourful framed prints, was gloomy and depressing. A tightly rolled carpet leaned dejectedly into a corner. The carpet had served to cover most of the apartment's green shag. Exposed, the shag looked every bit as ugly-grim as the day she'd moved in.

The bare walls cried out for a fresh coat of paint. In the bedroom stood the few lonely boxes of possessions she hadn't sold or already moved over to Willows'. The boxes contained clothing she had outgrown, or that had gone out of style, as well as a dozen pairs of unwanted shoes, and a few serviceable but also unwanted odds and ends. Cleaning out her closet, she had been surprised and a little dismayed to learn that she owned three hair dryers, not one.

Parker finished cleaning the kitchen while Willows carried the boxes down to the car. She'd left an opened bottle of wine in the refrigerator, and they sipped from disposable plastic glasses while they waited for the landlord to arrive. He'd insisted on inspecting the apartment before returning Parker's damage deposit – half a month's rent plus ten years' accrued interest. Fair enough. But where was he?

Parker checked her watch. "I told him three-thirty. It's quarter to four. Where is he?"

Willows shrugged. He sipped some wine. Parker had rented a heavy-duty carpet cleaner from a Safeway, but the bile-green shag carpet in the living room had laid down and died a decade or more ago.

At twenty past four, a key turned in the lock. The door swung open and the owner, a bland, determinedly middle-aged man named Owen Hackler, strolled in. Hackler had told Parker when she'd first rented the apartment that he owned five buildings, all of them three-storey walkups. Hackler had inherited his mother's house and promptly sold it, using the cash as down payments. During the first two years, Hackler had done all his own mainte-nance work, as well as holding down two full-time jobs. In the third year, selective renovations and drastically increased rents had produced a positive cash flow.

In the fifth year, he'd sold the smallest of the buildings. Benefiting from grossly inflated land values, he netted just under a million dollars, and paid out the other four mortgages. Parker estimated Hackler's worth at somewhere between six and eight million dollars. Hackler's wealth had honed his hunger for more wealth. Every year he raised the rent the legal maximum. He never did a penny's worth of repairs until he was nudged by a court order. He was so reluctant to return damage deposits that he had become locally famous. If Parker had expected trouble, she wasn't disappointed.

Hackler wandered around the apartment for a solid fifteen minutes, taking notes. Occasionally he pointed his cheap disposable camera at something or other that only he could see, and feigned taking a picture. When he'd finally played out his little charade, he cleared his throat, checked his indecipherable notes and said, "I believe you owe me one hundred and twelve dollars and fifty-eight cents, Miss Parker."

Parker hated being called Miss Parker. Hackler was well over six feet tall, but she stepped towards him, getting in his face, so close she could smell his lunch. "I don't owe you anything, Hackler. You owe me three hundred and fourteen dollars and twelve cents."

"I beg your pardon?"

"I phoned the Rentalsman's office. I gave them the numbers and they did the math. Pay up."

Hackler's face puckered. "I got to paint. Look at the carpet; it's a mess!"

"It was a mess when I moved in. I've painted the place myself, three times in the ten years I've lived here. I'm not responsible for normal wear and tear, and you know it."

"Well, that's your opinion . . ."

"It's the law," said Parker firmly.

"The law?" Hackler was surprised. He appeared never to have heard of such a thing.

Willows put his arm around Parker's shoulder. The gesture of solidarity was unmistakable. He said, "There are all sorts of laws, Mr. Hackler. A man in your position could go crazy, trying to keep up with all of them."

"What are you saying?"

"Write the cheque."

Hackler smiled, and turned his minuscule charm on Parker. "Okay, fine. I'll send it to you in the mail."

Parker shook her head. "That's not good enough. I want it now. Right this minute."

Hackler sighed, and slowly reached for his chequebook. He had to borrow a pen. He had to be reminded to return it.

Willows drove down Burrard to Broadway, made a left and drove west until he got to the Salvation Army retail store. Parker helped him carry in the boxes. Carrying two instead of one, she lost her balance and dropped them both. The contents erupted across the sidewalk. One box was stuffed with unwanted sweaters. The other was filled with shoes and boots, boots that were made for walkin'. Parker wondered if her travelling days were over. She hoped so. She hoped next time she moved, it would be to a retirement home.

Or, better yet, a graveyard.

7

Wayne knew April was out hunting for somebody like Lewis, but that didn't mean he was going to be happy she'd bagged him. Wayne didn't like surprises, no matter how predictable they might be. April wanted Lewis to be just perfect. Since Wayne was a cleanliness freak, she meant to do everything she could to improve Lewis's personal hygiene. She led him back into the bathroom, dropped the toilet seat and sharply told him, as if he were a recalcitrant puppy, to *sit*.

Lewis sat.

She told him to open wide, and wider.

April had never flossed anybody's teeth before. It was hard work. Really hard work. And not that pleasant, actually. Add dental hygienist to the long list of jobs she wasn't interested in, should she happen to be reincarnated.

Lewis was cooperative but very sleepy. When she'd finished with the floss, she made him rinse his mouth with Scope. Then she kissed him, just a quick smooch. Tasty. She told him to smile, and stood back, hands on hips, admiring her handiwork.

What next? His fingernails were fine. She got a box of Q-tips and assiduously cleaned a few scraps of wax out of his ears. The wax was golden and creamy. April rubbed it between the tips of her fingers until it had disappeared into her skin. She combed

Lewis's hair, and then she plugged in her Lady Braun and carefully shaved him.

It was nice to be with a clean-shaven man. Wayne was all beard. He had hair all over him. He shaved his neck with a straight razor, but his beard and sideburns covered his whole face, almost. He kept it trimmed of course, didn't let it grow down to his belly button like those weird ZZ Top guys. And another thing, Wayne had gained a lot of weight, fifty or sixty pounds, since April had first met him. He was a pretty big guy, six-four, three hundred and twelve pounds, and he had a gut hanging off him that didn't exactly make her wild with desire. When he was riding around on one of his big Harley-Davidson motorcycles, his *hawgs*, he looked just fine. But he never rode his Harley into bed, did he?

April unscrewed the cap from Wayne's aftershave, and then, just in time, came to her senses. If Wayne smelled his lotions on Lewis, there was no telling what he'd do. Well, yes, there was. He'd go crazy. He'd do bad things, which couldn't be undone. Things he would apologize for a few days later, when he'd finally cooled down. Not that his apologies meant anything to April, because by the time he got around to falling to his knees, she'd already have forgiven him anyway.

Lewis, doped-up and drowsy, was led back to bed. Exhausted, he nodded off. April lay down next to him. His hair smelled faintly of pepper spray, and Wayne's shampoo, weird organic stuff that came in inconvenient Mylar bags. Wayne bought shampoo from his hair stylist, a thin woman named Audrey Kong, who was deeply into body-piercing, good Scotch, and guys who drove Harleys. Wayne was two out of three, so far. April had coolly decided that, if he ever came home with a chunk of stainless steel hanging off his face, she'd zap him until he looked like that stuff that collects on the grill of a barbecue, torch his motorcycles, grab the on-hand cash, and run like hell.

That last part, running like hell, would be absolutely necessary, even if she'd killed him. Because Wayne, that miserable, happy-go-lucky sonofabitch, wasn't the kind of guy who'd stay dead.

April lay in bed with Lewis for half an hour or so, admiring him, and then got up and went into the kitchen. She tore the plastic wrapper off a brand-new syringe, cooked up an extra-diluted hit of heroin, and hurried back into the bedroom.

Lewis was dead to the world.

April sprayed the crook of his arm with a local anaesthetic. His skin was pale and almost hairless. His veins, fat as worms, lay just beneath the surface of his skin.

April knelt beside him. She held the syringe up to the light and, very deliberately and slowly, depressed the plunger, so all the air was expelled and a tiny spurt of liquid erupted from the point of the needle.

She had been calm, but now April was swept up in a tremendous rush of excitement. Her heart rate accelerated. Her vision blurred. Her hands shook uncontrollably. Lewis was so wonderful. Such a handsome man. He was exactly what she'd wanted. She'd been anticipating this moment for so long. She had dreamed about it, night after night. Lewis was all hers. She'd never realized how incredibly thrilling it would be, to take control of a life, guide someone through whatever door she chose to open.

She had worked so hard, to nab Lewis. Wayne thought he was so smart. He'd laughed at her. He hadn't believed in her. Well, he'd believe in her now. He needed a Lewis. Somebody who could be manipulated and then disposed of. And look, there he was! She couldn't wait to see Wayne's face. He was going to be so *pleased* with her.

Hopefully.

She repeatedly pressed the tip of the needle against Lewis's arm, dimpling the pale flesh.

April pressed her thighs together. Now was the moment. She took a deep breath, and tried her very hardest to hold herself steady as she poked at a bulging vein. The needle was unbelievably sharp. April's concentration was intense. She bit down hard on her lower lip.

A rush of blood swirled into the syringe's barrel, and she exulted in the certain knowledge that she had hit a vein.

Fascinated, she stared at the bloom of crimson as it migrated into the barrel. It was a cloud, a beautiful, feathery, amazingly delicate and complicated, miniature, sunset-red cloud. April tried to remember the names Wayne had told her. Cumulus, those were the great big ones, big as mountains, that towered up into the sky. Wayne had explained that they were so big because they *accumulated*. He was so smart, the way he explained things to her. Cirrus, those were the ones like feathers. Wayne had asked her if she'd ever wanted to run off and join the circus, so she could wear glittery clothes with lots of feathers. Nimbus. She wasn't too sure about that one. Jack be nimbus, Jack be quick . . .

She kissed Lewis's fingers.

If she mainlined him, he might die. But then again, he might not. But if he died, then what? He'd have been wasted, ditto her hard work. How would she get him off the bed and out of the house, if he died? She studied him. Wayne clocked in at a little over three hundred pounds. Lewis, soaking wet, was about one-sixty, tops. Even so, no way she'd get him out of the house in one piece.

April withdrew the needle from the vein, and plunged it somewhat petulantly into Lewis's biceps. *Skin popping*, it was called. As slowly as was humanly possibly, she depressed the syringe's plunger. A tributary of heroin flooded into Lewis's flesh. He moaned softly.

She kissed his smooth, freshly shaved face. He was so handsome he could've been a movie star, or a model.

She decided to buy him some clothes. A suit, maybe. It would be fun to dress him up, and undress him.

Lewis's breathing was slow but steady. His eyelids fluttered. Was he dreaming? April thought about how sweet it would be if she could slip into his dream. She imagined him strolling across a flowery meadow. He was wearing corduroy pants and a white shirt with the sleeves rolled up. He had his hands in his pockets, and he was chewing on a blade of grass. She ran up behind him, surprising him. No, it was better if she was sitting under a tree, in the dappled sunlight, perhaps reading a book. And he was walking through the field of flowers and he looked up and saw her, and it was as if he'd been struck by a bolt of lightning.

April shut her eyes. She saw that she was wearing a frilly white summer dress, and a straw hat, and that she was irresistibly beautiful.

Lewis saw her and broke stride and turned involuntarily towards her. He was smiling.

Both of them saw right away that they were made for each other. Love at first sight. How romantic.

April's eyes popped open. She'd been lap-dancing at a cheesy downtown bar when she'd first met Wayne. By then, Arturo and all the rest of Wayne's associates were long gone, Wayne having learned the hard way to depend on nobody but himself. He'd been sitting there, alone at a ringside table, drinking pint mugs of beer. Looking, from April's point of view, pretty cool in his black leather Harley-Davidson jacket, faded jeans and sexy black leather chaps. His shiny, pointy-toe, black, size-twelve stomper boots up on the table next to his helmet, a Bell Eagle shorty.

He'd asked April what time she got off work, and she'd said, Never. Wayne had thought that was pretty funny. He'd enjoyed a good belly laugh, his beard splitting open so you could see his teeth. He had nice white teeth. April liked that about him, and the sound of his laugh, hearty and unrestrained. He had a nice smile, and the most beautiful, velvety-mauve eyes.

He'd asked her if she had a boyfriend.

Yeah, she had a boyfriend.

Wayne asked her how much money she made. Lying a little, okay, lying a lot, she told him she was pulling in two or three grand a week. Wayne asked her if she enjoyed her work. She told him that, when she'd started in the business, turning the guys on had been kind of a thrill. For the first few nights. But ever since then, she admitted, stripping had been just plain hard work. More grind than bump, you might say.

Wayne told her he needed a . . .

He frowned. He scratched his beard, his stubby fingers disappearing into the shrubbery right up to the first knuckle. He wore a death's head gold ring with ruby eyes on the little finger of his left hand. April could see that he was thinking.

Housemaid and companion, that's what she'd be. His housemaid and companion. He'd pay her a thousand a week, in cash, plus he'd put another two-fifty a week into a pension fund.

Pension fund?

For her retirement, Wayne patiently explained, in the unlikely event she ever wanted to move on.

April had to admire his attitude. She totted it up on a napkin, with a Bic pen she borrowed from a waiter.

Five thousand a month. Not exactly chickenfeed, especially since she wouldn't be paying any taxes. Better yet, her leech boyfriend, Nicky, wouldn't get a single penny of it.

But, housemaid? What was a housemaid, exactly?

Wayne told her she'd be doing a little bit of this and a little bit of that, and not a whole lot of anything. A pair of Finnish sisters dropped by twice a week to clean and sometimes cook. Mostly he did his eating in restaurants and he was out of town a lot.

He quaffed a pint of beer at one gulp and snapped his fingers, loud as a small-calibre gunshot, for another.

April had another question. What was a companion, exactly?

Somebody to talk to, said Wayne. Somebody to watch TV with, or maybe do a little gardening. He had a big yard, they could do some planting, daffodils or whatever . . .

It wasn't, from April's point of view, a very appetizing proposition. Wayne saw he was losing her. He said that, in daytime, they could sit out in the backyard in the shade of the weeping willow, listen to the birds and watch the horses trot down the street, clouds drifting by way up there in the blue sky. Did she like horses? It was a horsy neighbourhood, rural, in a way, zoned for pastures and barns and what have you . . . One of his neighbours had a couple of horses. He could buy one, if April thought she might like to ride.

April wasn't into horses. She hadn't been into horses when she was a little kid, and she sure as hell wasn't into horses now. Not even to bet on them. She told Wayne she appreciated his generosity, and that he seemed like a really nice person, but it was a big step, so she'd have to think about it. His eyes darkened. He shoved his big hands deep into his beard and gave himself a vigorous, protracted scratch.

He drank another pint of beer, wiped himself clean with the back of his hand. He gave her a look that said she was making a mistake, but there was nothing he could do about it, too bad.

April said she'd see him around, she hoped he enjoyed the show. Wayne mumbled something, used his teeth to rip open a bag of cashews.

As she was turning away from him, he seemed already to have forgotten her.

April spent the rest of the night flitting from bar to bar, doing that lap-dance thing, hustling, working hard, making money. She took taxis until, finally, Nicky showed up. By then she'd worked half a dozen joints and netted one hundred and ninety dollars in tips, plus appearance money. Nicky wasn't too impressed, but at least he didn't slap her around or punch her.

If Wayne hadn't been so big and so hairy and so full of confidence, she'd probably have forgotten all about him in the time it took to light a cigarette. If he hadn't looked so deeply into her soul with his lovely, velvety-mauve eyes, she definitely would have forgotten about him by two in the morning, when she finally called it quits.

Thinking, wrongly, that the night was over . . .

Lewis moaned, bringing April back. Was he okay? He looked just fine to her. His forehead was damp, the roots of his dark hair lank with perspiration. He was a little pale, maybe slightly feverish. Not dying, though. No, not overdosing. She was sure he wasn't dying, because she had taken such care to dilute the heroin.

But what if he *was* dying?

April leaned over Lewis. She rested her splayed hand lightly on his chest, over his heart.

Was his heart beating?

She didn't think so. If it was, she couldn't feel it. She pressed the side of her head against him. There it was, *ba-boomp, ba-boomp*.

Suddenly it stopped. She'd lost it. Where was it? April frantically moved her head around on Lewis's quiet chest. His heart had stalled, and he seemed to have stopped breathing.

April slapped him. She pried open his mouth and clumsily blew air into his lungs.

Lewis went, *murrph!*

She kissed him. Spontaneously, without a moment's thought. He had a shapely mouth. His lips were soft but firm. She liked the lingering taste of his mouthwash, toothpaste, the soft echo of her breath in his lungs, coming back at her.

But no matter how enthusiastically she kissed him, that cold fish wouldn't kiss her back.

Frustrated, not sure whether she felt slighted or not, April gave up and went into the kitchen. Wayne had told her no drinking allowed, but she desperately needed somebody to talk to, and where was Wayne now? Probably hunkered down with his back to the wall at a corner table in some smoky, pulse-pounding, low-life bar, a cigarette dangling from the corner of his downcast mouth, as he schemed to murder somebody.

April saw him clearly. He was glowering indiscriminately out at the crowd. His meaty hands rested on the table, his thick, wrinkled, chrome-scarred fingers wrapped around a bottle of Bud Lite. The Bud's label had been picked into a thousand tiny pieces.

Or maybe the picture was all wrong. Maybe Wayne was actually out there murdering somebody, making that long list of his just a tiny bit shorter. One thing for sure, though. Drinking or murdering, he'd have a butt hanging out of his mouth. Ambition was a major source of stress. She couldn't blame him for falling back into the habit, especially when he was away from the comfort and relative safety of his own home.

April mixed herself a pitcher of martinis. She got a martini glass down from the cupboard, a fresh pack of contraband Marlboros from the bedroom closet. Where was her lighter? Where she'd left it. She went outside, into the gathering dusk. A slice of moon hung low in the sky. The weeping willow, in silhouette, looked like an unbelievably monstrous mushroom. April slumped into a plastic replica Adirondack chair.

Wayne, clumsily attempting to seduce her, had spoken of clouds drifting across the sky, and the soft whinnying of horses.

April liked listening to the frogs. There were ditches all along the roads. Proper ditches, deep and wide, fringed with greenery, speckled with algae that was absolutely the most fantastic shade of green. In the summer, the ditches were jam-packed with frogs. Bullfrogs, and they were the chattiest, most talkative and sociable creatures April had ever known. She loved listening to them, and she worried for them when they suddenly fell silent. There were creatures out there in the dark, predators, who loved eating frogs. Coyotes. Feral cats. Raccoons.

Not that it had anything to do with frogs, or nature in general, but April also loved watching the airplanes. The airport was only a few miles away, on the other side of the river. The planes came in from the east and from the west. During the daylight hours they were fat and ungainly; at night they were bright stars gliding out of the night. April loved the sound of them, that low, shuddery rumble that must make the frogs sit up straight, and wonder just exactly what was out there.

April smoked cigarettes and drank martinis and listened to the frogs and watched airplanes and slapped at mosquitoes until she was sick and tired of the whole show.

8

Parker had hired a couple of guys with narrow minds and broad backs to move her few valuable pieces of furniture to Jack's house. To the house she must soon start thinking of as *her* house. Willows' nineteen-year-old son, Sean, had said he'd be home all day. But when the movers had arrived with her furniture, there was no one there. They'd waited for a while, and then unloaded the furniture and left it on the front porch. Willows and Parker had moved it inside themselves, piece by piece. Willows' furniture had to be rearranged to accommodate the new things. It was kind of fun, or not, depending on your attitude. Willows had scraped a knuckle, and cursed.

The furniture that had been replaced by Parker's belongings was temporarily stored in the garage. Getting everything out the door and down the steps and around the side of the house and across the lawn and through the awkwardly narrow gate and into the garage was another sweaty learning experience Willows would gladly have done without. By the time they'd finished he was bruised and bleeding, and had a minimum three-Aspirin headache. Parker, on the other hand, somehow managed to look fresh as an uncut daisy.

In the cool dimness of the garage, Willows sagged onto his suddenly retired sofa and leaned back against the lumpy cushions.

He closed his eyes, and didn't open them until he heard the sharp hiss of a beer being opened. Parker was standing in front of him, offering him a can of Kokanee. He thanked her, rolled the cold metal across his forehead and then sipped with disciplined gentility.

"Thank you."

"You're welcome. I'm going to the store. Want anything?"

"Not that I know of."

"Don't fall asleep, okay?"

"Promise," said Willows. Parker leaned over him and kissed him on the mouth and went away.

Willows sat there, enjoying the moment. There was something very appealing about hanging around in garages. He had no idea why. Maybe it was just one of those *guy* things. He drank some more beer. In the middle distance, an electric lawnmower whined unsteadily.

A small brown bird flew into the garage and made an abrupt U-turn without losing speed, and went out again.

Willows realized that he had somehow become complacent about his surroundings. The house didn't look anything like shabby, but the white trim could do with a coat of paint. Moving Parker's furniture had allowed him to see everything with a sharpened eye. He was shocked to realize how beaten up and worn down his own furniture had imperceptibly become. Well, teenagers were hard on furniture. So were cats. So, for that matter, was he. Standing in the garage, he fingered a dubious stain in his sofa's middle cushion. He and Claire were planning a garage sale, but was any of this stuff really worth anything? He'd talk it over with her. Maybe they should phone the Salvation Army or some other charitable organization, and just get rid of the stuff. He sipped at his beer until the can was empty, then shut and padlocked the garage door and strolled across the yard towards the house.

Annie was in the kitchen, making a milkshake. She'd filled a glass with chocolate ice cream and milk, and now she was mashing the ice cream with a spoon.

She smiled at her father as he entered the house. "Hi, Daddy, how's it going?"

Annie had blossomed into a lovely young girl – or woman, Willows wasn't sure how to categorize her. Annie was considerate of others and had a strong sense of herself. She continued to do well in school, had plenty of friends, and was blessed with a naturally sunny personality. But what Willows most admired about her was her social conscience. Annie knew right from wrong. She had powerful convictions, and wasn't afraid to speak up and defend them.

Despite all that, she was still a teenager, inescapably crammed full of conflicting emotions, and an equally overwhelming need for the twin demons of security and independence.

Willows returned her smile. "Hi, honey. Home from school already?"

Annie licked her spoon clean and pointed at the wall clock above the refrigerator. "It's way past five, Daddy."

Time flew, when you were humping worn-out furniture. Willows resisted the temptation to ask Annie why she was so late getting home from school. Probably she was cramming for a quiz or an exam. No, now he remembered why she'd come home late.

He said, "How'd your sax lesson go?"

Annie shrugged. "Okay, I guess." She grinned impishly. "It's harder than it sounds."

"You ought to start taping episodes of *The Simpsons*. You might pick up some hints from Lisa."

"Thanks a lot, Dad."

"You're welcome. I don't suppose Claire's back yet?"

"Where'd she go?" The cop's daughter, already an expert at casual interrogation.

"Out," said Willows. "I take it she's still there?"

"Don't ask me. I just got here." Annie drank some milkshake, licked her lips. "Sean phoned. He said he's sorry he wasn't there when the moving guys showed up; he had an appointment with Dr. Foster that he'd forgotten about."

Willows nodded his thanks. Almost a year ago to the day, Sean had been shot during an armed robbery at the convenience store where he was working the graveyard shift. The wound had caused serious bone and tissue loss and extensive nerve damage. Sean's outpatient therapy had recently been reduced to one session a week. His doctor, a sports-medicine specialist, had worked up a series of muscle-strengthening physical exercises, and saw him regularly. Willows said, "I'm going to take a quick shower. If Claire gets home, tell her we're going out for supper."

"Where?"

"I don't know, I hadn't really thought about it." Willows made a production of thinking about it now. He folded his arms across his chest, rested his chin in his hand, and frowned heavily. Annie rolled her eyes. He said, "You in the mood for Chinese food?"

"Sure!" Annie's face lit up. She was a big fan of stir-fried rice, Szechwan ginger beef, lemon chicken, hot pots . . . All the usual suspects.

In the shower, as the steaming water beat down on his aching back, Willows decided, not for the first time, that he wasn't getting enough exercise. He'd carried his half of a sofa the length of the backyard and his back hurt like hell. Claire, on the other hand, had gone off to the store whistling cheerfully, not a hair out of place. There was an eight-year difference in their ages. From where he was standing right that moment, it looked as if the gap was widening. Not that he was flabby, or even overweight. It was just that he lacked tone. At least he wasn't losing his hair, thank God. He wasn't really growing *old*. All he needed was a little more fresh air, and regular exercise.

Downstairs, the front door banged shut.

Sean.

He adjusted the temperature of the water so it was a few degrees hotter, and turned so he was standing directly beneath the spray. Where was Claire?

Parker was on her way back from the local greengrocer's, where she'd bought two bouquets of flowers: five virginal white and five passionate red tulips. She'd paid for the flowers, tucked them under her arm and walked out of the store and suddenly found herself trembling uncontrollably. She recognized immediately that she was suffering from an acute nervous reaction brought on by the simple act of buying the flowers. The tulips were symbolic of her love, and her deep commitment to Jack.

Fine, but what was she committing herself to, exactly?

Jack's children, Sean and Annie, seemed to have weathered the divorce. But they still had a lot of growing up to do. Sean was still recovering from the trauma of being shot and nearly killed, and he had a long way to go, years and years perhaps, until he was fully recovered from his physical and emotional wounds. Annie was a sweet child, but she was going to be a handful in the next few years. Much worse, Jack couldn't see it coming. Parker wondered how much divorce-related "acting out" Annie was going to do, and how much of her anger would be aimed at Parker.

But all of that was relatively small potatoes. Parker loved Annie, and Sean, as if they were her own children. There was no doubt in her mind that she'd be able to handle any problems that came up. The children she was truly concerned about were the ones she wanted to have with Jack. Unbelievably, she had committed herself to buying a half-share of his house, and living with him, without settling the incredibly crucial issue of children. It wasn't that Jack didn't want more children. On the contrary, sort of. Theoretically, he was all for it. The problem was, *when*. Parker was in her mid-thirties. Her biological clock was steadily ticking away. She'd read about women who'd given birth in their early fifties, but she didn't want to be in her mid-sixties when her surly teenage child turned on her. The sooner the better, that was the way she felt about it. The clock was ticking, and who could say with any degree of certainty when the alarm might go off? She wanted children. Two, at least, and preferably four or five. No, that was too many. Three, then.

She wanted to make love to Jack and not have to worry about the time of month, dependability of contraceptives, the risk of pregnancy.

She wanted to *be* pregnant. She wanted to experience all the joys and sorrows of motherhood. Well, Jack certainly knew how she felt, all her matronly ambitions. She'd made it clear to him. But, so what? She had to tell him again, be gently forceful with him, help him reach the decision they'd both, in the long run, be happiest with.

In the car, Parker took a small mirror from her purse and checked her lipstick. Six months ago, she'd carelessly dropped her holstered Glock into her purse. The heavy pistol had cracked the mirror's fake tortoiseshell frame and chipped the glass. Every time she used it, she swore she'd buy a new one the first chance she got. There was a Shoppers Drug Mart only a few blocks away. Why not now?

Because it was late. The kids would be starving. Jack, too. If he hadn't already started cooking when she got home, she'd suggest they go out to dinner.

She felt a lot better, now that she had clarified her thoughts, and acknowledged her fears, and worked out a simple but effective way to deal with them. Communication, isn't that what all the experts said was the secret to a successful relationship?

But sometimes the most satisfactory conversations were the ones you had all by yourself.

9

The TV perched on the fridge blared inanely as April mashed half a dozen – six nights' worth – of the small yellow pills she took when she absolutely had to get a good night's sleep. The pills were so powerful that they made her want to curl up on the kitchen floor and fall unconscious just looking at them. She hoped she wasn't about to feed Lewis a fatal overdose. Maybe she'd mix half the powder into his stew, and wait for a little while, see what happened. If he didn't conk out, she could pour the rest of the powder into his beer, or wine, or whatever.

If that didn't work, maybe she could sneak into the garage, borrow one of Wayne's precious box wrenches or a ballpeen hammer, and give Lewis a gentle whack on the head. April smiled. She'd think of something. Some crazy thing. Didn't she always? Of course she did.

Her last night as a lap-dancer, she'd come out of the bar and Nicky was parked on the street, the Caddy's engine rumbling, a peppy tune from the movie *Showgirls* blaring from the car's speakers. Nicky's idea of a sophisticated joke. He'd bought the fifteen-year-old car for one thousand dollars and had spent at least twice that much on the stereo. The Caddy was a high-fidelity sound system on wheels. The ugly damn beast weighed as much as an elephant, got about ten miles to the gallon, and burnt a quart of oil every time you started the engine. But all Nicky cared about was the big fins, the chrome, the shape of the taillights.

April's mental bitching was cut short when she noticed Wayne leaning casually against a slightly off-vertical parking meter. His smile was a mile wide. He pushed away from the meter and started towards her, burly arms extended. He meant to hug her! April couldn't remember the last time she'd been hugged. Nicky sometimes gave her a friendly pat on the rump, on those rare occasions when he wasn't actively pissed off at her. But a hug? Never.

She realized how desperately she needed to be hugged. To be cherished for herself, for who she was, rather than how many crumpled bills were stuffed in her sequined purse. She was starved for affection. How had Wayne known?

She melted into his arms. He enfolded her. She hadn't fully realized how huge he was. He loomed over her. Looking up, all she could see was beard. He smelled good. Home cooking, cigar smoke, brandy, and the rich scent of honest sweat. April vanished into him. He was all around her, encompassing her. He was her safe harbour. She felt like a kitten, snug and warm on the family hearth.

The *Showgirls* tune rattled the windowpanes and then there was nothing but broad-band silence. Nicky was always doing that, turning the volume knob the wrong way. Would he ever get it right? Maybe, if he lived long enough.

The Caddy's door creaked open and slammed shut. Nicky's steel-capped boot heels grated on asphalt.

April heard the scrape of the key in the trunk, a dull click as the trunk popped open.

Wayne tried to step away from her. She clung tightly to him, not wanting to let go. He gently disengaged, and turned and strode towards the gleaming overripe-plum-coloured flank of the Caddy.

Nicky had originally intended to use his new number-one wood. But the club had cost him several hundred dollars, and he was loath to risk damaging it. Maybe the putter? Better not, because he was sure to tighten up, check his swing. He settled on a five-iron. His favourite club. He'd take a dinner-plate-size divot outta that punk's skull . . .

Wayne yanked Nicky away from the trunk, spun him around.

Nicky had to tilt his head slightly to look the guy in the eye. He was big, but Wayne was bigger. And heavier. Nicky stepped back. He was acutely conscious that his back swing was a little too rapid, but felt it was understandable, given the circumstances. He bent his right knee as he whipped the club around.

The air was bruised by the hard smack of accelerating metal impacting on vulnerable flesh.

Nicky's physiognomy buckled. It was as if he had metamorphosed in a split second from a more or less standard-issue human being into an animated three-dimensional cartoon character. His sallow, unshaven cheeks collapsed. His hair rose up off his sweat-drenched scalp. His mouth was full of snaggly teeth, and his eyes bulged so much that they threatened to fall right out of his head.

April, too, was a little startled.

Wayne moved plenty fast, for a big man.

He'd caught the head of the five-iron in his meaty fist. Now he rotated his wrist, and pulled. The club leapt out of Nicky's two-handed grip. Wayne bent the shaft until it snapped. Nicky, sucking wind, sounded an awful lot like an overworked sump pump. He pulled a rusty Tijuana switchblade. Wayne dropped the two pieces of the shattered club in the gutter. He hit Nicky in the belly with an economical left hook. Nicky folded like a cheap suitcase. But he gamely held onto the knife, you had to give him that much.

Wayne said, "April ain't your sweetheart no more, get it?"

Nicky tried to stab Wayne in the knee. His movements were sluggish and entirely predictable. Wayne disdainfully slapped away his arm and popped him with a stiff overhand right. His fist couldn't have moved more than six inches, but the punch was power-packed. The back of Nicky's skull shattered the Caddy's curbside taillight. His flailing elbows dented the fender. Yellowed teeth clattered on the pavement like a pair of desperately thrown dice. He uttered a garbled wailing sound, high-pitched to low, that was like the death rattle of a mortally wounded set of bagpipes, and sat down hard on the pavement. His shirt was splattered with blood. He was unconscious, or near enough to unconscious not to be concerned about it. His knuckles grazed the oil-stained asphalt. His head lolled slowly forward until it settled onto the curb.

A small crowd had gathered. April recognized several of her fellow indentured workers. They eyed her jealously.

Wayne grabbed a handful of lapel and lifted Nicky clear of the road, lowered him none too gently into the spacious trunk. Then he went around to the front of the car, killed the engine and walked back and tossed the keys in the trunk and carefully shut it.

Somebody in the crowd said, "Man, that guy licked Nicky like he was a two-cent stamp!"

April saw her ex-boyfriend about a week later, on the BCTV noon news. The illegally parked Caddy had been towed to a chain-link-and-razor-wire-wrapped compound. The tow-truck's unintelligent driver readily admitted he'd heard Nicky's frenzied screams but assumed the racket was due to mechanical problems. He explained to the viewing audience that he'd diagnosed a broken drive shaft or maybe a thrown rod. Nicky's face was streaked with gore and puffed up to approximately twice its normal size. He blamed the towing company for his injuries, and righteously squawked that he was going to sue their miserable asses into bankruptcy. But his eyes had a furtive, hunted look, and he gratefully settled, on the spot, for a sum equal to the towing and storage charges, plus one hundred goodwill bucks.

The camera zoomed in on him as he duct-taped a ragged square of red plastic over the Caddy's shattered taillight lens. Asked about his plans for the future, Nicky muttered a few words about friendlier climes, as he scrambled into the car and fired up the big V-8 engine. The Caddy and superficially-attractive-but-perhaps-overly-persistent BCTV reporter vanished in a roiling black cloud of forty-weight smoke.

April, jiggling the little vial of yellow pills, said, "Thus endeth Nicky."

Wayne filled the kitchen doorway and then he was through it. April didn't try to hide the fact that she was startled.

"Jeez, Wayne! How long have you been here?"

"Just drifted in this very minute." Wayne shrugged out of his jacket, slung it over a chair. His nostrils flared. "Somethin' smells better'n a dead horse. What's for supper?"

"Beef stew." April eyed his new freckles. "What's that stuff on your hands? Wayne, is that *blood*?"

Wayne frowned. He stared down at his hands for a moment and then lifted one to his mouth, gave it a lick. His frown deepened. He got that dark, glowering look in his eyes that April had learned to dread. "You say somethin', honey-pie?"

"Not really." April hit the remote. *Baywatch.*

Wayne, switching gears, said, "You could be on that show."

"Get out of here!" April was pleased. She tried not to show it, but really, what was the point.

"You're so beautiful."

"I am not!"

"Yes you are." Wayne went over to the sink. He squeezed a dollop of Sunlight detergent onto his open palm, turned on the taps, and began to wash himself. Glancing at April over his shoulder, he said, "I go crazy with desire just lookin' at you. I gotta squeeze one eye shut, to avoid sensory overload." He turned off the taps, used a dishtowel to dry his hands. "C'mon over here and gimme a smooch."

April wandered over, pursed her lips, and received a cursory peck on the cheek.

Wayne said, "You ever miss him?"

"Who?"

"Cadillac-trunk boy."

"Are you kidding me? Miss him? Don't make me laugh!"

"But do you?"

April shrugged. "Not much. Sometimes." She whistled tunelessly, and kicked out her foot, suddenly restless as a wayward child.

Wayne said, "It's okay."

"Is it?"

"I understand."

"You do?"

Wayne looked her in the eye. He said, "I know every last little thing about you, baby. Parts tiny as the cogs in a watch." He vented the low rumble she'd eventually learned to identify as an amused chuckle. "I know what makes you *tick*, sugar-lumps."

And he did, too. He knew her inside out and upside and down, from top to bottom and backwards and forwards. He knew her too darn well, when you came right down to it. In a way, his constant insights into her motivation and behaviour were kind of frustrating. She'd open her mouth and he'd provide her with a deadly accurate line of dialogue. She'd cock her hip or flash an eye and he'd know what was bothering her and, every last nut and bolt, what he had to do to make things right.

Frustrating?

No, it was a lot worse that. It was downright irritating.

How could she ever be on equal terms with somebody who was always one up on her?

April turned up the gas under the big stainless-steel pot. The stew began to bubble. She turned the gas down a smidgen, and then cut half a loaf of French bread into fat slices and put the bread in a bowl.

"Want the bread heated up?"

Wayne grunted. April put the bowl in the microwave, punched buttons. Thirty seconds on high heat ought to do it. She uncorked a bottle of red wine and poured a half glass into the stew.

Wayne said, "Damn, but I'm hungry. Nothing like hard work to give a man an appetite." A sudden thought lit up his face. "Not that I'm through yet," he added.

"You going out again?"

"You don't want to know."

April's mouth was dry.

The microwave beeped. The machine advised them, via its miniature electronic message board, to enjoy their meal.

She thought, Stew needs bread just like I need Wayne. But then she found herself wondering if she had it backwards, if maybe it wasn't Wayne who was the truly needy person in their relationship.

10

Lester Rules' dingy two-room apartment was located a block off Main Street, directly above a corner store locally famous for the huge quantities of potent Chinese "cooking wine" it sold to the area's inhabitants – the mostly down and mostly out. The building was falling apart; sheets of lead-based paint scaled off the wooden siding, and the siding itself was pulling away from rust-pinched nails. The owner, under threat of imminent demolition, had patched the leaks in the roof and recently brought the sprinkling system up to code, but otherwise hadn't spent a penny on the building in the past fifteen years.

Inside, there was more scaling paint, the pervasive smell of damp, and mould, and intensive rot.

At the top of the stairs a dead lightbulb dangled from a frayed cord. Willows reached up and flicked the bulb. It was loose in its socket. He screwed it in. Forty watts, but it would do. There were at least a million ways for a cheap landlord to save a buck, and that was just one of them. Parker turned off her flashlight, saving the city a few precious pennies that she doubted would be spent on social housing. Her stomach was bothering her. Maybe it was the Chinese dinner, which she was still digesting.

The door to Lester Rules' apartment was wide open. A uniformed constable stepped aside as Willows and Parker made their

way down the narrow hallway towards him. The cop held a delicate bone-china teacup in his massive hand. His eye on Parker,
the cop said, "You just missed the paramedics."

"Who called them?"

The cop jerked his thumb. "Woman down the end of the hall.
The door was open, she looked inside, saw the body."

Parker said, "Get her name?"

"Marjorie Berg. You want to talk to her, she's more than ready."

Parker smiled.

The cop, emboldened, said, "She offers you a cookie, don't make
the mistake of turning her down."

"How's the tea?"

"Hot and sweet." The cop almost said, "Just like me." But didn't,
though he let Parker read the message in his eyes, as Willows
brushed past him.

Lester Rules' tiny apartment was furnished with a swayback
single bed, a tallboy bureau, and a wooden kitchen table and three
mismatched chairs. If Lester had owned more furniture, there
wouldn't have been any place to put it. A slump-shouldered refrigerator and ancient gas stove crowded up against the far wall. The
door to the bathroom was off the hinges. The tub had been white,
but now it was green. A tap dripped steadily into a cracked and
badly stained pedestal sink. The floor in both rooms was covered
with linoleum so old it had lost all its colour. Rules didn't appear
to have owned a broom.

Popeye Rowland, Willows' second-favourite Medical Examiner,
sat at the table in the least uncomfortable of the three kitchen
chairs. As Willows and Parker walked into the apartment he wriggled his bushy black eyebrows, encouraging his pince-nez to fall
out of his left eye socket and into the cupped palm of his hand.
He turned the disc of glass over, and put it carefully away in a
fitted leather case. He slipped the case into his pants pocket.
Dolefully, he said, "Got some bad news, folks."

"What's that?" said Parker.

Popeye reached out and gently gripped her arm. "Steel yourself, young lady. Be brave. Be strong."

Popeye was wearing two pairs of throwaway latex gloves, and who could blame him – Lester Rules was an addict, and the HIV infection rate among the approximately one thousand injection-drug users crammed into the city's downtown eastside was an estimated 25 per cent. Parker wore black leather. She disengaged from Popeye's wrinkly fingers one by one. "You're going to tell me he's dead, aren't you?"

"Deader than Ringo Starr."

"You're thinking of John Lennon," said Parker.

Popeye shrugged. He'd never been able to tell them apart; why start now.

Willows said, "Time of death?"

"His time came when his time was up," said Popeye with heavy-handed playfulness.

Willows held his temper in check. "Could you please be less specific, Popeye?"

"I'd say he died late this afternoon. Or maybe early this evening."

"Cause of death?"

"This trained professional is willing to hazard an educated guess that the poor guy suffered a self-inflicted drug overdose. Heroin, most likely." The M.E. sighed theatrically. "But for all I know, he might've pumped a solution of rat poison into his vein. Forgive me for flaunting my hard-earned medical knowledge, but I'm here to tell you that people do the weirdest goddamn things."

"Art Linkletter," said the cop by the door.

"You're hereby promoted to Chief," said Popeye.

The M.E. was no Sherlock. He was barely a Watson. The squalid little room was littered with schoolboy clues. Burnt paper matches and a bent, fire-blackened spoon lay on top of the bureau. So did several balls of tinfoil, and a small bottle of bleach. A syringe was clenched in the dead man's hand. The plunger had been fully depressed, and there were traces of blood in the barrel. A frayed shoelace was tied tightly around the corpse's grossly swollen right arm, an inch or two above the elbow. The tiny puncture had leaked a thin line of blood.

If that wasn't more than enough evidence to point the M.E. in the direction of a heroin overdose, there was more.

Rules' face was barely large enough to contain his smile. He looked as if he'd gone to Heaven, and *then* died.

Willows crouched. Rules was about five-foot-six, on the thin side of emaciated. He needed a shave, and a haircut. He was probably past due for his weekly shower. Willows took his wrist in his hand. The flesh was cool, and yielding. Rigor had come and gone. Willows checked Rules' watch against his own.

Popeye said, "You were hoping for a cracked crystal, minute and hour hands and maybe even second stopped at the precise time of death, weren't you?"

Willows ignored him. Lester's watch was a virtually indestructible Timex Ironman. There was almost no chance that it had stopped ticking at the time of death. But though Willows would never admit it, Popeye was at least partly right. For as long as Willows could remember, there'd been a running bet among the homicide detectives that, sooner or later, a victim's watch would be stopped by a blow at the time of death. Every detective in the squad added a dollar a month to the kitty. After eight years, when the total reached five hundred dollars, Inspector Homer Bradley had reluctantly accepted custodianship. Now the pot was well over a thousand dollars, and was prized as much for the hundreds of old one-dollar bills it contained as for the cash value of the money.

Willows said, "He's wearing his watch on his left wrist, so he must be right-handed, correct?"

Parker nodded her agreement.

"So why did he tie off his right arm?"

Popeye snorted. His definition of a detective was a guy who was smart enough to put *both* his feet up on his desk. Homicide evidence was meaningless, outside a medical context. The M.E. firmly believed that 99 per cent of a detective's work was done for him, while he slept, by highly trained followers of Hippocrates, fellows much like Popeye himself. He snapped shut his black leather bag and started for the door.

Popeye was single, unattached. A lonely guy. His habit was to linger at crime scenes. Willows said, "You're leaving already?"

"There's two more of these unlucky fellows three blocks away, and another over by Commercial Drive. It's going to be a long and busy night, Jack. We'll all be glad when it's over."

Willows found Lester's wallet in the right-side back pocket of his pants. More evidence that Lester was a righty. The wallet was stuffed with cash. Willows counted five hundred dollars in crisp new twenties with consecutive serial numbers. He held a bill up to the light. It looked authentic to him – but then, he was no expert. Lester owned no credit cards. He had a social-security card, and government-issue picture ID, but that was it. The wallet yielded a condom in a shiny Mylar wrapper, indicating that Lester was an optimist; though it was impossible to determine whether he'd hoped for sex, or drugs.

Willows' groping fingers stumbled across a small black-and-white photograph with piecrust edges. The picture was of a boy about five or six years old. He was sitting behind the wheel of a split-windshield Ford. A '52, Willows believed. The boy had both hands on the wheel and his smile was a mile wide. Could that be Lester, in happier days? Definitely. Willows slipped the photo back into the wallet.

Parker was over by the window, looking out at the night. A patrol car was parked on the far side of the street, the cop behind the wheel punching buttons on his computer, his face lit up by the washed-out, pale grey glow of the screen.

The bone-china cup rattled against the saucer, as the cop by the door lit a cigarette. Willows glared at him. Trailing a cloud of smoke, the cop backed into the hallway.

Parker turned away from the window. Lester Rules was well known to the police. He was a street-level dealer, and had a record long as an orangutan's arm. Lester, like many of the city's career addicts, sold dope so he could afford dope. Given his background, his sudden lack of future was entirely predictable.

Parker had conducted a desultory search of the small room, but now, spurred on by Willows' observation that Lester Rules was wearing his watch on the wrong wrist, she started in all over again. Aside from the clothes he was wearing, Lester owned three shirts and four pairs of socks and three pairs of underpants and two pairs of pants.

Parker found a paring knife under the mattress. She didn't blame Lester for taking precautions to defend himself. There was no telephone in the apartment, and in this neighbourhood, no matter how loudly you screamed, there was no guarantee anyone would bother to hear you.

Parker found an envelope taped to the back of one of the bureau drawers. The envelope contained three five-dollar bills. She pulled the bureau away from the wall. Dust.

Willows was in the bathroom, poking around.

Parker checked inside the refrigerator. Lester had been a light eater, apparently. She looked inside the oven, and discovered that Lester was sharing his apartment with an extended family of cockroaches.

It had taken them only a few minutes to search the apartment, and they had done a thorough job. There were no signs of a struggle, or any other indications – other than the shoelace on the wrong arm – that there was anything amiss.

Parker said, "What d'you think?"

Willows took one last look around. He said, "I think Lester overdosed, and died."

"What about the watch?" said Parker.

Willows shrugged. The watch bothered him. But not that much. He put away his notebook.

Parker said, "That cop must've finished his tea, by now. Why don't we take Marjorie's cup back to her."

"See if we can fiddle a cookie," said Willows.

Parker decided not to say anything about the cockroaches.

Marjorie Berg was in her eighties, thin and spry, as bright-eyed as a kitten. Her breath smelled of brandy. She wore a bulky wool sweater and tartan pants, sensible shoes. Her clothes were a size too large for her, but the sweater was clean, her pants were pressed. Her apartment was no larger than Lester's but it was as spotlessly clean as a surgery. The walls and ceiling were white, and had been recently painted. There were several framed pictures of family and friends. The floor was carpeted, and the heavy oak furniture, though it dated from the thirties, had been lovingly cared for. A clay pot of miniature daffodils stood on the table, next to an open book.

Marjorie clapped her hands lightly together and asked her two guests if they'd like a nice cup of tea. Her voice was slurred, and she was a little unsteady on her feet.

It wasn't just the daffodils that were potted, observed Parker.

Willows hesitated, and was lost, swept away by Marjorie's obvious desire to play the good hostess, despite the hour. The kettle had just boiled. It was no trouble, really . . .

Marjorie made the tea. She offered them a wee medicinal drop of brandy, and was not the least put out when they declined. She poured a staggeringly generous shot into her own teacup. The oven door was opened on a fresh batch of chocolate-chip cookies.

They sat at the table. Marjorie volunteered that her husband had been a logger. His name was Bill, and he'd died fifteen years ago. She pointed out several pictures. Parker acknowledged that Bill was a handsome fellow. Marjorie had been a receptionist. She benefitted from a minuscule pension, and somehow always managed to make ends meet.

Between her second and third cookies, as Marjorie poured her a fresh cup of tea, Parker asked her how well she'd known Lester Rules.

Not at all, as it turned out. Lester was the secretive type, though you couldn't say he kept to himself, because his friends were always coming around, at all hours of the day and night. Marjorie didn't know any of them by name.

She hadn't heard a struggle, or anything like a cry for help. She'd had no idea Lester was a drug addict or that he was a small-time dealer. She'd noticed, passing his open door, that his apartment was always a mess. Men! Especially bachelors! The building was old, and infested with cockroaches. Lester didn't seem to mind. She'd seen a huge, shiny bug in the hallway, right outside his door . . . By now, Marjorie was a long way past a little bit tipsy. Her words increasingly slurred, she said she wanted to attend Lester's funeral, if there was a service.

Parker promised to let her know.

Marjorie fumbled half a dozen warm cookies into a paper napkin and pressed them into Parker's hand. She looked up at Parker with her clear blue eyes and said if she'd ever had a daughter, she would have wanted her to turn out just like Claire.

Parker thanked her, and gave her a quick hug.

Driving back to 312 Main to do the paperwork, Willows and Parker agreed that, despite a few minor discrepancies in the crime scene, Lester Rules had almost certainly died as a consequence of an accidental overdose.

They couldn't have been more wrong.

11

April wore a black lace push-up bra, a black leather mini-skirt, a heavy black leather Harley-Davidson motorcycle jacket, and the jaunty black leather cap Wayne had bought her for her last birthday. The cap was an exact replica of the one Marlon Brando had worn in the classic movie, *The Wild One*. Wayne owned the video. April couldn't even begin to count the number of times he'd watched it – and she didn't mean just the exciting parts, either. He always watched the whole thing, from beginning to end, right through the credits. And it was in black and white! There was just no accounting for some people's tastes. She had to admit that Marlon was pretty cool, though. The guy had been a hunk, fifty or sixty years ago.

April stuck her fingers deep into her second king-size martini, and fished around for the last of the olives. She speared the olive on an artificial fingernail, and carried it dripping to her mouth, licked away the last few drops of booze. She pretended to be unaware that Lewis was watching her closely as she popped the olive into her mouth, and chewed noisily.

Lewis said, "Good?"

"Yummy!"

Lewis wore Wayne's terrycloth bathrobe, the one with the petit-point Harley on the back. Wayne had paid an elderly woman eleven hundred dollars to stitch the motorcycle on the back of the robe, and if you asked him, he'd tell you it was worth every penny, and mean it. And he was right, in a sense, because the woman's hourly wage had worked out to considerably less than she'd have earned flipping burgers at McDonald's.

April lit a Marlboro. She offered the pack to Lewis, sparked her lighter for him.

They sat there at the table, April starting her third vodka martini and Lewis with his very first beer. Lewis was a little high now, but not too bad, nowhere near nodding off, April hoped.

She said, "How're you feeling?"

"Okay." Lewis thought it over for a while. Or maybe he was thinking about something else. "Not bad," he amended.

"You look good."

Lewis absorbed that one without flinching.

April tried again. "Handsome."

Lewis pulled hard on his Marlboro. The smoke went deep into his body. Half a minute later, he exhaled.

"So tell me more about your family," said April. "Got any brothers?"

Lewis shook his head in a lateral plane.

"What's that supposed to mean?"

"Nope."

"Too bad. Sisters?"

Lewis frowned.

April said, "Got any sisters, Lewis?

He held up three fingers. After a long while he said, "Three."

April was fairly sure that he'd already claimed to be an only child, but let it slide. Maybe he'd been afraid of what she might do to them, kidnap them or whatever, and now he was starting to trust her. She said, "Are they pretty?"

"Yeah, sure."

April, burning with jealousy, drank an inch of martini. "What're their names?"

He shrugged.

"Hey! Wake up!"

"I dunno."

"Yes you do!" April was on her feet, her leather jacket's chromed zippers and buckles flashing bright as her eyes. "Don't you bull-shit me, Lewis!"

"Kathy. Elizabeth . . ." You only had to glance at Lewis to see how hard he was thinking.

April impatiently stomped her pretty foot.

"And Veronica," said Lewis heavily. He took another long pull on his cigarette, noticed the beer, sipped.

"Veronica?"

Something in April's voice roused him. "What about her?" he said belligerently.

April wasn't sure. All she knew was that she was angry, and she didn't know why, which made her even madder. Veronica was a stupid, stupid name. It was so old-fashioned. Until now, the only Veronica she'd ever heard of was the rich one in the Archie comics, although now she came to think of it she believed Veronica had her own comic book, or at least shared one with Betty.

Come to think of it, Betty was short for Elizabeth. Lewis had said one of his sisters was named Elizabeth. Betty.

Was he fucking around with her?

April grabbed the jar of olives and unscrewed the lid and tossed it aside. She jabbed viciously down with her index finger, impaling an olive. Her fingernail had pierced right through it and was sticking out the other side. If the olive had been a migrating salmon, she'd have killed it. Not that she cared for fish. She put her finger in her mouth and pursed her lips and withdrew her finger, leaving the olive behind. She studied her fingers as she chewed on the olive. The nails were sharp as knives. If she leapt across the table she'd take Lewis completely by surprise. If she wanted to, she could rip his stupid eyes out before he had time to blink.

April speared another olive, and then another, and another. Olives were sinfully full of calories. She ate another, and another, until she'd started to loathe herself for her lack of self-control.

Now she was okay. She wasn't angry at Lewis any more. For now, he was safe.

She said, "What's she look like?"

"Who?"

"All of them, but especially Veronica." April drained her glass and picked up the sterling shaker and poured herself a refill. "Tell me about Veronica."

"She's . . . the oldest."

"Good. How old is she?"

Lewis mulled that one over for a while. Finally he said, "Twenty-nine."

"That's pretty old, Lewis. She married?"

He nodded.

"What's her husband's name?"

"Ron."

"What's he do?"

"Accountant." Lewis dropped the stub of his cigarette hissing into his beer.

"Any kids?"

"Not that I know of."

"How come?"

Shrug.

"They live in the city?"

"Saskatoon."

"Too bad," said April enigmatically. "So tell me, what's she look like? Is she a blonde like me?"

Lewis said, "Yeah, I think so . . ."

April grilled him like a steak, until she'd learned more about his trio of sisters than he'd known he could tell. Then she made a fresh batch of lovely martinis, got Lewis another Budweiser from the fridge, fired up Marlboros for both of them, settled back down in her chair and started to tell him all about her own dysfunctional, totally screwed-up family. She had just finished describing her straight-from-hell mother when the front doorbell chimed the opening bars of "Hotel California."

There was a brief silence. Lewis glanced worriedly at April. She put her finger to her eternally pouting lips, shushing him. He heard the scratch of metal on metal, key on lock.

Now somebody was pounding on the door with his fist. The sound of the blows, and April's shouted name, rattled through the house.

Lewis said, "Who's that?"

"Wayne."

The name was vaguely familiar. Lewis frowned, got it. "Your boyfriend?"

April shrugged with feigned carelessness.

"Why don't you let him in?"

"Why should I?"

Wayne had traded in his fists for his boots. He was apparently determined to kick the door to splinters. The thunderous crash of boot on door was not much short of apocalyptic.

Lewis helped himself to a Marlboro. He said, "Maybe you should get dressed."

"I *am* dressed."

"Well then, maybe I should get dressed."

April's reply was lost to history, for in that moment the door crashed open and there was the sound of a large body hitting the floor at speed, and then a torrent of foul oaths, and then a silence more dreadful than everything that had gone before.

Heavy footsteps stomped towards them.

April's pointy, diamond-studded tongue lightly touched her lips. Her sharp nails dug into her thigh. She flushed, and began to hyperventilate.

Wayne burst into the kitchen. He was so enormously large that it was as if the room had been inhabited by an eclipse. He took in the situation at a glance. Ignoring Lewis, he scooped up April in his arms and kissed her passionately.

"How's my baby?"

April tugged at her skirt. "Put me down."

"Glad to see me?"

"Put me down!"

"Who's the twerp?"

"Lewis, meet Wayne." April had held on tight to her martini glass. She sipped and sighed. "Wayne, meet Lewis."

Wayne sat down at the table. He hauled April onto his lap. He wore black leather Harley-Davidson gloves, a black leather Harley-Davidson jacket and matching Harley-Davidson chaps, a black T-shirt emblazoned with a large Harley-Davidson logo, heavy black motorcycle boots, a devil-black "shorty" motorcycle helmet, and aviator-style Harley-Davidson sunglasses. He shucked the gloves and jacket and reached across the table, helping himself to Lewis's Budweiser.

A pair of tattooed Harleys, authentic in every detail, graced Wayne's thick left and right arms. He wore several heavy gold biker rings, and a Harley-Davidson wristwatch.

Lewis furtively checked for Harley earrings. No dice.

"What the hell you lookin' at!"

Wayne's natural tone of voice was similar to that of a mortally distraught warthog. At full bellow, he should have required a noise-pollution permit. Lewis quailed. He looked like a man who'd been shot dead half an hour earlier, and just that moment figured out what had happened to him. He sank low in his chair. His eyes skittered around the room, finally settling on April.

Wayne shouted, "Don't look at her, punk!"

Lewis squeezed his eyes shut and then covered them with his hands. He began to cry, his body shaking uncontrollably, tears of anguish leaking between his palsied fingers.

April screamed, "Now look what you've done!"

Wayne was instantly contrite. "I'm sorry, honey. It's just that . . . who in hell is this guy, anyway?"

"None of your business!" snapped April. She lit a cigarette, and exhaled into Wayne's face. The pale blue smoke clung to his beard as early morning mist clings to a heavily treed mountaintop. She said, "He's the guy I told you I was going to get for you."

"The fall guy?"

April's tone was caustic. "That's not exactly how I'd refer to him in his presence."

Chastised, Wayne stomped over to the fridge and yanked open the door and scooped up three cans of Budweiser. His gold rings flashed as he made a fist and brutally punched the refrigerator door shut. He popped open a beer and quickly emptied it. The second can met an identical fate. He opened the third can, and paused to wipe a tideline of foam from his beard.

April pointed towards the refrigerator. "Look what you did."

"What?"

"You dented the door, you big ape."

Wayne smiled. "Yeah?" He sounded pleased.

"You're so *proud* of yourself, aren't you?"

"I guess so. Come to think of it. Wouldn't you be?"

April snorted in disgust. "You kick the door all to hell, bull your way in here like a goddamn storm trooper . . ."

"I broke the door down because you wouldn't open it and my key didn't fit the goddamn lock." Wayne's fist came down on the two empty cans, flattening them thin as coins. "You changed the lock, didn't you?"

April nodded. She poured herself another martini.

Wayne was perplexed. "Now why in hell'd you go and do a crazy thing like that, for God's sake?"

"Duh . . ." said April, rolling her pretty eyes.

"Back off, honey. All's I'm doin' is asking."

April thought it over, decided to bear the conversational burden just a little bit longer. She said, "You were gone a long time. Where were you?"

Wayne glanced across the table at Lewis, who had stopped crying but continued to shudder spasmodically.

"Forget him," said April. "He's harmless."

"You know where I was," whined Wayne. "Like they say, takin' care of business. Bumping people off, to be exact."

April had finished her martini. She put her pretty feet up on the table, and wriggled her toes. Too sweetly, she said, "Do you happen to remember how long you were gone, before you finally came home tonight?"

Wayne mulled it over. His fingers picked at his beard.

April said, "Three days, Wayne. Then you come waltzing in, shovel some stew into your gut, burp twice, and walk out. You enjoy your meal? You never even bothered to say boo."

Wayne made his face go all contrite.

"I thought you were dead," explained April. "Murdered, or fallen off your motorcycle, smeared all over the goddamn asphalt, your keys stolen by some drug-addled psycho biker friend of yours, on his way over with a bunch of his slack-ass buddies, thinking to take an unfriendly poke at lonely, helpless little April."

"I got no friends, biker or otherwise," protested Wayne.

"Okay, point taken. But there's people you ride with who *think* they're your friends, aren't there? You dumped your bike, these same people'd dip their greasy thieving hands into your pocket before you'd stopped breathing, wouldn't they?"

"Maybe," admitted Wayne.

"Be over here in a shot, wouldn't they?"

Wayne's teeth chewed worriedly at the fringes of his beard. He showed the whites of his eyes. Finally he reluctantly said, "Yup."

"So tell me, you still mad I changed the locks?"

"I dunno . . ."

"Wayne!"

"Okay, okay . . . I'm *sorry*." Wayne reached over, effortlessly picked up the chair April was sitting on, and lowered it onto his lap. He put his arms around her. "Miss me, babe?"

"Of course I did," said April. She trailed a proprietary hand over Wayne's grossly bulging gut, and then stretched a shapely leg across the table and rumpled Lewis's hair with her foot. "I missed you like crazy," she said, "right up to the minute I grabbed my brand-new loverboy!"

12

Addicts were dying like flies, all over the city. Siren after siren wailed the same hopeless tune. The morgue was jumping, the only sour note being that gurneys and clean sheets were in short supply. Teams of exhausted homicide detectives worked far into the night, knowing full well that all they were getting was the cream. In the morning, and in the gruesome days to follow, plenty more corpses were bound to rise to the surface.

In their race to the ultimate finish line, Melvin Ladner had finished six to eight hours behind Lester Rules.

"He's still warm," said Popeye Rowland. The M.E. swept his hand over Melvin Ladner's eyes, expertly shutting them. He rested his pudgy palm on Melvin's forehead, as if in belated benediction. "Warm as toast." He smiled. "Which figures, if you think about it, because he *is* toast."

Mel Dutton took a moment to switch lenses – from the 28-mil wide-angle to an 85-mil more suitable for portraits. He straddled the corpse, took several carefully composed shots, and then let the camera hang from the strap around his neck as he got out his pen and notebook, and wrote down the date and case number, Melvin Ladner's name and occupation, the model Nikon he'd used, as well as the lenses and *f*-stops, brand and speed of his colour film.

Mel Dutton and Popeye Rowland were so physically alike – both of them short and bulky and balding – that they might have been brothers. But Popeye was a cynical, squinty-eyed pragmatist, whereas Dutton had worked hard to cultivate the image of a sensitive *artiste*.

Dutton glanced around. Popeye was industriously cleaning trace elements of blood from his thermometer – and who could blame him? Parker and Willows were in the kitchen, probably checking out Melvin's cupboards with an eye to a tasty bacon-and-egg breakfast. Or, in the case of Parker, bacon and bean sprouts.

The uniform by the door was lip-reading the sports section of yesterday's paper.

What mattered was that no one was paying any attention to Mel Dutton.

A couple of hotshot drug-squad cops, Ken DelMonte and Tony LoBrio, would be arriving at any moment, if the crackle of the radio could be believed. But all that mattered was that DelMonte and LoBrio weren't here now, they weren't here yet.

Dutton seized the moment. He saw his window of opportunity, and jumped through it. Bending, he lifted Melvin Ladner's left eyelid, and then straightened and peered anxiously through the Nikon's viewfinder.

Ladner lay on his back, legs crossed at the ankle and his arms spread wide. His face was split by an ear-to-ear smile. The bloody hypo was still inserted in his swollen arm. It looked as if Ladner had died laughing. What a shot! Dutton decided to call the picture *Winker*.

He delicately fine-tuned the focus, and was no more than a split-second away from taking the shot when he noticed that Ladner's eyelid had slid shut.

"Son of a bitch!"

Willows appeared in the kitchen doorway. Popeye glared over his burly shoulder. The uniformed cop rattled his paper.

Dutton adjusted his beret. "As you were, folks. Minor technical problem, a mere glitch. Nothing to concern yourselves about. Holster your weapons, resume duties . . ." Dutton fiddled with the

Nikon until interest had faded, then swiftly bent and pried the eyelid open.

"Now stay put, damn you!" he hissed.

The Nikon had an autowinder. Dutton fired off three shots in half as many seconds. Then, always the pro, he lowered Ladner's left eyelid and raised the right, and finished off his roll of film.

If you were going to do something wrong, do it absolutely right.

In the kitchen, Parker found a .38 Colt snubnose revolver wrapped in a plastic bag that had been hidden in a box of Raisin Bran.

Willows said, "Two scoops of raisins and one scoop of thirty-eight Specials. No wonder it's such a popular cereal."

Parker flipped open the cylinder. Six rounds. The revolver was fully loaded.

Willows said, "That's a good sign. It means nobody's been shot."

"Lately."

"That's good enough for me," said Willows. The cookie jar was full of stale cookies. He emptied the sugar bowl into the sink. Sugar. The bread box held an unopened loaf of sliced rye and a little less than half a loaf of cracked whole wheat. Willows squeezed the bread to death. His interest had been piqued by Parker's discovery of the illegal firearm. But now, already, he was fading. He yawned. He'd been up all day and now most of the night, and tomorrow didn't look any slower than yesterday.

Poking around in a dead man's apartment was tedious and emotionally draining work, especially when the corpse was a junkie. Injection addicts hid their "works" everywhere you could think of, plus a whole lot of places you'd never think of. Needle-stick was always on a cop's mind when he was dealing with addicts. Kevlar gloves were available, but they were so bulky and thick that if you wore them during a frisk, the perp could hide a cannon between his legs, and never get caught.

He swung open a cupboard door on a dozen or more stacked tins of Campbell's tomato soup.

Campbell's was his own preferred brand. But a dozen tins seemed a bit excessive. Maybe Ladner had taken advantage of a case-lot sale. Maybe, but probably not. Willows carefully examined the tins one by one. Detecting nothing unusual, he peeled away several labels. As far as he could see, the tins of soup were merely tins of soup. He pulled open drawers until he found Ladner's can opener, and opened up a tin. The contents looked and smelled and had the consistency of tomato soup. He probed with a spoon. Nothing. He opened a second can, and then another, and another.

Soup, soup, soup.

Parker drifted past. She said, "What've you got there?"

Willows dipped his index finger into a tin. He sucked the finger clean, smiled, and said, "Soup."

Parker nodded. She said, "Do I hear something?"

Willows tilted his head. Somewhere not far off, a telephone was faintly ringing.

Parker said, "It's in the bedroom."

"I don't think so." But Willows followed her out of the kitchen and down a short hallway and into the bedroom. The ringing was definitely louder. There was a phone on the bedside table. He picked it up, and got a dial tone.

Parker said, "It's coming from the closet."

The closet door was open; Willows had taken a quick look in there, patted down Ladner's off-the-rack sharkskin suit, shirts, a tartan sports jacket in all the colours of the rainbow, a soiled and permanently wrinkled double-breasted raincoat. He'd found nothing of value.

But when he pushed all the clothes down to the far end of the rack, there was a woman huddled in the corner, her hands and feet bound by miles and miles of bright orange outdoor extension cord. The cellphone had been forcefully stuffed into her mouth. She appeared to have asphyxiated. Or simply died of fright.

Willows couldn't believe he'd overlooked her. A full-grown corpse. In a closet. A very small closet. The light dimmed. He glanced behind him. Parker said, "DelMonte and LoBrio are in the kitchen."

Willows nodded wearily. The damn cellphone was still ringing. Or rather, *warbling*. The bright green readout on the phone's tiny screen lent the woman the complexion of a Granny Smith apple. Ken DelMonte crowded the closet doorway. His Mag-Lite zeroed in on Willows, and then the corpse. The sickly-sweet smell of breath mints wafted across to Willows.

DelMonte said, "That's the weirdest-looking phone booth I've ever seen. Hey, Tony!"

"What's up, Ken?" LoBrio brusquely shouldered his way past Parker, followed the Mag-Lite's path to the woman's gaping mouth. "Who's the babe?"

"Ask me anything but that," said DelMonte. He nudged the woman with the steel-capped toe of his boot. "Jack, whyn't you do the right thing, and introduce us to your new friend?"

Willows was wearing latex. He got a thumb-and-finger grip on the phone and pulled. He'd expected resistance, but the phone, trailing several gossamer threads of saliva, slipped easily out of the woman's mouth.

Her mouth eased shut.

Willows flipped open the phone, lifted it to his ear. A man's voice said, "Madeleine, you there?"

"Who is this?" said Willows.

The caller disconnected.

"Wrong number?" guessed LoBrio. "Listen, I'm into drugs, not murder, so maybe you can explain something to me. Why in hell would anyone try to swallow a telephone?"

Willows backed LoBrio up as he exited the closet, phone in hand.

"Maybe she's got call forwarding," said DelMonte.

The telephone was a Motorola StarTac 6000. It weighed three-point-one ounces, and featured a built-in rapid charger and three ringer-tone choices. It was registered to Madeleine Kara, whose home address was identical to that of Melvin Ladner.

"Think they knew each other?" wondered DelMonte.

"We were hoping you could tell us," said Parker.

"Oh yeah, right." DelMonte and LoBrio exchanged a few nudges and winks.

"Should I tell them?" said LoBrio.

DelMonte shook his head. "No, you do it."

"You sure?"

"Not in the least."

"Okay, fine. Go ahead."

DelMonte lit a cigarette. "Melvin and Madeleine. They were kind of like M&Ms, know what I mean?"

"Not really," said Parker.

"You hardly ever saw just the one of them," explained DelMonte. "It was like they were joined at the hip."

"Good choice, you want my opinion." LoBrio winked at Parker, caught her reaction, and pretended he had something in his eye that was irritating him.

"Madeleine did a little hooking," said DelMonte. "But only when times got tough. Otherwise, her one true love was Melvin."

"Melvin deals," explained LoBrio.

His partner punched him on the forearm. "Who said you could give away the juicy parts?"

"Your wife."

"True," said DelMonte. "So, Mel's a mid-level dealer. Sells to the sidewalk salesman. He's a couple rungs up the ladder from Lester Rules, guys like that."

Willows said, "You know people who knew Melvin?"

"Bet your ass," said LoBrio. "You looking for us to play the part of middlemen, you got no problem, probably. Me 'n' Ken, we been around so long, we almost made it back to where we started."

DelMonte glanced at his partner, shook his head, and sighed with infinite weariness. He said, "The important thing, what you should know about Melvin, he was a dealer, but he wasn't a junkie."

"Maybe a little coke, now and then," said LoBrio.

"I give you that, but he never injected."

"Never."

"Never?" said Parker.

"He had a fear of needles. Melvin mainline? No way."

"Somebody murdered him," said DelMonte.

"What I just said, Ken."

"Tell it like it was, partner. If you can't keep up with the rest of us, the least you can do is keep up with yourself."

Willows said, "Who wanted Melvin dead?"

"Nobody we know," said LoBrio a little too quickly.

"Except us," amended DelMonte.

Inspired by a sudden insightful inspiration, LoBrio snapped his fingers. "And God, probably."

"Amen to that, brother."

Vancouver's a great city, but it's short on all-nite diners. By three in the morning, the opportunities for a hot meal are severely limited. Willows suggested the Denny's on Broadway. Parker exercised her veto.

"How about you drive us home, and I'll cook."

"Is there anything in the fridge?"

"If you're in the mood for an omelette."

No sale. Willows hungered for a half-pound of well-done sirloin, a monstrous baked potato smothered in sour cream, a token vegetable, and a stiff drink. But he knew from too-recent past experience that his appetite and his stomach were often at odds.

He said, "An omelette would be fine with me, Claire."

Willows enjoyed the ride home. The city was renowned worldwide for its spectacular ocean setting and mountain views. But his favourite time was in the small hours of the morning, when the office towers were ablaze with light, but eerily quiet.

The signal at Burrard and Broadway turned red when they were half a block away. He braked, checked for traffic and found none, lit up the dashboard fireball and cruised through the intersection.

They slowed twice for four-legged pedestrians; a family of five raccoons the first time, and then a solitary skunk. Half a block off Dunbar, Parker spotted a pack of coyotes streaking across the road. The city zoo had been shut down, except for the aquarium, but there was no need to go any further than your front porch to observe wildlife.

The raccoons, who had a special knack for overturning garbage cans, were a nuisance. Skunks smelled, but nobody expected anything more of them. It was the coyotes that caused the most resentment. They hunted in packs, were threateningly large, and seemed to dine exclusively on house cats. People loved their pets. Willows had bought thirty linear feet of one-by-eight-inch cedar board, and constructed a pair of plain-but-sturdy open-ended "boxes," escape hatches for Barney or Tripod to slip into, in a tight situation. Even so, whenever the cats decided to spend the night outdoors, he worried about them.

It was twenty past three when he pulled up in front of the house. Parker had dozed off, and he had to wake her. By now his appetite had faded and all he wanted to do was fall into bed.

Fall into bed and forget forever that he'd overlooked one hundred and twenty pounds of corpse tucked into a very small closet.

Was he losing his touch? No, he'd lost it. The only question now was whether he could get it back.

Neither of the cats greeted Willows and Parker as they made their way up the front walk and onto the low front porch. Willows unlocked the front door. Still no cats. He found them in the den, curled up on the sofa next to his son, Sean.

Sean was watching television. He told Willows he couldn't sleep, that his arm was bothering him. Parker looked in for a moment, saw that the situation was under control, and went upstairs to check on Annie and then go to bed. Willows asked Sean if he'd like a cup of cocoa.

In the kitchen, he made cocoa for Sean, and fried-egg sandwiches for both of them.

Between bites, Sean confessed that there was something else nagging at him. Annie was going out with a kid from another high school. Sean knew the boy by reputation, and didn't think much of him. There was a rumour that the guy had fathered a child and abandoned the girl he'd made pregnant. Willows knew nothing of this. He promised he'd have a talk with Annie.

The movie ended at 4:00 a.m. Sean had to turn up the volume a few notches to catch the last few minutes of dialogue over the gentle drone of Willows' snoring.

13

They were out in the backyard, that unlikely trio, April and Lewis sitting in Wayne's dark green plastic Adirondack-style chairs around a metal-and-glass table topped off by a large pastel umbrella. Wayne liked the plastic chairs because they were comfortable, and if stuff got spilled on them, salsa, for example, or blood, it washed off nice and easy. One swipe with a damp rag and you'd never know a sloppy eater had passed by, or a mortally wounded man, either.

Wayne was downwind a few feet, towering over the gas barbecue. He wore a tall chef's cap and an apron decorated with a repeating motif print of meat cleavers and splatters of blood overlaid with the phrase COME 'N' GIT IT!

Lewis had eyed the apron and his mouth hadn't exactly watered.

It was getting on to dusk, the air damp and sweet, smelling of fresh-cut grass, and horses. The slow-moving waters of the south arm of the Fraser River were about a quarter of a mile away. Lewis could smell the river, or at least he thought he could. The airport crowded the far side of the river. Incoming and outgoing flights were a constant. Every half hour or so the sound of a 747 made the ground tremble, and set the willow tree's branches dancing.

The airplanes didn't seem to bother the area's multitude of frogs. The ditches, some of them so big they were swimmable, were full of the cute little critters. Presumably they'd acclimatized. Wayne was their real enemy, their deadly enemy. About six o'clock, he'd snuck out of the house in a matte-black wetsuit, face mask, a snorkel. Prior to exiting the house, armed with a high-tech carbon fibre crossbow, he'd wandered into the bedroom.

At the time, Lewis was lying on the bed. He'd shot up no more than an hour before, was still nice and high, feeling he was a wonderful person. He was watching cartoons on TV. An animated roadrunner raced off a cliff. Lewis was having a hard time making much sense of the plot, but he was sure enjoying all those brilliant colours that flashed across the screen.

He jerked upright as much as the handcuffs would allow, the chains rattling, his heart suddenly using his chest for a speed-bag.

"Don't be alarmed," said Wayne. His voice was unaccountably garbled, and he had to repeat himself twice to be understood. Haltingly, he explained that he was headed for the ditches, and that he was looking for his swim flippers.

"The ditches?" said Lewis, uncomprehending.

"To hunt frogs," explained Wayne, twice. "Froggies," he said in a deep bass voice. Perhaps hoping to make himself even clearer, he raised his burly arms above his head and bowed his trunk-like legs. All in all, it wasn't a bad frog imitation, given that he was handicapped by his size and the distinctly unfrog-like bushiness of his beard. Not to mention his manic, blazing eyes. Bulging out his cheeks, he uttered a lifelike croak, and then another. He kept croaking, croak after croak. He was an incredibly talented mimic. The music of bullfrogs filled the room, drowning out Wile E. Coyote's scream of dismay as he toppled off a mile-high cliff. Smiling, Wayne opened his mouth and fished around in there for a minute with his stubby fingers, produced a piece of pink metal almost as big as his tongue, triangular in shape, but with blunted ends.

"Frog-caller," he said. "Sent off for her after I saw advert on late-night TV. It was one of them 800 numbers, and I'm here to tell you I'm real glad I made that call. Had to wait six to eight weeks for this cute little gadget to make it through the mails; she came all the way from Roanoake, Virginia. Cost me thirty bucks, but it's worth every penny."

"You use it to call frogs?"

"In season. I mean to say, mating season. You might not think so to look at them, but frogs 'r' smart as whippets. I've hunted deer, black bear, elk and moose. None of 'em's intelligent or wary as your average backyard bullfrog. And they don't taste near half so good, neither! But when it comes time to get laid, well, what can I tell you that you don't already know. When they're horny, them bitty green things can't think no straighter than a hula-hoop!"

"Huh!" said Lewis.

It wasn't much of a response, but it was the best he could do.

Wayne shoved the frog-caller back into his mouth. Practising his croaks, he passed from view.

Splat! went Wile E. Coyote.

Wayne must have eventually found his flippers, because he was wearing them now, as he clumped around the barbecue, flipping grilled frog's legs and contentedly sucking on a large can of Budweiser.

On the far side of the neighbour's sagging rail fence, a couple of nondescript ponies stood quietly. The fence wasn't much to look at, but it was topped off with an illegally installed electrified wire. From time to time a robin or a blackbird, or perhaps a small hawk, would alight on the wire, and sizzle, and die. It was entertainment, of sorts.

The smallest of the horses wore a saddle. Not long ago their owner had appeared wearing a bulky black sweater, jodhpurs, and a pair of knee-high black leather boots with vestigial spurs. She was a large woman, cumbersome and dull-eyed, topped off by a mop of frizzy bottle-blonde hair and armed with a whip.

The woman had ridden for precisely half an hour, in cramped circles. Two or three times per rotation she would exhort the horse to slow down. Her voice was shrill and irritating as a mosquito hawk's. Eventually she dismounted without fanfare and disappeared back inside her house. If she'd enjoyed herself, it was a well-tended secret.

"Pretty, aren't they?" said April, following Lewis's line of sight. He shrugged.

April nodded agreeably. "I know what you mean. The way they're standing there, so quiet and unambitious, it's like somebody must've snuck up behind them and scooped out their brains. I'm not saying they're all that smart to begin with." She paused in her monologue to strike a match and set fire to the Marlboro that had been jumping around in the corner of her animated mouth. "Ever been bit by a horse, Lewis?"

"Not that I remember."

"Now *that* smarts!" said April. She chuckled at her own joke, and exhaled a cloud of smoke. "It's when they're in motion that they really come alive. Cantering, trotting, at full gallop. Who cares, just as long as they're moving. The way their tails flow out behind them, and those long legs, four of them, and they *never* get all tangled up, no matter how fast they go. And they can go like hell, Lewis!"

Lewis slapped at a mosquito. There were thousands of them. He was slathered in repellant, but they were so famished and desperate for blood that they didn't seem to care. Lewis, a city boy, had never given much thought to mosquitoes. Up until that evening, they'd been nothing more than bugs. Now he saw them as airborne hypodermic needles, silent and deadly. Wayne didn't seem bothered by them. Probably the vicious little bastards couldn't penetrate the wet suit's thick rubber. Or maybe the fact that Wayne periodically disappeared into a self-inflicted cloud of Raid was responsible for the fact that he was so unappealing.

April leaned across the table, picked up Lewis's empty Budweiser, and gave it a shake. "Want another beer?"

"Yeah, thanks."

She dipped into the foam cooler, got him a beer and even opened it for him. She raised her martini glass. "Cheers!"

"Jeers," mumbled Lewis.

"Hey, don't be like that. Wayne's a party animal. He happens to notice your lower lip dragging on the ground, he's liable to stomp all over your face."

Lewis smiled weakly.

"I'm kinda surprised he hasn't already killed you," said April. "It's a lucky thing for you that he's so inner-directed." She cocked her head in a way that was supposed to make her look cute but not too bright, and gave him a daffy smile, so he'd know she wasn't entirely serious. "Perk up, handsome. Enjoy yourself, why don't ya?"

Lewis was trying. But he couldn't stop thinking about Wayne, how the biker had looked as he'd come stumbling up out of the ditch and over the fence and through the weedy backyard. Wayne had spent almost two hours hunting frogs. He was covered in mud and algae. The crossbow was slung over his back. His sack, made from a leg cut from an old pair of pantyhose, bulged with perforated amphibians.

Wayne emptied the sack onto the table. Here were froggies that would no more go a'courtin. Froggies that would go no more to the coconut show. Had Lewis a little more education, he'd have been reminded of the more horrific paintings of Hieronymus Bosch.

There was a cutting board, and a small, chrome-plated meat cleaver.

Wayne tested the meat cleaver's edge against the ball of his thumb, and easily drew blood. Satisfied, he tossed several corpses onto the cutting board, and began to hack away at them, separating the legs and piling them on a plate. He was, indeed, a natural-born butcher.

Lewis's stomach churned.

April said, "Say, are those frogs *bothering* you?"

He managed to nod weakly.

"Well, why in heaven's name didn't you say so?" She jumped out of her chair, snatched up the de-legged corpses and piled them high on the cutting board and picked up the board and carried it around to the side of the house. Lewis heard the clatter of garbage cans. She was back in jig time, briskly rubbing her hands. "That better?"

From the barbecue, Wayne called out for Lewis to "C'mon over here and gimme a hand!"

The frog's legs were already done. The flesh was puffy and white, the stubs of shattered bones tantalizingly charred. Wayne flapped six huge T-bone steaks down on the grill.

"That's a lot of meat," observed Lewis.

"I'm hungry," snarled Wayne. He lowered the barbecue's domed lid, grabbed Lewis's arm and led him back to the table.

April wore impossibly tight-fitting gold Mylar shorts, a gold Mylar halter top, matching open-toed shoes with squared-off three-inch heels, a floppy-brimmed straw hat she'd painted gold. She'd used the same shiny gold paint on her toenails and fingernails, and she had a lovely tan, especially considering that summer was still just around the corner. She had prepared a dill-and-green-pepper dip that Wayne noisily approved of. Between the two of them, they made short work of the appetizers.

His mouth full of hot frog, Wayne told Lewis to flip the T-bones.

Lewis got up without thinking about it. He went over to the barbecue and lifted the lid and turned over the six massive steaks, one after another.

The barbecue was marginally closer to the fence than the table. The electrified wire was about chest height. Wayne had his back to him. The wire might burn him, but it wouldn't kill him. On the other hand, Wayne surely *would* kill him, sooner or later. Him or April. Even if he didn't make it over the fence, the frizzy-haired woman would hear him screaming, call an ambulance. He'd be wounded, but saved. What was there to think about? Why was he loitering?

No reason, really.

Except he had a craving deep inside him for heroin, and a strong hunch April was going to shoot him up pretty soon.

Not that he was an addict. Yet.

He shut the barbecue's lid and went back to the table and sat down. The light was fading fast, softening Wayne's hard edges, lending April's lightly tanned body a ghostly, luminous quality. Wayne loved to talk motorcycles, but April wasn't interested, so Wayne started talking about his second-favourite subject, which was Wayne.

He'd left home just short of age fourteen, via a stolen Ford that belonged to his mother. A bad start had led to a predictable middle. He confessed, as he poured an inch of Wild Turkey into his Harley-Davidson mug, that he was a recovered junkie and alcoholic. Well, who could blame him? He'd never had a chance. His father had bailed out of the relationship, which was criminally casual to begin with, about three cigarettes after the moment of conception. Wayne's mother, not quite sixteen, was an unrepentant lush, full of unrepressed rage. She'd given him up for adoption, but there'd been no takers. He'd ended up at Granny's. His presence was not appreciated.

Now, he explained, as April served plates full of hot meat, baked potato, and Caesar salad, he worked hard at staying calm. Doing that Zen thing. His life was full. He collected Harleys, and enjoyed tinkering with them. He owned a large number of pistols and hunting rifles, and he was a damn fine shot.

Wayne talked firearms right through his third steak and second baked potato. He chewed and swallowed, fixed his beady eyes on Lewis. Leaning over and jabbing him in the chest with his fork, not intending to wound or maim but simply emphasizing his point, he said, "And there's something else you should know about me, Lewis."

"What's that?" said Lewis, getting the words out just as Wayne blindsided him with the empty Wild Turkey bottle.

"Tell you later, bud." Snickering, Wayne hoisted Lewis over his broad shoulder, and carried him into the house, through the kitchen and into the bedroom. April had tagged along, and was watching him closely, so Wayne gently lowered Lewis onto the bed, instead of dumping him like a sack of potatoes.

Against his better judgement, Wayne hung around while April stripped Lewis naked.

"He sure is skinny."

"Yes he is," said April, still caustic. "And if you keep whacking him unconscious at the dinner table, you can bet that he isn't going to gain a lot of weight."

"Not that it makes any difference," Wayne pointed out.

Ignoring him, April prepared a syringe, and slipped the needle into the big muscle in Lewis's thigh. When she had finished administering the drug, she turned out the bedside light, plunging the room into darkness.

Wayne said, "Hold on a minute." There was a furtive rustling sound and then the spark of a lighter. A long, thin blue line of hissing fire lit up Lewis's supine body; Wayne had deployed his miniature propane burner.

April took the torch from Wayne. Careful not to scorch him, she slowly traced the outline of Lewis's body with the burner's hissing, hot blue flame.

"He's beautiful, isn't he?"

Wayne wasn't looking for an argument. Not tonight, after all the trouble Lester Rules had caused him. He said, "Yeah, sure."

Scathingly, April said, "Know something, Wayne? You're fucking pathetic!"

Wounded something awful, Wayne spent the next couple of hours in the attached garage, fooling around with his new Anniversary Edition 1200 c.c. Sportster. The bike only had a few hundred kilometres on it, looked and rode as if it had just come out of the showroom. Worse, he couldn't even change the spark plugs, for fear of voiding the warranty. He turned on the radio and got a bundle of clean rags and a can of polish and went to work on the chromed spoke wheels.

Not that he was complaining, but sometimes he wished April was a little less complicated. Trying to figure her out was about as easy as grabbing a handful of steam. He hoped she wasn't getting emotionally involved with little ol' Lewis. April was precious to him. He loved her almost as much as he loved life itself.

Almost, but not quite.

14

Inspector Homer Bradley's cramped but tidy office on the third floor of 312 Main had gradually become, during the course of more than ten years, a second home to him. Bradley was getting perilously close to the mandatory retirement age of sixty-five. Recently, increasingly personal photographs of family and friends had appeared on the walls, next to the faded rectangles of parchment that charted Bradley's slow but inevitable progress through the ranks.

But except for the expensive Haida-carved cedar humidor his cigar-loathing wife had given him as a farewell gift, following a particularly acrimonious divorce fuelled by particularly acrimonious divorce lawyers, Bradley's cherrywood desk was all business.

He signed a document with no hint of a flourish, pushed aside a berm of paperwork, capped his pen, and looked up.

Willows and Parker sat with no hint of impatience in the two wooden chairs by the door. Not long ago, a year or two, maybe, there was no way Willows would have been able to sit down, stay still. Was Jack getting old? No, it was too soon, even for a cop. He did look tired, though. Bradley clipped his pen to his shirt pocket, leaned back in his chair and, careful not to muss his thinning hair, clasped his hands behind his head.

"Detectives Parker and Willows. If you're here because you need somebody to co-sign your mortgage, forget it."

Parker cringed. She'd forgotten all about yesterday morning's appointment with Mary Sanderson, the Bank of Montreal loans officer. Christ.

Willows said, "I phoned Jerry Goldstein, called in some heavy markers." Goldstein was a VPD technician who'd been assigned to the E Division RCMP crime lab about a year earlier. The overtime was phenomenal. "Jerry analysed the trace heroin found in the hypos used by Lester Rules and Melvin Ladner, using the Heroin Signature Program. Preliminary results indicate the heroin originated in Nigeria."

Parker said, "The dope's 66-per-cent pure."

Bradley lifted an eyebrow, registering his surprise. Street heroin was usually about 34-per-cent pure. No wonder so many junkies were going belly-up from overdoses.

Willows, reading from his notes, said, "According to Jerry, the heroin's been diluted with talc, which is nothing unusual. But there are also various other contaminants, including scopolamine, cocaine, and dextromethorphan."

Bradley nodded.

Willows said, "It's a toxic mix, Inspector. We're not looking at accidental deaths. Lester Rules and Melvin Ladner were murdered. It's probably safe to assume at least some of the other victims injected from the same batch."

"Jerry working on that?"

Willows nodded. "Yeah, but it's going to take time. Weeks, if we're lucky."

Bradley said, "We had three deaths last night. A body turned up in an efficiency apartment on Comox about twenty minutes ago. Spears and Orwell are working on it. The victim's name is Paul Ames. He worked for an advertising agency, was considered very conscientious, but didn't show up for work yesterday, or answer his phone. His girlfriend works for the same company. She used her key, found Ames in the bathroom with a needle sticking out of his arm. Add 'em up, *if* they're all murders, we're deep into double digits." Bradley reached for the phone. He said, "The chief's going to want to organize a task force." He shuffled papers, selected a file from a stack of identical files, withdrew a single sheet of paper. "That's a copy of the list of victims, up to but not including Ames. Keep it – you may want to revisit some of the crime scenes."

Both Willows and Parker had been thinking along the same lines. Bradley said, "Anything else?"

Willows glanced at Parker. She shook her head, no.

"Full speed ahead," said Bradley, picking up the phone. He was dialling the Chief Constable's extension as Willows and Parker left the office.

Nobody had bothered mentioning it, but all three cops had been thinking that the end of the month was right on top of them, and that an unknown number of tenants weren't going to be paying their rent on time. Inevitably, delinquent rent would result in a number of apartments being entered by irate landlords. When that happened, chances were excellent that the death toll of over-dosed heroin addicts was going to skyrocket.

Parker shut Bradley's pebbled-glass door as they left the office. She said, "Jack . . ."

Willows slowed down, let her catch up. Except for the civilian personnel down by the door, the squadroom was empty.

Parker said, "Jack, we've got to schedule a new appointment with Mary Sanderson."

Willows frowned.

"At the bank," said Parker, reminding him.

Willows was on the move again, striding purposefully towards his desk. "Call her, explain the situation. She's already done the math, made a decision." Willows picked up a pencil and put it down an inch away from its original location. "Tell her we'll drop by sometime this afternoon, if we can make it. Otherwise, we'll get it done tomorrow. Be charming, and vague, okay?"

Willows pushed away from his desk.

"Where are you going?"

"To make a copy of the victim list. Especially for you. Back in about thirty seconds."

Parker dialled Sanderson's number, and explained the situation as tactfully as she could. Sanderson assured Parker that the rescheduling was not in the least bit inconvenient. She understood that murder took precedence over mortgages, and cheerfully agreed to juggle her calendar in their favour, whenever Parker was able to arrange a new appointment.

Parker decided not to sweat it. After all, what could Willows' ex-wife do if her cheque arrived a few days late? Not much, from Mexico.

Willows' sturdy grey metal desk and Parker's identically modest desk butted up against each other, head to head. They sat there in the otherwise empty office, facing each other, studying the chronologically arranged list of victims.

Tom Klein	Melvin Ladner
Marcia Chang	Madeleine Kara
Russell Green	Maggie Collins
Warren Fishburg	Toby Clark
Sandy Newton	Ralph Lightman
Neil Winwood	
Lester Rules	

Willows added the name Paul Ames to the bottom of the list. He was certain he didn't recognize any of the names, or addresses. Most junkies were thieves. How could it be otherwise? Dope cost money, and addicts never had enough of either. Willows assumed that, with the wild-card exception of Ames, most if not all of the victims had criminal records. But they'd have been busted for petty crimes like shoplifting, theft from autos, purse-snatching, and break-and-enter, not murder.

Claire's head was bent over her own copy of the victim list, her glossy black hair casting her face in shadow. She'd been on the phone, a minute ago, when he was at the copy machine. Had she already called the bank? He wasn't about to ask. He couldn't stop looking at her.

"Claire?"

She glanced up.

He said, "I love you, Claire."

Parker couldn't hide her surprise, and didn't bother trying to hide her intense pleasure. Willows told her frequently that he loved her, but he'd never spoken of his love while they were on duty. Whether that was due to wariness about departmental regulations and politics, or Willows' own sense of propriety, was unclear, and unimportant.

Parker glanced quickly around the squadroom and then reached across her desk to squeeze his hand.

She said, "I love you, Jack."

Willows smiled. He picked up his pencil and pogo-sticked it across his copy of the victim list. "Recognize anybody?"

"Not a soul."

"We need DelMonte and LoBrio."

"I hate to admit it, but you're right."

Willows dialled DelMonte's internal number. The phone rang and rang, and was finally picked up.

"DelMonte."

"Ken, it's Jack Willows."

"Hold on a minute." DelMonte neglected to cup his hand over the receiver. "Hey Tony, guess who I got on the line?"

"Your wife? Probably wants to know how come I'm always so late getting to the motel, right? Tell her I don't look forward to it any more, maybe she should put another ad in the paper."

"No, it's Jack!"

"Jack who?"

"Jack Willows, the homicide detective!"

"Get outta here, what's he want with a couple of low-life cops like you and me?"

"Good question!" DelMonte came back on the line. "What's the story, Jack? Finally coming out of the closet?"

Willows told DelMonte about Jerry Goldstein's analysis of the Nigerian heroin.

"You're saying what?"

"That some of the victims may have been murdered. Deliberately slipped an overdose of toxic heroin. Tell me if you recognize any of these names." Willows started to read slowly down the list, but DelMonte cut him off.

"I got a copy, Jack. Yeah, me 'n' Tony knew maybe half of them. Let's see now . . . Okay, these are the ones we were familiar with, had busted or dealt with in one way or another. Tom Klein, Warren Fishburg, Marcia Chang, Sandy Newton, Lester Rules, and, last but not necessarily least, Melvin Ladner and Madeleine Kara."

"You see a connection between them?"

"Other than the fact that they're all dead? Not off the top of my head. The women all did a little hooking, from time to time. Far as we know, none of them hustled for a pimp. Klein and Chang shared that lovin' spoonful. Ditto Ladner and Kara."

"They were living together?"

"You got it, Jack."

Willows said, "If you think of a connection . . ."

"You'll be among the first to know," said DelMonte amiably, a split-second before he slammed down the phone.

Willows hung up. Parker gave him an enquiring look. He said, "No surprises. Remind me to call back, next time I need a laugh."

Parker said, "Why don't we revisit the crime scenes, take another look around. Start with Melvin Ladner, work our way back. Make sure we didn't miss anything on the first pass."

"Sounds good to me."

Parker drove them to Melvin Ladner's apartment, stopping en route so Willows could grab a take-out cappuccino. The sky had been clear when they'd arrived at 312 Main, but now there were clouds massing on the southern horizon, and a stiff breeze carried the threat of rain. Willows, a native Vancouverite, was looking forward to a little damp weather. It hadn't rained all day. All that blue sky had left him feeling restless and parched.

Parker pulled in to the curb directly in front of Ladner's apartment block. In the harsh light of day, the building looked a lot worse than it had the night of the murder. Peeling paint, crumbling stucco. Crooked brown stains indicated ongoing water damage. The place was falling apart so convincingly it might have been built by fast-buck developers during the past few years, rather than half a century ago.

The door to the building wasn't locked. Parker followed Willows up two flights of linoleum-clad stairs and down a broad hallway. The bright yellow crime-scene tape and police seal were still intact. Willows used Ladner's key to unlock the door. The hallway smelled damp and musty. Inside, it was worse. A crudely drawn outline of Melvin Ladner's last pose had been drawn on the threadbare carpet in blue chalk. Seen in only two dimensions, Melvin looked as if he'd danced off the planet. A tightly folded square of paper lay on the floor between the chalk outline and the sofa. Parker wriggled her fingers into a throwaway pair of latex gloves, and picked the paper up. Willows was interested. She squinted to read the tiny printing. The paper contained detailed instructions for the use of a roll of 400 ASA black-and-white film.

Willows said, "What was Dutton shooting?"

"Four hundred. I saw him stuff the box in his jacket pocket when he reloaded his Nikon."

The other night, Willows had searched the kitchen and Parker had searched the bedroom. This time they did it the other way around. Willows had started in on the bathroom when he was interrupted by a timid knock on the door.

Parker got there first. She swung the door open and found herself face to face with a clenched fist.

The fist's owner, a portly man in his late sixties, apologized as he hastily lowered his arm. "My heavens, excuse me! I'm so terribly sorry!"

Parker smiled. The man wore baggy blue-and-white-striped coveralls and a matching engineer's cap. His face was cherubic: pink cheeks and a soft white moustache, bushy white eyebrows. Around his neck he wore a red bandanna with white polka-dots. If he'd told Parker his freight train was double-parked out front, she'd have been happy to believe every word.

She said, "Can I help you?"

"Name's Billy Tobin. I'm the super."

Parker introduced herself, and Willows, who was loitering.

Tobin's eyes, piercing blue yet somehow lacking a greater intelligence, said, "You're the police?"

"Both of us," said Willows. Parker had flashed her badge. Now he did the same.

"You're detectives?"

"Yes, Mr. Tobin, we're detectives."

Tobin nodded. He briskly rubbed his nose with the flat of his hand. "Investigating Mr. Ladner's unfortunate demise, are you?"

Willows nodded.

"The reason I'm asking, I got some mail for Mr. Ladner, and I was wondering what to do with it."

"What kind of mail?" said Parker.

"Well, let's see now . . ." Tobin reached behind him, and withdrew two envelopes from the baggy back pocket of his coveralls. He held the envelopes up in front of his face, at a precise distance.

"This one, it's his eviction notice. I know that for a fact, because I sent it off to him myself. The man's rent was a full month overdue, and he just plain didn't give a fig, if you'll excuse my language. I gave him plenty of warning, you can be sure of that. Verbal and written, all according to the law."

"What about the second letter," said Willows with just the slightest hint of impatience.

"'Scuse me?"

"The second letter."

"Telephone bill. How they'll handle the situation is anybody's guess. I suppose they got some kind of routine they follow. Go after a close relative, due process, something along those lines."

Willows said, "Nice meeting you, Mr. Tobin." He turned and started back to the bathroom, to finish poking around in Melvin Ladner's no-name-brand toiletries.

"No, wait a minute! I been saving the best for last!"

The third piece of mail had Melvin Ladner's name typed on the plain white envelope in capital letters. There was no address and no stamp.

Billy Tobin said, "You'll notice there ain't no address? How the postman figured out where in hell to deliver it is way beyond me. Maybe they got some kind of X-ray machine, can see inside so they know who *wrote* the letter." He rubbed his nose again. "Though how that would help them is a puzzle in its own right, from where I'm standing."

Parker, still wearing her latex gloves, held the letter by the edges. Not that there'd be any fingerprints, other than Tobin's. The envelope had not been sealed. Parker thanked Billy Tobin for his help, and briefly but very slowly explained why they'd like to fingerprint him.

"For comparison purposes? I don't get it. You're saying you think me and the fella that sent this letter might have identical fingerprints? I thought that was impossible, and anyway, I don't get the point."

Willows told Tobin not to leave the building for the next few hours.

"Don't worry about it, I ain't going nowhere!"

Willows shut the door, and locked it. Parker gingerly opened the envelope, and withdrew five Polaroid photographs.

A close shot of Melvin Ladner's needle-stuck arm.

Melvin dying.

Melvin dying.

Melvin dying.

Melvin dead, dead, dead.

15

Something smelled really, really ugly. In near-total darkness, Lewis gingerly sniffed the air. Was it the frogs? Had Wayne slipped a bunch of dead, horribly mutilated frogs into bed with him?

He tried to sit up, and discovered he was manacled, wrists and ankles, to the bed.

Bourbon, was that what he smelled? He vaguely remembered being basted with a bottle of Wild Turkey. Now it was all coming back to him, and he wished it wouldn't. His head pounded. His mouth was dry. He lifted his head, and saw that a crust of blood lay on his shoulder. Gruesome. His hair against the pillow felt as if it had been gelled to death. He arced his body and twisted his head towards his groping right hand. His hair was incredibly sticky, matted with dried blood and alcohol. His gently probing fingers encountered a hard, smooth, slightly curving surface. Had his head been fractured? Was this a piece of his skull? He warily untangled the fragment from his hair, tilted back his head so he could look at it.

Glass. Nothing but a piece of glass. He fell back, exhausted.

The bedside lamp snapped on. Wayne stared down at him. "Man, you stink something awful. Where's the remote?"

Blinking against the light and his thumper of a headache, tears streaming down his cheeks, Lewis peered blearily up at him.

Wayne snatched the remote off the night table. "Gotcha!" He

turned towards the television, and a moment later the screen flickered, then blossomed like an enormous, unnaturally shaped flower. Wayne flipped through the channels.

Tight-packed names and numbers, hundreds of them, scrolled down the screen.

"Hong Kong stock market," said Wayne. "I'm gonna be rich, or I'm gonna be sorry." In silence, he watched the numbers roll by. Lewis found the steady advance and retreat of the well-organized lines oddly soothing. He was mildly irritated when Wayne toyed with the remote, activating the set's picture-in-picture capabilities. Down in the bottom right-hand corner of the screen, a small screen appeared. *Baywatch.* One of Lewis's favourites, in his previous life.

Sand. Surf. Potential tragedy. Pamela Anderson Lee, her three-piece body clad in a scanty one-piece bathing suit, juggled her way across the screen in exquisite slow motion. Talk about special effects! She splashed into the water, did a little swimming, grabbed a scrawny, freckle-faced kid, turned around and swam back to the beach. Hauled him out of the water, bent over him. The kid was apparently revived by her cleavage. Tragedy averted.

Wayne said, "You read about her in the paper?"

He was waiting for an answer, looming again, breathing hard through his furry nose.

Lewis said, "Not that I remember."

"Accused Tommy Lee of attacking her. This's at their Malibu Beach house? Man, how'd you like to live in Malibu with Pamela? Anyhow, she said he hurt her back, and broke her fingernail. Broke her fingernail! Cops charged him with assault. Bail's a million, U.S. Guy's already on probation, a battery charge."

Lewis shut his eyes, and tried to tune Wayne out. No dice. He hummed loudly, trying to create white noise. Wayne saw what he was up to, and cranked up the TV's volume.

"I ain't saying he's guilty. All I'm saying, my advice to you, gratis, never marry a drummer!"

"Okay," said Lewis.

Wayne played with the remote. The VCR mounted beneath the TV clicked into life, and the scroll was replaced by a video of April and Wayne dining on what appeared to be a seaside hotel balcony.

It was a splendiferous sunny day. Beyond them, the gently curving horizon clung tightly to a glittery blue sea.

"That's the Mediterranean," said Wayne. "Greece. It's where we honeymooned. Ten days, man. I never saw a cloud, not one. It was just like the travel agent promised – all souvlakia and salads and sunshine."

"Terrific," said Lewis.

"I never had so much fun in all my life," said Wayne. He was excited, pumped up by a flood of memories. His deeply sunken eyes were bright as olives freshly dipped from the jar. His blunt fingers clawed at his beard.

He said, "April means so much to me."

A few hairs came away in his fingers. He studied them intensely, and then flicked them away. The window on the far side of the room was wide open, curtains drifting in the breeze.

Wayne said, "I ain't touched a blade in more'n three years. April likes me hairy. The hairier the better."

Wayne pointed at Lewis, his index finger rigid and trembling, as if he meant to run him through, pin him to the bed for all eternity. "Stay put. I'll be right back."

Lewis lay there, manacled and hopeless.

True to his word, Wayne was only gone a few minutes. He returned to the bedroom armed with a pack of Marlboros and a six-pack of beer. He uncuffed one of Lewis's legs, shifted the leg aside and sat down, lit up, and popped the tab on a Bud.

Lewis said, "Where's April?"

"Out back, cleaning the barbecue. I told her you'd be glad to do it, but she said she was in the mood." Wayne puffed on his cigarette, gulped some brew. "She's the cleanest woman I ever met. Showers or takes a bath twice a day, minimum. Can you believe it?"

"She looks clean."

"Damn right. She *is* clean." He finished the Budweiser, opened another. "Clean as a kitten!" he insisted with false jollity.

Lewis said, "I thought you told her there was no smoking allowed in the house."

"There's a lot of rules around here that apply to everyone but me. You got a problem with that, you'd be pretty damn stupid to say so."

The conversation, such as it was, lagged.

Wayne said, "Could *I* have a cigarette?"

"Yeah, sure." Wayne stuck a Marlboro in the corner of Lewis's mouth, fired up his Harley-Davidson lighter. Lewis pulled smoke into his lungs. He coughed, got himself under control.

Wayne said, "April mention what she's got in store for you?"

"You're turning me into a drug addict, aren't you?"

"Not me, pal."

"What are you going to do to me?" It was a question Lewis hadn't meant to ask. He tried to stay calm, but it wasn't working. The Marlboro fell out of his mouth, and rolled away into the fetid sheets. He hardly noticed. He'd begun crying again. He was crying uncontrollably, sobbing like an orphaned child. He couldn't stop. He didn't want to stop. He felt no sense of shame, only a terribly deep and endless unnamed fear.

Wayne said, "Hey, take it easy." He pawed Lewis's shoulder. "There, there."

Lewis felt it overtaking him again, his need, his craving, his insatiable desire.

Where was April? Where was his sweet baby nurse, his beloved April, with her lovely needle?

Lewis's stomach was in knots. His body twisted and turned, straining against the handcuffs.

It was time! It was time!

Where in hell was his goddamn heroin!

16

Bradley had all four teams of homicide detectives working on the Lester Rules murder, and related cases. The drug squad was also heavily involved, LoBrio and DelMonte at point. Willows couldn't recall a case that involved so many murders. The fact that the vast majority of the victims were not solid citizens added to the complexity of the situation.

The suspect list was going to be impossibly long.

The financial cost to the city, in overtime alone, was going to be horrendous.

Willows and Parker had found hand-delivered Polaroids at the homes of Melvin Ladner, Warren Fishburg, Sandy Newton, and Ralph Lightman. In every case, several pictures recorded the victim's last moments on this mortal coil. Pressed, Ken DelMonte had admitted that Fishburg and Lightman were street-level dealers, and had worked for crime kingpin Jake Cappalletti. Sandy Newton was a possible. DelMonte, and LoBrio, had heard rumours but had no hard evidence. All DelMonte could tell Willows was what he already knew. Female drug dealers were a rarity at any level.

Sandy Newton, benefitting from brand-new friends in very high places, had leap-frogged to the front of the line.

The ex-hooker/suspect drug dealer's autopsy was scheduled for twelve o'clock. Noon *sharp*. Willows and Parker arrived at the morgue a few minutes late, and were mildly relieved to discover that the festivities had not yet begun.

The pathologist, Christy Kirkpatrick, had been cutting bodies for as long as Willows had been a cop. Kirkpatrick, like Bradley, was closing in on mandatory retirement. It was a thorn in his side. "What am I expected to do for the rest of my life," he complained to Parker, "buy a penknife and a truckload of lumber, and *whittle*?"

Kirkpatrick was a tall man, well over six feet, though time and his occupation had given him a permanent stoop. His red hair had long ago faded to silver, but his hand was as steady as it had ever been. He was out in the hallway, smoking, and drinking tea from a paper cup, when Willows and Parker arrived.

Kirkpatrick lifted a heavily freckled arm in greeting, exhaled a cloud of smoke, and sipped at his tea.

Willows said, "Waiting for us?"

"Pathologists wait for no man. Our schedule's too crowded. Lucky for us, our patients rarely complain." Kirkpatrick indicated the double swinging doors leading to the morgue. "Go ahead, I'll be with you in a minute. But you better steel yourselves, detectives. There's a damn repulsive morality play going on in there."

Mystified, Parker and Willows pushed open the double swinging doors.

Sandy Newton lay supine and naked on a stainless-steel table. A pale blue sheet lay in a crumpled heap on the white tile floor at the foot of the table.

A pale green homicide detective leaned over the body, hat in hand.

Willows said, "Bobby?"

Bobby Dundas spun around, startled and confused. Like a traffic light, his face turned from green to red. His puffy red eyes skittered from Willows to Parker. Bobby had obviously been crying. Bawling his eyes out, from the look of him. His camel-hair coat was streaked with tears.

Parker said, "What're *you* doing here?"

Bobby shrugged. He started to put on his hat and saw that it was brimful of used Kleenex.

"Friend of yours?" said Willows.

Bobby mulled it over, his damp eyes full of rapidly whirling cogs. It took him a while, but in the end he decided against.

"Not really," he said, too casually. "I met her a couple times, here and there, when I was in vice. Dropped by hoping a visual might trigger some memories, lead to something . . ."

Willows and Parker exchanged a quick glance. Bobby had been caught off balance. An accomplished liar, he was clearly lying. What was going on?

Willows said, "It work?"

"What's that?"

"She trigger any memories?"

"Nah!" Bobby coughed, and wiped his nose on his sleeve. "Waste of time!"

Another lie, but who was counting.

No way Bobby would ever admit that he and Sandy Newton had been lovers. The first time Bobby met Sandy, he busted her for soliciting. He'd been new to the force, on the job less than six months, a rookie, working undercover. He was standing behind Sandy, cuffing her, when she'd suddenly groped him. He'd staggered backwards, shocked, and tripped and fallen flat on his ass on the rain-drenched asphalt. Sandy could've kicked him in the head, driven her five-inch stiletto heel right through his addled brain. Instead, she offered him a hand up, and a freebie. Any way he wanted it, now or at his convenience.

Bobby scrambled to his feet, brushed off the seat of his pants. "Are you trying to bribe me?"

"No, I'm offering you a deal. It's up to you to decide how you want to handle it." She smiled, and provocatively cocked a hip. "You aren't interested, take me to jail."

Bobby was no fool. He smelled complications. A few hours later, after he'd got off shift, he met Sandy at a downtown bar.

Surprised to find her where she said she'd be, and on time. "Time is money," she told him. "There's nothing more punctual than a whore, except maybe a brain surgeon or an orthodontist."

She asked Bobby what he wanted to drink, told the waiter to put his Heineken on her tab.

Bobby felt himself sliding into her life. Somehow, for reasons he couldn't even begin to pin down, he didn't care. Maybe it was that his fiancée had just dumped him. Maybe it was something else.

Sandy Newton was six-one, an inch taller than Bobby. She was twenty-three years old, for now. She charged two hundred and fifty dollars an hour, two-hour minimum. Her all-night fee depended on the variety and frequency of services required, but her base rate was two thousand dollars. A green-eyed natural blonde, she was two-thirds leg, and dressed accordingly.

Bobby lacked many qualities, but made up for it with a surplus of vanity. But despite his exalted opinion of himself, he knew that Sandy was a thousand miles out of his league.

She wanted something from him. Something large.

As he worked his way through his third Heineken, she got down to it.

There was this guy, called himself LaMer Ocean . . .

"LaMer Ocean?"

"It's, like, a joke."

"What's his actual legal name?"

"I don't know. Benny something or other, maybe."

"He's black?"

"Not that I noticed."

"A local guy?"

"He is now. Skipped out on his probation, via the I-5."

"He tell you what he did?"

"Cut a woman."

Bobby nodded. LaMer had rolled his Lexus down the interstate from Seattle, and put together a string. He wasn't the first Yankee pimp to move across the border, and he wouldn't be the last. Sandy wanted out, and no wonder.

She said, "What're you thinking?" Toying with the long red straw that had come with her drink. Flirting with him, batting him around with her eyes.

He wasn't going to pretend he was immune to her immeasurable charms. No way a healthy male could inoculate himself against a woman like that, so why pretend. But he had his career to think about. His precious cop life. She could do him some serious damage, if she ever turned against him.

He said, "Where does LaMer hang his hat?"

"Actually, at the moment, he's staying at my condo."

False Creek, the south side. LaMer, busy with his remada, rarely made it home before dawn. Or so Sandy said. During the ride over, Bobby worked out how he'd handle the situation. There would be a handful of warrants out on LaMer. Bobby could arrest him, fingerprint him, identify him and send him back to whatever jail term awaited him. But that would leave a mile-wide paper trail. Better to work out a deal with LaMer. Cuff him and drive him over the border, let him go. What option did the pimp have, but to cooperate? None. He was bound to see the light.

He and Sandy waited in the dark, in the living room with its big picture window overlooking the water and the deceptively bright lights of the city. The stereo played softly, as they made small talk. From time to time, Sandy fetched him a beer. It must have been three or four hours after they arrived that she turned on the gas fireplace, and made a decisive move on him. He fended her off for at least a couple of seconds. They made love on the carpet and then in the bedroom, Bobby hobbling after her in hot pursuit, his pants around his ankles.

They were in the shower, getting started all over again, when LaMer breezed in the door.

Bobby heard the jangle of his keys, and then LaMer was in the bathroom with them, standing at the toilet, in a good mood, taking a noisy whiz, asking after Sandy, wondering how her night had gone, where she'd left her fuckin' purse.

"It's in the bedroom, LaMer."

Along with Bobby's suit, underpants, badge and pistol. The toilet flushed.

LaMer said, "You wan' me wash your back?"

"No thanks, LaMer."

"You sure, baby?"

"I just need a few minutes to myself right now, okay?"

"Okay, baby!"

Bobby eased open the shower door. No LaMer. Stark naked and dripping wet, Bobby padded after him. Detouring through the kitchen, he snatched a breadknife off a blood-stained wooden cutting board. He caught up to LaMer in the bedroom. Intent on dumping the meagre contents of Sandy's purse onto the rumpled kingsize bed, LaMer apparently hadn't noticed Bobby's clothes. He noticed Bobby, though, and the knife.

"What're you doing in here? Sandy bringin' tricks home? That stupid bitch! You a thief?"

LaMer stepped forward. He kicked Bobby so hard he lifted him up off his feet. The pain was unbearable. Bobby fell onto the carpet, moaning piteously. LaMer pried the breadknife out of his hand, rested a knee on his throat. "You gonna cut me up, is that what you were gonna do, you *putz*?"

LaMer drew back his arm. Would he, had he lived a few seconds longer, have sliced Bobby's throat from ear to ear?

Bobby never found out, because Sandy had slipped into the room, helped herself to his snubnose .38, put the barrel up against the back of LaMer's head, and pulled the trigger. Twice.

Bobby relieved her of his weapon. He double-bagged LaMer's ruined head in Safeway plastic, and then he and Sandy headed back to the shower to wash away the blood and gore.

Bobby, as he soaped her down, kept expecting somebody in a uniform to kick in the door, or at least knock.

It didn't happen. Sandy promised that, if he didn't arrest her, she'd be grateful forever. Bobby had no idea how long "forever" might turn out to be. He knew one thing, though. He'd rather be a cop than a convict.

He and Sandy zipped LaMer into a cheap sleeping bag, dumped him in the trunk of Sandy's Dodge Intrepid, drove him across the border and dumped him in a drainage ditch on the outskirts of Blaine.

Ever since, Bobby had wondered if he'd done the right thing, or if Sandy would eventually roll over on him. Like many hookers, she aged precipitously. The faster her career nosedived, the more Bobby worried about his own fate. When he learned that Sandy was a heroin addict, he looked her up, offered to get her into a clinic, and emptied his savings account to prove he was serious. He'd thought, more than a few times, about bumping her off.

And now here she was in the morgue, all her passion stopped, and he was out of harm's way at last.

Bobby had expected to feel overwhelming relief, tinged with maybe a *soupçon* of guilt. To his relief, he felt nothing, not even a lingering regret for the better life they might have shared. Then, to his intense surprise, he suddenly found himself bitterly regretting his utter lack of common human emotion.

For a brief unguarded moment, Bobby knew himself for the empty husk he was, and hated himself, and everything he could never hope to become.

He'd wept, and wept.

Willows said, "You knew her pretty well, did you?"

"Not really."

Willows asked a few penetrating supplemental questions. Bobby blew a fuse, cursed and screamed until he ran out of wind, then bent to kiss Sandy Newton chastely on the forehead, and stormed out of the morgue.

Willows said, "Is it possible he loved her?"

"No chance," said Parker, and she was absolutely right.

Bobby loved Bobby. What tormented him was the certain knowledge that it was the only meaningful relationship he'd ever have.

17

Wayne scrutinized Lewis a little too closely as Lewis stepped into the shower.

Lewis pretended not to notice. He turned on the water, adjusted the taps, bent his head and let the spray wash pieces of bottle out of his hair.

From the other side of the frosted-glass shower door, Wayne said, "Are you *normal*?"

Lewis had been reaching for the shampoo. The question froze him.

"Hey, you still in there?"

Lewis nodded. How clearly could Wayne see him through the frosted glass? He said, "What d'you mean, normal?"

"Normal. Are you normal. Are you *normal*. Is it something you have to think about? Answer the question, Lewis."

Lewis said, "Yeah, I'm normal. I mean, as far as I know. Nobody's ever said otherwise."

"When April picked you up, were you seeing anybody?"

Seeing anybody. What cloud had Wayne stepped off, before he drifted down to earth? Lewis squeezed a pale yellow worm of herbal shampoo into the palm of his hand. He thought about Elizabeth. Liz. His partner in crime. Did she miss him? Had she called the cops, hooked up with somebody else, moved back to Saskatchewan . . .

Lewis worked the shampoo into his hair. He tried to picture her, conjure up an image. She was slim, pale. Her hair was . . . short, out-of-control? Her eyes were . . .

Wayne pounded on the glass. "You still in there, dreamboat, or did you escape down the drain?"

Lewis said, "I had a girlfriend. Her name was Elizabeth." He'd almost said Liz, but Elizabeth sounded more stable, somehow.

"Living with her, were you?"

Lewis nodded. He said, "Yes."

"Shared an apartment, a bed . . . Must've been nice. What part of town d'you live in, you don't mind me asking."

An alarm situated midway between Lewis's ears rang shrilly. What wretched egg was Wayne bent on hatching? Lewis rinsed his hair. No way he was giving up Liz, even if he couldn't remember what she looked like.

Wayne was standing there, towel in hand, when Lewis finally came out of the shower. He noted the blood trickling from a cut between Lewis's thumb and index finger, and asked him what had happened.

Lewis said, "I cut myself."

"On what?"

"A sliver of glass from a Wild Turkey bottle."

"Oh, man! I'm so sorry!" Wayne scuttled out of the bathroom, returned in jig time with a first-aid kit. He fussed over the selection of bandages, gauze, pressure tape, little tubes of antiseptic jelly. But at least he didn't offer to kiss it better. Dressed in his bathrobe, Lewis ministered to himself.

Wayne was in a talkative mood. He grabbed a fresh six-pack of Budweiser from the fridge and shooed Lewis into the backyard. It was a sunny, reasonably warm day. They sat at the picnic table, Lewis in his robe, Wayne in heavy black motorcycle boots, oil-stained jeans, a black T-shirt and his sleeveless black-leather Harley-Davidson vest. He shook a Marlboro from a pack, offered the cigarettes to Lewis, fired up his Harley-Davidson lighter and held the flame steady for his guest. He popped the tab on a couple of cans of beer, and pushed one across the table for Lewis. They sat there in the sunshine, quietly sipping and smoking.

Lewis anxiously said, "So tell me, is April still outside?"

"Miss her, don't you? Or maybe it's Nurse April's needle that you miss." Wayne's sneer trailed away into a bitter, weirdly twisted approximation of a smile. "She's gone shopping. For groceries. We're outta orange juice and coffee, Raisin Bran, and Christ knows what else. Just about every goddamn thing you can think of. Hey, don't get me wrong. I'm not bitchin'. April does her itty-bitty best, and that's all a reasonable man can ask of any woman. But I'm telling you, sometimes I get so goddamn frustrated . . ."

Wayne guzzled his Budweiser, sighed contentedly. Grasping the empty can top and bottom, he rotated his hands in opposite directions. The can magically shrank in size, seemingly screwing itself into itself, until finally it wasn't much larger than a satellite photo of Danny DeVito.

Wayne tossed the can aside and got started on his second beer of the morning.

"See, April's well-intentioned. She does her best. But she has a limited attention span, her mind tends to wander, she's forgetful." Wayne frowned at a perky robin that had gracefully alighted on a fence post, and was preening itself with studied indifference. "What I'm trying to say, April has a history of being prone to sudden attacks of loneliness that do not last. From time to time she goes on the prowl for that thing called love. I blame myself. In certain areas, I find myself wanting. Not that it's any of your business. What concerns you is that April's well-intentioned, but has a notoriously unsteady heart."

Wayne sat there, dead silent, giving his arrow time to sink in all the way to the feathers. He flicked away his cigarette butt and lit another. "Tell me something. Do you care about April at all, in even the smallest of ways?"

What was the correct answer to this question? Was there a correct answer? Lewis tried to make eye contact with the robin. Not that he expected divine guidance; he was merely stalling.

"Are you taking advantage of her?" said Wayne. "Are you abusing your relationship?" He rapped the table with his fist. "Hey, look, I never claimed I was Mr. Perfect. But if I don't pass judgement on you, who will?" He took a long pull on his cigarette, and exhaled a large cloud of dirty blue smoke that sailed grimly across the yard and disappeared into the branches of the weeping willow.

"I want you to be happy," Wayne said. "I know that might not be possible, or even likely, given the circumstances. She nabbed you, plucked you out of your cosy little world. Turned you into a junkie. I don't know what you're thinking. I can't see into your brain. Not that I want to. You got a poker face, man. In another world, you could've been a real successful cigar-store Indian. Maybe you resent what happened to you. I wouldn't be surprised. I mean, you got a right, some might even say an obligation, to stay in touch with your emotions."

Lewis had no idea what Wayne was talking about. It was as if he was regurgitating vaguely remembered sentences chosen at random from a poorly written article he'd stumbled across in a trendy self-help magazine.

Wayne said, "You're going to have to try a lot harder, in all areas of your life, if you're going to have any chance at all of cutting the mustard. Understand?"

"Understood," said Lewis.

"I'm gonna give you and April a little more time to get things sorted out, come to an understanding."

"How much time?" wondered Lewis aloud, as he struggled to comprehend at least the basic rules of whatever weird game Wayne was playing.

Wayne said, "I'm not making any promises. I want April to be happy. See, I *love* her. I *care* about her." Wayne cracked his third can of beer. "Something you might not understand, Lewis. When a man loves a woman, I mean really loves her, then all he cares about, all that's important to him, is her happiness. He'll do anything to make her smile. *Anything.* And if the thing that makes her happy also happens to be the same damn thing that breaks his heart into little pieces, that's okay, it don't matter."

Wayne's face, as he spoke, suddenly fell in upon itself, distorted like a partially deflated balloon. He roughly knuckled his eyes. Was that why they suddenly filled with tears? He was weeping, crying a rivulet, and then a full-bore river.

Lewis sat there on the far side of the table, aghast. Finally Wayne regained rudimentary control of his emotions. He thrust a trembling, muscle-bound finger at Lewis's face. "I know who you are. A fucking thief! A low-life thief! Nothin' but a punk! It was up to me, I'd rip your lungs out, and eat 'em for dinner!" Lewis, vividly recalling how Wayne had dealt with the frog population, believed every word.

Severe internal turbulence had played havoc with Wayne's heart. He sat there, chest heaving, his furry cheeks bulging and collapsing as he huffed and puffed, settling at last into an uncertain calm.

He started in on yet another beer, slammed down the can, and rose up out of his chair, grunting and snuffling. Lewis watched him shamble over to the weeping willow. The zipper of Wayne's jeans whined briefly, like an overheated mosquito. Wayne leaned against the tree's sturdy trunk. He urinated copiously, not bothering to shift his boot when the amber flow suddenly and unpredictably altered course.

A screen door banged open.

Lewis turned, hoping for April. The frizzy-haired blonde neighbour, hands on ample hips, leaned towards them from her back porch.

"Don't I keep telling you not to do that?" she shouted at Wayne. "What the hell's the matter with you, anyways?"

She thrust an accusatory finger at him.

"This's your last warning! Next time, I'm calling the cops!"

Wayne spun around so his back was to her. He hurriedly zipped up, uttered a shrill screech, and howled piteously as he reversed the zipper. Moaning softly, he finished tucking himself away. He strolled with mock-casualness to the electrified fence.

He clasped the wire. A pleasantly unpleasant tremor ran through him. He gritted his teeth and said, "I apologize if I shocked you, ma'am. I got severe bladder problems. Most bikers do, as I've patiently explained to you on more than one occasion."

"You and your damn motorcycles."

The screen door slammed shut. Wayne let go of the fence and strode back to the table. He thumped down into his chair. "I gotta stop doin' that. What's wrong with me?" He punched himself on the side of his jaw. His head snapped sideways.

Lewis said, "When's April coming home?"

"Good question."

Wayne shook a plump, hand-rolled cigarette liberally laced with heroin from his pack of Marlboros. He leaned across the table and stuck the cigarette between Wayne's parched lips, sparked his lighter. Lewis sucked the smoke into his lungs, his bloodstream, the vast arterial roadmap of his body. The world brightened. Suddenly feeling perky, he leaned back and enjoyed the spectacle of the contrail-filled sky.

"That's better, huh?"

Wayne watched Lewis closely, hunting for symptoms. Miosis, severe constriction of the pupils, occurred in just under two minutes. Lewis was slumped in his chair, admiring the willow tree.

"It's just a question of time," Wayne said, "until April loses interest in you. When that happens, you're gonna end up exactly like my good buddy Lester Rules."

Lewis had no idea who Lester Rules was, or what had happened to him. Nor did he care about Lester, or anything else. Except the robin. Where had he flown off to, that pretty bird?

18

The last call Sandy Newton ever received on her StarTac cellphone was traced to a woman named Kathy Brown.

Questioned, Ms. Brown defined herself as a therapist specializing in "buried memory" syndrome. Ms. Brown's compact offices were located at the top of a four-storey staircase, in an unfashionable, badly neglected building on the expanding fringes of Gastown, a brick-lined tourist trap to the north of the downtown core, down by the tracks. A low-slung woman who favoured androgynous clothing, and apparently cut her own hair, Ms. Brown volunteered that Sandy Newton had uncharacteristically missed two consecutive appointments, and had not returned calls to her home or cellphone.

Kathy Brown was rigorously questioned. In the interests of justice, she agreed to let the police photocopy her late client's confidential files. But she was unable to provide detectives with any useful leads.

Christy Kirkpatrick's autopsy proved conclusively that Lester Rules had died, as many heroin addicts do, of asphyxiation. He'd choked on his own vomit.

However, scorch marks on Rules' body strongly suggested that he had been tortured before he'd died. This was a new twist. Kirkpatrick was buried in work. He hadn't even scheduled autopsies for the other victims. But he had given them a cursory visual examination, and determined that Tom Klein and Warren Fishburg had suffered third-degree burns in the area of their genitals. Willows and Parker, en route to a Chinatown restaurant for a lunchtime brainstorm with Tony LoBrio and Ken DelMonte, mulled over many enticing possibilities. Were the men tortured for spite, or fun, or merely for profit?

The four detectives had agreed to meet at the On-On, a local landmark renowned for good eating, moderate prices, and dependably cheerful waiters. LoBrio and DelMonte had arrived early, and were parked, backs to the wall, in a semi-enclosed corner booth at the far end of the restaurant. Both men wore jeans, Nikes, and expensive black leather jackets that were identical except in the detailing.

The restaurant had seen better days. The place needed a coat of paint. The tables and chairs were battered and scarred. The linoleum floor was badly worn. The lighting was inadequate. But Willows liked the double glass doors, the old-fashioned glass counter, the ancient, but unfailingly courtly, Chinese who manned the cash register, the tinny music that came from cheap speakers mounted high up on the walls. Most of all, he liked the gaudy decorations that had been hung from the ceiling about five years earlier, and never come down.

"Nice jackets," said Parker as she and Willows entered the booth. "Kind of similar, aren't they?"

"I told you it was gonna be a problem," said DelMonte to LoBrio.

LoBrio shrugged.

DelMonte said, "Price shouldn't have been the major consideration. Didn't I say? You still got the receipt? I'm taking mine back."

"Do whatever you want, Ken."

"I will. For a change."

Willows said, "You ordered yet?"

"Just got here. We're still waiting for menus."

A waiter drifted past. LoBrio tried and failed to catch his eye.

"See?" said DelMonte. "What'd I tell you."

"About what?"

"Bein' a tightwad cheapskate." In direct contravention of recently imposed city bylaws, DelMonte lit a cigarette. Waving his cigarette at LoBrio, switchbacks of smoke curling into the air, he said, "I told you, didn't I? Stiff one waiter, you stiff 'em all."

Another waiter drifted past. And another, and another.

"He spilled my black bean soup on my goddamn Rockports!"

"Hey! Calm down. Jeez. It was an accident. These guys are all related. The way you glared at him, you're lucky you didn't end up with a meat cleaver sticking out of your obstinate skull."

"Don't be ridiculous."

DelMonte's chair shrieked as he stood up.

"Where you going?"

"There and back." DelMonte strolled down the narrow passageway between the restaurant's semi-private booths, and disappeared into the kitchen. He returned a few minutes later, looking unduly pleased with himself.

"What'd you do?"

"Took care of business. Made it right."

"What'd you say?"

"I said, Here's twenty bucks, to make up for the last time me and my contemptibly penurious partner ate here."

"What'd the waiter say?"

"He said, 'Thank you.'"

"Well, yeah. Twenty bucks. But he didn't know why you gave him the money, did he?"

DelMonte dropped his cigarette on the spotless linoleum floor and squashed it underfoot. "I got a thing for Chinese food, Tony. You know it and I know it. You think I'm gonna enjoy my meal, knowing there's a good chance it's got something in it doesn't belong?"

A waiter wearing black pants and a limp white shirt dropped four menus on the table.

LoBrio said, "The usual."

"Ditto for me," chimed in DelMonte.

The waiter scrutinized Parker. "A diet Coke," she said. "In an unopened can, please."

"Ditto," said Willows.

A different waiter was back in a few moments, with the two Cokes and four unopened bottles of Kokanee beer.

LoBrio uncapped two bottles of beer, handed one to his partner. He leaned back in his chair, waggled the bottle at Willows and Parker. "You're not hungry, don't want to eat? No problem. But we split the tab four ways, understood?"

"Fine with me," said Parker.

DelMonte lit another cigarette. He'd smoked it all the way down to the filter when the food arrived. Chop suey for LoBrio; lemon chicken, ginger beef, crispy noodles and stir-fried rice for DelMonte. LoBrio was adept with his chopsticks. DelMonte employed stainless-steel cutlery he produced from an inside jacket pocket.

Predictably, DelMonte did most of the eating and his partner did most of the talking.

"Okay, at your request and on your behalf, in the best interests of the department, and because you're gonna owe us a huge favour, we did a little discreet poking around, snapped some bones . . ."

"Metaphorically speaking," interjected DelMonte, responding to the look of alarm in Parker's luscious, chocolate-brown eyes.

"Oh yeah, absolutely!" LoBrio rested his hand on Parker's arm, offering her comradely reassurance. "We don't actually *hurt* people."

"We merely threaten them," said DelMonte. He lit a cigarette, drank some beer, and plunged his fork into the ginger beef.

LoBrio said, "What we learned, the late but not great Tom Klein, Warren Fishburg, Lester Rules, and Madeleine Kara, Russ Green, Toby Clark and Sandy Newton . . ."

"And Maggie Collins and Neil Window," prompted DelMonte.

"Winwood, Neil Winwood. Anyway they were all dealing, all of them."

"In what quantities?" said Willows.

"Minuscule." LoBrio sipped at his beer. "We're talking dime bags."

"Lester was doing okay," said DelMonte. "Fishburg, too."

Willows said, "What about Melvin Ladner?"

"Melvin was living relatively large, having climbed a rung or two up the ladder. Until his untimely demise, he dealt to Tom, Warren, and Lester."

Parker said, "Hand me a napkin, Ken."

DelMonte continued shovelling food into his mouth as he pushed the chrome-plated napkin dispenser across the table.

"Thank you."

"Is that how you get to be a homicide cop," said LoBrio, "by being so polite?"

Parker industriously wiped the top of her Coke can clean, and popped the tab.

Willows said, "Who did Melvin Ladner work for?"

LoBrio grinned mischievously. He drained his beer and opened the last two bottles, pushed one across the table to his partner.

DelMonte spread his knife and fork wide. "The guy who owns this restaurant."

"Sammy Wu," said LoBrio.

DelMonte flicked cigarette ash at the floor. A direct hit. He yelled, "Hey, Sammy! You on the premises, Sammy? Got a minute to talk to a couple of your old pals from the drug squad?"

The wall of silence that met this riposte was timeless and inscrutable.

"I guess not," said LoBrio.

"He was here earlier."

"Bullshit."

"No, really. I'm sure he was working in the kitchen, when I went back there to take care of that waiter you stiffed."

"He was in the kitchen?"

"Eviscerating a cat. An alley cat. A marmalade."

"Get outta here!"

DelMonte speared a particularly succulent chunk of ginger beef, popped it into his mouth. "This's really good." He genially waved his fork at Parker. "Sure you don't want some?"

"Thanks anyway."

"So polite," said LoBrio.

Willows snapped the tab on his Coke. "Tell us about Sammy Wu."

LoBrio shrugged. "What's to tell? Almost nothing, because that's exactly what we know about him."

"It ain't that bad," said DelMonte.

"No, it's worse. Wu's a real slippery carp. The guy's been busted more times than . . ."

"Than what?" said DelMonte. "Than G.E.'s sold refrigerators? Sylvania's sold lightbulbs? Madonna's been a virgin?"

"That last one," said LoBrio. "But the thing is, Wu's never gone to court. If that sounds like sloppy police work, it's time to clean the wax out of your ears. What always happens, gaudily lighted vehicles appear from outer space, and yank our witnesses."

"At least, that's what we *assume* happens to them," said DelMonte. "The truth is, we don't actually know the details of their fates."

"Gruesome details," interjected LoBrio.

"However," said DelMonte, "I do have a new theory pertaining to their sudden and unscheduled disappearances."

LoBrio was genuinely interested. He said, "What's that, partner?"

"I'm thinking *cats*."

"No! Get outta here!"

"Evisceration. Slice and dice. Cubism. And then, voilà! You got your delicious portions of ginger beef!"

"Yeah? Really?" LoBrio scooped up his chopsticks. "Mind if I try a bite?"

"Help yourself, partner."

LoBrio, when he'd finished licking his chops, explained that the network of mid-level dealers was unbelievably complex; mazes within mazes, gangs within gangs. To complicate matters, turnover within the industry was nothing short of phenomenal. People kept dying.

For decades, there had been unsubstantiated but infuriatingly persistent rumours that Sammy Wu, along with virtually all the other top-of-the-ladder dealers that worked within the confines of the city limits, were on the plump payroll of ageing West Coast kingpin Jake Cappalletti.

This last titbit came as no surprise to either Willows or Parker. Jake was the stuff of legends. They'd first heard about him during their stints in the academy. Jake had been a spectacularly successful crook since the Depression, where he'd earned a ton of money wholesaling booze 'n' broads. A year earlier, Jake had been a prime suspect in a high-profile VPD investigation into the kidnapping of a local stock promoter. During a brief-but-entertaining shootout, Jake's chauffeur was killed. Willows and Parker had failed to implicate Jake in the kidnapping or any of several related murders. They were still steaming over their failure to put Jake away.

"Summing up," said LoBrio, "I'd say the next step was to locate Sammy Wu, or somebody else on his level. Talk to the guy, reason with him, snap a few bones if you have to, see if he comes up with any ideas as to who might be bumping off Jake's low-level talent."

"Or . . ." said DelMonte.

"Or you could go straight to Jake. Point out that it'd be in his best interests to cooperate, before the killer makes it all the way to the top of the ladder."

"Jake won't talk," said DelMonte. He picked at a last scrap of lemon chicken, wiped his knife and fork clean on a handful of paper napkins, wrapped them in several more napkins, and slipped them into his inside jacket pocket.

"We're done," said LoBrio. "Twenty apiece should cover the bill, including tip."

Willows had already calculated the tab. To Parker he said, "I'll get it." He opened his wallet, dropped a ten and a five on the table.

DelMonte said, "It's like that, is it?"

"Exactly like that," said Willows. Since he hadn't finished his Coke, he took it with him.

19

A horn blared endlessly. Lewis, his bathrobe flapping in his wake, stumbled along behind Wayne as the foul-mouthed biker hurried outside to see what the hell was going on, and hopefully pound some thoughtless creep into something akin to mush.

April had parked the leased Jaguar at a rakish angle across the gravel driveway. Her boots were up on the steering wheel, and this accounted for the racket.

She lifted her feet off the wheel as Wayne, gravel crunching underfoot, stormed towards her. Into the choking silence he yelled, "Pull down your skirt, April!"

"Don't look, if it bothers you so much." But April demurely pulled her skirt down to her knees. She smiled past Wayne at Lewis. "Hi! Nice outfit! You look like a movie star!" She peered more closely at him. "Oops!"

Wayne said, "You're late. Where were you?"

"Nowhere. At the Safeway, that's all."

"Shopping," said Wayne heavily.

"You are *so* suspicious! Yes, shopping! This really nice checkout boy in a cute red vest helped me carry my groceries to the car, and then he said he had an hour off for lunch, and would I like to spend some time with him, so we could get to know each other, or was I in a hurry to get home before my ice cream melted."

Wayne slumped against the car.

"How could I say no? I mean, I didn't *buy* any ice cream."

"So, where is he?"

"I don't know what you mean."

"The checkout guy. Is he in the trunk?"

"No! Certainly and absolutely not. How could you even think such a thing?"

Wayne jerked a thumb at Lewis, who stood shivering in a patch of sunlight.

"That's different. You know it is." April's adorable little fist thumped the steering wheel. "That's so *unfair*. You kept making hints. You as much as ordered me to go get him, for God's sake!"

Wayne made desperate, inadvertently comical shushing motions all through her little speech. April had been checking her lipstick in the Jag's rearview mirror, so she hadn't noticed.

Lamely, a wary eye on Lewis, Wayne said, "Well, yeah. I guess you could say I encouraged you to go hunting. But I didn't know you were gonna actually do it."

Lewis said, "You told her to go and *get* me?"

"Well, no. Not exactly. Not you in particular."

Wayne took his time firing up a Marlboro. He said, "Don't feel singled out. Nobody's been picking on you."

Lewis walked unsteadily over to Wayne and bummed a cigarette from him. He went over to the Jag and opened the door, leaned past April and plugged in the cigarette lighter.

He said, "I feel sick."

She stroked his hair. "I just bet you do, you poor thing."

"You're late."

"I know I am, and I'm *so* sorry."

The lighter popped out of its socket. April helped Lewis fire up his Marlboro. Smoke leaked out of Lewis's mouth. Wayne said, "You better get back inside, Lewis."

April's jaw tightened. "First things first." She used the remote to unlock the trunk, waved Lewis out of her way and pushed open the door. Her skirt rode high up on her slender thighs as she eased out of the car. She sauntered around to the trunk, opened it wide, snapped her fingers and said, "C'mere and give me a hand."

The trunk was full of plastic Safeway bags full of groceries, but no cowering, red-vested Safeway employees.

Lewis grabbed a few bags and headed back down the driveway towards the house. Wayne trudged after him with the several bags that were left. April slammed shut the Jag's trunk.

In the kitchen, Wayne discovered that one of the bags was leaking Neopolitan ice cream. Gobbets of the stuff lay in an easily followed trail that led from the front door and along the broad, carpeted hallway that split the house more or less down the middle, and emptied into the kitchen.

Stuffing shrink-wrapped chunks of meat into the freezer, he said, "I thought you told me you didn't buy any ice cream."

"I must've forgot."

"What a fucking disaster! Take a look in the hall, go see what you did to the rug."

"It's just ice cream, Wayne. You act as if it was nuclear waste." April shoved a clear plastic bag of McIntosh apples into the crisper. "If we had a dog, everything would already be cleaned up."

"*If we had a dog?* Well then, why don't you go *get* a dog."

"Maybe I will."

"*Fine*," said Wayne.

"But right now," said April, "Lewis needs me. He needs to shoot up. I mean, look at him. He's a wreck!"

This time, ex-addict April made Lewis do all the work. It was time for him to fly solo. She'd patiently shown him how to heat the spoon, dilute the heroin, manipulate the hypodermic, let slip the air, plump up a vein, slide in the needle. If he was going to take his addiction seriously, he'd better learn how to take care of himself. Hadn't she repeatedly warned him that this moment was coming? She sat cross-legged on the bed, and chewed her way right around a McIntosh apple's diminutive equator, as Lewis put all his hard-gained knowledge to work.

She watched, fascinated, as Lewis depressed the plunger and the drug squirted into his vein.

"Better?"

He nodded. He felt great, for now. Soon enough, he'd nod off. April led him through the house to the front door, yelled at Wayne that she was taking Lewis for a drive. No reply from Wayne. She was careful to lock the door behind them, led Lewis down the sun-dappled driveway and opened the Jag's front passenger door for him.

"Where are we going?" mumbled Lewis, not really caring.

April fastened his seatbelt, shut the door, walked around to the far side of the luxurious automobile and got in and started the enormous, gas-guzzling twelve-cylinder engine.

Traffic was light to moderate. There was nary a cloud in the sky. April stopped at a Chevron station, and had the car gassed up. Feeling lucky, she bought ten 649 lottery tickets.

April followed South-West Marine to Commercial, turned left and headed north, crested the big hill that ran on an east-west axis from one end of the city to the other. They dipped down to Fourth Avenue, cruised past an unassuming industrial district and ended up, not forty-five minutes after they'd begun their journey, at 1205 East Seventh, the Vancouver regional branch of the SPCA. The cinderblock building was painted a washed-out blue. Inside, it was warm and comfortable. A wire rack held information pamphlets pertaining to various breeds. To their left there was a low wooden counter, computers, a cash register. A notice board was buried in black-and-white photocopies of beloved pets that had gone astray.

Lewis listlessly followed April down a short hallway and into an open courtyard. Two dozen spacious wire-mesh cages held roughly thirty mostly lackadaisical dogs. The vast majority were of indeterminate, that is to say mixed, breed. The cages were smooth concrete boxes. Each held a large bucket of clean water. If the dogs so desired, they could pass through a low doorway into an area that was heated and out of the weather.

Slips of paper on the cages provided minimal information on the occupants.

The first cage held a spayed pit bull/lab cross named Josie and a neutered shepherd/collie cross named Bob. During her life as a stripper, April had heard countless bad-taste jokes about the sexual proclivities of shepherds, but she had never believed any of them, until now. Was it actually possible? The place was swarming with volunteer labour, so she supposed she could ask. But the thing was, she wasn't sure she wanted to know.

She knelt, and rubbed her thumb and index finger briskly together. "Here Josie, here girl!"

The pit bull/lab eyed her for a moment, and then, very carefully, turned in a half-circle and sat down with her back to her unwelcome visitors.

April vented her charm on Bob, with similar results. "Okay, fine. If you want to be stuck-up, suit yourself. Just don't come whining to me when it's your turn to take gas."

Most of the other dogs, though there were close to three dozen of them, were oddly similar. Crossbred, but without purpose, the children of anonymous parents driven by pheromones and a base, inflexible will to reproduce, they were the sad progeny of chance desire, and fleeting passion. Though they varied in size and colour and even temperament, none of them could be considered fetching. What they had in common, most of them, were stumpy legs, dull eyes, and tails that were rather longish, in proportion to their chunky bodies.

A few seemed to have been drugged. Perhaps they had simply lost their lust for life. One brute snarled incessantly at a flock of sparrows cavorting in a nearby tree. Several spent the scant time remaining to them barking forcefully but without apparent reason.

April failed to read the printed warning on one cage and nearly lost a finger to a justifiably maladjusted afghan/cockapoo.

She came very close to overlooking a pair of dalmatians that were reclining at the back of their pen, in the heated area of the

compound. According to their scanty information sheet, the dogs
were fourteen and eight months old. They were unrelated. Both
had been spayed, which, if she properly understood the jargon,
made them bitches. The dogs had been given up for adoption by
their previous owner. The spotty dogs were designated "house-
trained" and "not good with children." April, with Lewis lagging
along behind, followed big red arrows around a corner and down
a corridor and past a metal-clad door to the heated run. There
they were. "Esmeralda" and "Conchita." What crappy names. She
knelt, and snapped her fingers. The larger of the pair, Esmeralda,
presumably, sauntered over and leaned against the mesh.

Lewis thought they looked like black and white jigsaw puzzles
that had partially melted. Ugly things.

April fished around in her purse, dipped the tip of her index
finger into a plastic bag of white powder, and then stuck her finger
into the unfortunate dog's wet black nostril.

Esmeralda staggered back, whoofed uncertainly, pirouetted in
tight, nearly concentric, circles, and staggered sideways. Her four
legs splayed out. She fell on her chin.

"Good girl!" said April.

Esmeralda's tongue left a wet smear of drool on the concrete as
she crawled determinedly towards her saviour.

"Be right back!" promised April.

At the reception desk, she flung down the information slips
she'd plucked from the mesh, and said she wanted to buy a couple
of dogs.

The woman behind the counter drolly asked her if she had any
particular animals in mind.

"The purebreds!" snapped April. She opened her purse. "What
do I owe you?"

"Excuse me?"

"For Christ's sake, how much do they *cost*?"

April soon discovered that the SPCA was a large bureaucracy.
There were rules, and plenty of them. She was required to prove

to the satisfaction of one and all that she lived in the city, had a fenced yard, loved dogs, was a responsible adult human being, would keep the dogs for at least a year, swear not to roll them over for a quick profit, sell them dead or alive to an institute of higher learning for purposes of vile research, or otherwise abuse or take advantage of them in any way.

Yadda, yadda, yadda.

The grand total, including collars, leashes, tags, the spaying and first inoculations, came to $246.57.

April didn't get it. What kind of scam were they trying to pull? How could an even number of dogs total out at an odd number of pennies? April angrily slapped her gold Visa card down on the counter, signed with a flourish, roused Lewis, and got out of there. What a bunch of crooks!

On the way home they paused at a pet-supply emporium. Lewis dozed blissfully while April purchased several twenty-kilo bags of dry dog food, stainless-steel feeding bowls, boxes of biscuits, durable rawhide chewing bones, and a brace of sturdy leather muzzles that had been manufactured in *España*, and would have looked right at home in a book about the darker side of the Inquisition.

She could hardly wait to show off her new pets to Wayne. But by the time they got home, he was gone.

And so, April discovered when she checked Wayne's closet, was another of his shiny bug-suits. Her stomach coiled in on itself. She experienced a sick feeling of inevitable disaster. Had she bought the dogs as replacements for poor, doomed Lewis? God, she hoped not! If it was true, how in the world could she ever again trust her subconscious?

20

Alice was in her late sixties, going on mid-seventies. Poor eating habits had made her severely overweight. Her feet were splayed. Her puffy ankles were wrapped in Tensor bandages. Her hands were red and permanently wrinkled. Her back was stooped under the weight of a long lifetime of hard, underpaid labour. Her dark eyes were tired and sombre, centred in whirlpools of wrinkly flesh. Her thinning grey hair was untended. Willows couldn't help wondering about the effect of all those years of close encounters with the myriad industrial-strength chemicals her work would inevitably expose her to.

Alice worked as a house cleaner, floating domestic help, for a Burnaby-based company called Minute Maid. She'd already explained to Willows and Parker that she had been cleaning Sammy Wu's luxurious downtown apartment twice a week, Mondays and Thursdays, for the past five years.

"He lived here for the past five years?" Parker hadn't believed the building was that old. But then, she could scarcely believe Sammy Wu had so recently been the topic of jovial lunchtime conversation, and was now reduced to lunch.

"No, he changed addresses many times. But he always took me with him. He appreciated my work." There was no hint of pride in Alice's voice. She was simply stating the facts, ma'am.

"Did you know him very well?"

"No, not at all."

"After all that time? I'm surprised."

"When I come, he's gone. Always. No exceptions." Alice paused, reflecting. "No, wait. One time only, he is here. He gives me fifty dollars, and sends me away."

"When was that, Alice? Recently?"

"No, many years ago." Alice shifted from foot to foot. She said, "Maybe I could sit down a minute."

"Make yourself comfortable," said Parker.

Alice settled deeply into an upholstered chair. She smiled. "I always wonder, is chair as comfortable as it looks? Now I know."

Willows said, "When you were cleaning Mr. Wu's apartment, did you ever find anything unusual?"

"Like what?"

Willows shrugged. "Anything at all, that you can think of . . ."

"He was a bachelor. No wife, no kids. He was a drinker. Vodka. He had many women visitors. I can tell you he liked to watch TV. The set was always turned on."

"He left the television on when he wasn't home?"

"Yes. Very loud."

"Anything else?" said Parker.

"He was a slug. Filthy. Disgusting. Dirty dishes everywhere. Clothes all over the floor. Empty bottles, filthy ashtrays. Sometimes, he would not clean up after his sex adventures." Alice fixed Parker with her beady little eye. "I never complained. Or shirked my duties. But this is too much. A dead body! There are limits. I am not going back in there. I refuse, and if I am fired, so what!"

"It's all right," said Parker. "We don't expect you to go back in there. It's a crime scene."

"Yes, I know. But it has to be cleaned up sooner or later, yes? I won't do it, that's what I'm saying."

"Fine," said Parker. She patted Alice's arm. "You must have had a key to the apartment."

"I have many keys. Many. But when I come to work, the door is already open. As I told the policeman."

"We need to hear it from you," said Parker.

"Okay, fine. The door is open. Wide open. I knock. No answer. I smell burnt meat. Okay, in I go, with all my equipment. I shut the door and lock it, so nobody bothers me. I turn down the TV sound, so it is not hurting my ears. I go into the kitchen, look in the oven. Nothing. The electricity is off. No heat. Now I am not worried. I go to work. First the kitchen, then I rest. Five minutes. Now the bathroom, and then the hall, the living room and eating area. I rest again. Five more minutes. I watch the TV. Then it's time for the bedroom. The door is open. I am picking things up off the floor, and I see him lying on the far side of the bed. He is naked. I never see a dead person, except my poor husband, in his coffin. But I know right away that Mr. Wu is dead. Very, very dead. Yes?"

"Absolutely," said Parker. She glanced at Willows. He apparently had no supplementary questions, for now. She said, "We'd like you to go to police headquarters on Main Street, to make a statement. An officer will drive you there, and then take you back to your car."

"What about my equipment?"

"You can take most of it. We'll need to keep the vacuum cleaner, but you can have it back in a day or two."

"That's no problem. My company has many vacuum cleaners. But I would like to ask you a question, if you don't mind."

Parker nodded encouragingly.

Alice said, "I only met Mr. Wu that one time, but he was very serious. So tell me, now he is dead, why does he look so happy?"

Sammy Wu lay on the carpet, belly up. Sammy was tall, but thin. His glossy head was turned towards the carpet. His right hand rested over his heart. The inevitable syringe lay on the carpet within a few inches of his unblinking eye. He was smiling broadly. Had he died laughing? Willows doubted it.

The bed was a mess. There had been no sign of forced entry, but Willows believed Sammy had been surprised in bed. There were signs of a protracted struggle. The sheets were blood-flecked, and badly scorched by an intense, tightly focused flame. Sammy had been severely beaten; his face and upper body were bruised and swollen.

He'd been burned, as had some previous victims. Probably with a portable propane torch. Teams of detectives were already canvassing retail outlets. Canada Tire, Radio Shack, independent electronics and hobby shops, department stores. The list of potential suppliers was just short of endless.

Willows prowled around the room. Alice had scrubbed the rest of the apartment to within an inch of its life, but the bedroom hadn't been cleaned, so there was a possibility it might yield up some fingerprints, or other useful clues. Otherwise, the bedroom was no different from the rest of the apartment. Furnishings were minimal. There were no photographs or artwork hanging on the walls, or anything else that might hint at Sammy Wu's private life or personality. The clothes in the closet were bland and impersonal – the kind of garments a plainclothes cop might choose if he was hoping to blend in, and not be noticed.

So far, Willows and Parker had been unable to find any evidence of a bank account, paid or unpaid bills. Sammy's wallet had been stuffed with large-denomination currency. The only piece of plastic he owned was a VanCity Visa card. They'd found no correspondence of any kind. There was a phone in the kitchen and another in the bedroom, but no personal phone book or Rolodex.

Willows fanned through the two thousand pages of B.C. Tel's fat Metro Vancouver directory, and found them unmarked.

Sammy didn't own an answering machine.

There was not the slightest trace of evidence that he had any close or distant friends. Ditto relatives. He hadn't appeared to have any social life at all.

Willows picked up the phone, punched in *69, and obtained, at a fifty-cent charge that would eventually be billed to Sammy's estate, the phone number of the last person who'd called him. Willows dialled the number and then wrote it down in his spiralbound notebook.

"Quick 'n' Easy Escort Service, Debbie speaking."

Willows said, "Hi, this is Sammy Wu. Listen, I can't recall the name of the woman who visited me recently, but I would like to meet her again. Is that possible?"

Delayed response. A keyboard rattled softly in the background.

"Debbie? Are you still there?"

"Sammy, can I phone you back in just a few minutes?"

"Yes, of course. My number is . . ."

"It's okay, I have it right here on the computer. You're still living in the apartment on Gilford?"

"Yes, that's correct."

"We'll get back to you in a few minutes, Mr. Wu."

Debbie disconnected.

Parker said, "What're you up to?"

Willows briefly explained.

"Quick 'n' Easy?" Parker laughed. "I guess that's marginally better than "Quick 'n' Painless.""

"Or Quick 'n' Painful."

The phone rang. Willows picked up.

"Sammy?"

"Yes. Who is calling?"

"This's Debbie. Holly was thrilled to learn that you wanted to see her again. She can hardly wait to get over there. Unfortunately, she's unavailable at the moment, but she could see you later this afternoon, if you like."

"Yes, Holly. Now I remember. Tell me, when will she be available to come and visit me?"

"Any time after four."

"Four o'clock would be most excellent," said Willows.

Parker rolled her eyes.

Debbie said, "Your computer file indicates that sometimes you like to be visited by two of our ladies. Are you interested in two ladies this afternoon, Sammy?"

"No, I don't think so." Willows had reacted instinctively; as a person rather than a cop. He debated changing his mind.

"How long will Holly be staying with you, Sammy?"

"I don't know. Two, maybe three, hours."

"We'll have to bill for three, but we can credit your account if she leaves sooner than you'd expected. Will that be all right?"

"Certainly."

"We'll need your credit-card number . . ."

Willows fished Sammy's Visa card out of his wallet. Debbie had a sweet voice, but she was agonizingly slow with numbers. Willows had to repeat Sammy's number three times, before she finally got it right.

Debbie had one last question. "We're offering our best customers a limited-time special, Sammy. As you know, Holly's a college girl. If you think you might be interested in including her special friend, Barbara, we could offer you a significant reduction over our usual rates. I mention this only because you sometimes enjoy two guests at the same time."

Willows said, "I'm tempted. Very tempted. But I am not so young any more, and Holly is such a handful . . ."

Parker feigned knocking him for a loop.

Debbie promised Willows that Holly would arrive at four sharp. She advised him to have a nice day, and hung up.

Popeye Rowland had been loitering in the doorway. Now he entered the room, verified that Sammy Wu was at least as dead as his general demeanour indicated. Popeye judiciously prodded the corpse. He lifted an arm and let it drop, noted the contusions and bruising, deployed his thermometer.

"Time of death?" wondered Parker.

"Premature. The guy's in his mid-thirties. Too young to die, even by today's standards." Popeye checked his watch. "Who was the babe in the living room?"

"What babe?" said Willows.

"In the blue pants."

Parker said, "That's Alice."

"Very nice. Any chance of an introduction?"

"Sorry, but she was just leaving."

Popeye gingerly withdrew his thermometer, wiped it clean on a disposable tissue, and held it up to the light.

"How much would you say he weighs?"

"Pretty close to one-fifty," said Parker.

Willows nodded his agreement.

"It's a little on the cool side in here. Sixty-eight, if the thermostat in the entry hall is accurate. And I see no reason why it shouldn't be." Popeye squinted at the thermometer. He reached out and briskly wiggled Sammy Wu's big toe. "My best guess is that he died not less than two and not more than three hours ago."

Mel Dutton was late, but not apologetic. He shooed the Medical Examiner out of his way, hastily snapped a minimum number of pictures, and hurried off to his next homicide – a heroin overdose in a bootlegger's house on Boundary Road, right on the edge of the city limits.

The IDENT squad, dressed in white coveralls and elasticized caps that might have been pinched from the set of *E.R.*, moved in. The body was bagged, and removed. The syringe was carefully bagged. Several large plastic bags were filled with sheets, blankets, and pillows. Sammy's clothes filled more bags.

Any and all surfaces that might conceivably relinquish a fingerprint were dusted with white or black powder.

The bedroom was exhaustively searched, and then, when the room had given up all its other secrets, the carpet was vacuumed, and the contents, including thousands of invisible dust mites, were dumped into yet another plastic evidence bag.

When the IDENT squad had finally left, Willows and Parker shut and locked the apartment door, and settled down to wait. The doorbell rang at one minute past four. Willows got up, went over to the door and opened it wide.

Holly sniffed the air and smelled cop. Willows saw in her eyes that she was about to turn and run. He took her by the arm and led her inside.

"I want a lawyer."

"No you don't." Willows guided her deeper into the apartment, sat her down in the overstuffed chair that Alice had so thoroughly approved of. He introduced Parker.

Parker said, "We're not vice, Holly, and we're not here to bust you."

"Yeah?" Holly was a little old for a college girl. Maybe she was a mature student. Her lightweight black raincoat came all the way down to her ankles. There was absolutely no way of knowing what, if anything, she wore beneath it. A heavily made-up drug-store blonde, she was all hair and eyes and lipstick.

Willows said, "D'you remember Sammy?"

"Not really."

"Don't remember anything about him."

"Nope. But I'm thinking about it. Mind if I smoke?"

"Go ahead."

The raincoat fell apart as Holly fished around in her pockets for her cigarettes. She had very nice legs, as far as Willows could see. Holly didn't seem to be the least bit concerned about the amount of thigh she was exposing. Willows supposed she had to endure many occupational hazards, and a lack of modesty was just one of them.

He thought about Tony LoBrio and Ken DelMonte. Both men had been with the vice squad for as far back as he could remember, until a few years ago, when they'd moved to drugs. They'd spent a big chunk of their lives dealing with hookers, women like Holly. He snuck another peek at all that thigh.

No wonder LoBrio and DelMonte were so damn crazy.

21

Wayne wasn't interested in the new additions to their happy little family. He liked dogs, but not necessarily dalmatians. Hadn't he heard somewhere that they were short-tempered and demanding, and tended to bite? Conchita and Esmeralda stared up at him as if they knew exactly what he was thinking. He didn't care. He'd had a murderously hard day. He wanted dinner. Hot food on a clean plate. And he wanted it now.

"Now, goddammit!"

In a pique of anger, he swung his booted foot at Esmeralda. The dog was agile. She leapt playfully aside, easily avoiding the blow, and then rushed in and nipped his calf, and darted away in a flash.

"Christ!" He wasn't bleeding, but the bite hurt like hell. He limped over to the refrigerator and yanked a shrink-wrapped kilo package of raw hamburger from the meat bin.

"What're you doing?" said April.

Wayne tore the package of hamburger in half and tossed the two chunks of meat to the dogs. Hamburger and wrappings disappeared in an instant.

"Good dogs," said Wayne. The dalmatians lowered their heads and eyed him warily.

He lit a cigarette, and idly watched April labour over the stove. She said, "That was supposed to be our dinner."

"Good."

"Take off the plastic wrap next time. They could choke."

Wayne made a mental note. The things a guy could learn, if only he paid attention.

April said, "What'll I cook now?"

"How about that pasta thing, with the shrimp?"

April smiled. It was one of her own recipes. She said, "You like that, do you?"

Wayne shrugged. "It'll do."

Out of the corner of his eye, he saw Conchita amble carelessly under the kitchen table, squat, and urinate copiously. The kitchen floor wasn't quite level. The puddle of urine became more and more elongated as it crept silently towards him, stopping only a few inches from the toe of his boot. A miscalculation. But dalmatians were smart; Conchita would get it right next time, if he gave her the chance.

Wayne said, "Toss me a Bud, honey-pie."

Urinating in the kitchen. He glared at Conchita. That was a game that two could play. He said, "Better make it *two* Buds, babe."

He sat at the table, thinking about his day's work. There had been a large mirror in Sammy's bedroom. That vain prick. Wayne had turned the Polaroid camera on himself, snapped a few action photos. He slid the photographs out of his shirt pocket.

Man, but he looked weird. Watching TV a few months back, he'd seen an ad for Intel processors, a bunch of guys or babes or whatever, dancing around in these shiny, Mylar-type laboratory coveralls, hoods, goggles. It struck him right off the bat that it was the ideal set of clothes for a man who was bent on multiple murder, and didn't want to leave any part of himself at the crime scene. He'd got April to hit the Yellow Pages, phone around town, find a supplier. It wasn't an easy task. You couldn't just drop down to Eaton's and buy one off the rack. Eventually some science geek out at the university gave April a Montreal phone number.

Wayne made the call from a downtown booth. The Montreal guy spoke pretty good English, which was a pleasant surprise.

Wayne asked for prices. The suits weren't cheap. He ordered one silver, two gold, paid with a stolen credit card, and had the suits couriered to a box number at a neighbourhood mail drop. No way the suits could be traced to him.

They said clothes make the man. Was that true? He didn't think so, not entirely. It wasn't easy, being a multiple murderer. Avoiding capture was a major, but not the only, consideration. He hadn't been blessed with the twisted credentials of a bona fide psychopath. To play his part, he had to work up some serious passion, stoke his internal fires until the conflagration was completely out of control. Even then, slipping the needle into those guys was no piece of cake.

That was a pretty good shot, the last picture he'd taken of himself, kind of prancing. Sammy in the background, his life already flown away somewhere, gone forever. Too bad he couldn't leave that one for the cops to find, show them his artistic side.

Wayne slipped the devastatingly incriminating evidence back into his shirt pocket and turned so he could look at April. She was almost as pretty as the day he'd met her. She still had that special power to drive him absolutely crazy. Still the juiciest peach on the tree.

He'd brought a set of lock picks with him, found to his surprise that Sammy's door was off the latch. Oh, happy day. He'd gone inside, shut the door behind him, shot the deadbolt, and fastened the safety chain. The chain, rattling against the door, had made quite a racket. But the TV was blaring away, fortunately.

Sammy wasn't in the living room/dining room. Neither was he on the toilet.

Wayne found him in the bedroom, lying on the bed, dozing. He shook him awake, showed him the pointy end of his stiletto.

Sammy hadn't wanted to take his clothes off. Wayne sympathized. He suggested starting with something easy, like his socks. Sammy didn't appreciate the advice. He'd rolled off the bed, scooted across the rug on his hands and knees, and squirmed headfirst into a corner.

He'd wedged himself in there with his spiderlike arms and legs at strange, obviously unnatural and clearly uncomfortable angles, his head bent so sharply Wayne couldn't believe he hadn't broken his neck. It was amazing, how small Sammy had made himself.

Wayne squatted down in front of him, only inches away. He tried to make eye contact, but Sammy was having none of it. Even so, Wayne believed he knew what was going on.

Sammy was entangled in a terrifying, utterly inescapable situation. He had only a few minutes to live, and he knew it. There was only one way out, and that was via extreme disassociation. So, at the moment, his body was mashed into the corner but the rest of him – his brain – was out to lunch. So, Sammy Wu was, but was not.

To be, or not to be? Hey, it's the nineties. The millennium's right around the corner. Why not have it both ways? Enjoy!

Wayne wondered what he must look like, from Sammy's point of view. A giant insect? Some kind of enormous, hulking bug? His jumpsuit a gleaming carapace, the green-tinted goggles a bug's incurious, hugely bulging eyes.

Sammy had scuttled around to the far side of the bed, tried to crawl under the bed, and then given up, run out of steam. He lay there on the rug, trembling, utterly silent, while Wayne undressed him. He hadn't come to life until Wayne sparked the propane torch.

By then it was too late for him to save himself.

April laid the table. Dishes, cutlery, glasses. The two of them would be eating alone, without the benefit of Lewis's company. Wayne was pleased. For April's sake, he'd tried really hard to keep an open mind, but in his opinion, Lewis wasn't a very likeable person.

April twirled a pasta-laden fork into her spoon. She said, "What're you thinking, Wayne?"

"Good food. Delicious. Very tasty. Nice sauce."

April nodded her thanks.

He said, "I don't like him."

"No kidding."

"He's vain, high-strung, jittery as a goddamn worm farm. Worse, he's got an addictive personality."

April chewed and swallowed. She put her fork aside and wiped her luscious lips with a paper napkin.

"Well, sure. Of course he does. He's weak. That's what I liked about him. It's why I thought he'd be useful to us."

Wayne was in no mood for smoothie logic.

"We got any more Buds?"

April tried to slam her napkin down on the table, but of course the aerodynamics were all wrong; the square of plain white absorbent paper fluttered harmlessly, like a good-natured butterfly. She stomped over to the fridge and came back with the rest of the six-pack. The cans crashed violently down on the table in a way that was entirely satisfactory. She attacked her pasta as if it was an enemy machine-gun nest.

Wayne cleaned his plate and went over to the stove for a second helping. Those shrimp sure were small. The oven light was on. Inside, the space was shared by a prefabricated pie and a loaf of French bread. He rescued the loaf, sliced it, dumped the slices in a bowl, returned to the table and resumed eating.

April said, "I forgot about the bread."

"No problem. What kinda pie you get?"

"Apple."

"Yummy."

Wayne filled his mouth with pasta, chewed and swallowed. Sharp tines gleaming, his fork hovered above his plate, suddenly stabbed down. He'd speared a shrimp, and now he hunted down and speared another.

How many shrimps could he make dance on the tines of his fork?

Three, four, six . . . Eleven . . .

Sammy had finally snapped, some delicate, fatigued, brittle part of him flying apart, interfering with all the other parts, running amuck. The guy couldn't have weighed more than a hundred and fifty pounds, but he'd charged Wayne with all the confidence and gritty enthusiasm of an NFL All-Pro linebacker.

Wayne swiped at Sammy with the torch, took out his eyelashes and melted a handful of hair.

Sammy kept coming. He was a bear on the rampage, flailing away, all teeth and claws. His gnashing teeth clamped down on Wayne's precious jumpsuit. Snarling, he wrenched his head sideways, and tore away a ragged chunk of material.

Wayne blew his stack. He left-handed the propane torch and hit Sammy Wu flush on the jaw with a straight right. Sammy's eyes rolled up in his head. His knees buckled. Wayne hit him again, putting every last ounce of his three hundred and twelve pounds into the blow. Sammy rose up on his toes, ballerina-like. Wayne got in another solid shot, striking Sammy a downward glancing blow as he collapsed to the floor.

Sammy lay there on the carpet. Extinguished like a candle in a hurricane. Wayne recovered the patch of material torn from his suit. His defences had been breached. But then, Sammy had been de-breeched.

Wayne's ominous chuckle sounded oddly frog-like.

His goggles were fogged up. He slipped them off, wiped them on a trailing edge of sheet, and put them back on.

Sammy just kept on lying there, motionless as a photograph of Sammy just lying there. Wayne snapped a few pics.

He got out his drug kit, and prepared Sammy's syringe.

April said, "Are you okay?"

Wayne's head snapped up. He was back in the kitchen, sitting at the table, the tines of his fork crammed with crumbling pieces of soft pink shrimpflesh. As far as he could tell, April hadn't moved an inch.

He said, "Yeah, fine. You got a problem with that?"

"Just asking."

Wayne shoved the loaded fork into his mouth, filled himself up with tiny mutilated bodies.

Disinterested but thorough, he chewed and chewed.

April said, "Want me to warm that up for you?"

"No, I've had enough."

Wayne miscalculated the required force as he pushed away the congealed pasta and deceased shrimp. The plate shot across the table and hit the floor, and shattered. The dogs pounced.

"Did you do that on purpose?"

"'Course not."

The dogs were in a frenzy, indiscriminately gobbling up belly-fuls of carbohydrates and splintered shards of plate. One of the creatures, it was impossible to say which, was bleeding copiously.

"Christ, now look what you've done!"

"What?" said Wayne. He kicked out, not trying to hurt the animals, so much as simply intending to make them keep their distance.

April yelled at him. Swore at him. Debased his ancestors. Queried the validity of his DNA sequences. She was a tigress. Once she got rolling, there was no stopping her. Wayne torched a Marlboro and leaned back in his chair to enjoy the ride. April was foaming at the mouth, speaking in tongues. Still, he got the gist. What a mean-spirited, foul-hearted bitch! She was just amazing, wasn't she!

Eventually, April ran out of wind, and venom. By then Wayne was down on his knees, lovingly tending to the wounded dog, Esmeralda. The cut was superficial, at worst. It had already stopped bleeding. Wayne said, "Aren't you *such* a good dog."

Esmeralda licked his beard, became confused, and backed away with her tail between her legs.

"I guess she don't like shrimp," hazarded Wayne.

"It's the tobacco smoke, you idiot. Want a slice of pie?"

Wayne didn't hear the question. He'd shifted back to Sammy's apartment, was sitting down on Sammy's bed. He fine-tuned his Radio Shack torch until the hissing, pale blue flame was thin as a razor.

Sammy Wu was not a particularly hirsute guy. Wayne knelt beside him and ran the torch up his leg, from ankle to pubic bone. The familiar stench of scorched hair was something he hoped he'd never get used to. He ran the torch into the scanty nest of Sammy's pubic hair, circled, and pulled away. The torch sputtered and died. He tried, unsuccessfully, to relight it. The flow of gas was weak. The damn cylinder was empty, and he'd forgotten to bring a spare.

Wayne got out his lighter, adjusted the flame as high as it would go, and painstakingly finished the ritual burning.

Had a team of paramedics burst into the room, kick-started Sammy with a dose of Narcane, and brought him blinking back from the bottom of his grave, and had Sammy asked Wayne what the hell he was up to with that crazy torch thing, Wayne would not have been able to provide him with a definitive answer.

He'd have said something along the lines of, "I dunno." Pressed, he might have admitted the possibility that it had something to do with his lack of sexual drive.

Something to do with the way his dad treated him when he was a helpless little kid, maybe.

Of course, he'd be flat-out lying like a rug.

"Want some ice cream with your pie?"

"Sure," said Wayne. April spooned a lump of ice cream onto his plate. He began to eat. The dogs watched him as closely as paint clings to a wall.

Wayne said, "I was thinking Lewis might be interested in my collection of Polaroids."

"So soon?"

"Yeah."

April toyed with her dessert. She swirled the ice cream into the pie until it was a gooey, unidentifiable mess.

"I was hoping to keep him around for a while."

"I know you were." He reached across the table and snagged a choice piece of her piecrust. "You kind of like him, don't you."

"Just a few more days . . ."

"What's the magic word, babe?"

"Please?"

The dogs had flopped down companionably, in close proximity to the refrigerator. Were they white, with small black spots? Or mostly black, with large white spots?

Wayne pushed away from the table. Was Lewis a sacrificial lamb, or April's new boyfriend? He said, "I'll think about it. Okay?"

22

The cafeteria at 312 Main had never made any of the local lists of ten best restaurants. Or fifty best restaurants. Or thousand best greasy spoons. On the other hand, unlike several of the city's finer dining establishments, the cafeteria had never suffered from an outbreak of *e-coli* resulting from undercooked or improperly handled meat.

Willows and Parker sat on either side of Bradley, who had made himself comfortable at the head of the table. Parker had availed herself of the hot water, and had dunked a teabag she'd had stowed in a plastic sandwich bag, at the bottom of her purse. There had been a brief-but-spirited conversation about the physics involved in a featherweight teabag's unlikely journey to the *bottom* of her purse. Willows was deep into his veggie burger, but not enjoying it very much. Bradley had finished his salad and just begun to tuck into his apple crumble. He paused, his fork poised midway between plate and mouth.

"What about the hooker – you already talked to her, right?"

Willows, his mouth full of God knows what, nodded agreeably.

Parker said, "Holly Wentworth. We didn't talk, we listened."

"Chatty, was she?"

"To say the least. I'm pretty sure she set a new land speed record. A real motor-mouth. I kept wanting to issue a ticket."

"Back to your roots," said Bradley. "So, what'd she give you?"

"Nada."

Willows drank some coffee. He said, "She gave me a headache."

"I stand corrected," said Parker. "In fact, come to think of it, she gave me something, too."

"That stick of Juicy Fruit," said Willows. His hamburger was falling apart in his hands. What a mess. Kind of like the case. He said, "How're we doing, big-picture-wise."

Bradley shrugged. He swallowed, used his fork to chase the last of his crumble around the plate. He was slowing down, losing his moves. Ten years ago, he'd have wiped up every last crumb with a single pass. It was all in the wrist . . .

He said, "Orwell and Spears are re-canvassing the victim's neighbours, hunting for witnesses. They've split the work load with Dan Oikawa and Bobby Dundas. Dan tells me Bobby keeps going AWOL."

"You talk to Bobby?"

Bradley nodded. "I sure did, but I wish I knew why."

Parker told Bradley about Bobby's odd behaviour at the morgue, prior to Sandy Newton's autopsy.

Bradley laid his fork down in the exact centre of his plate. "Bobby was *crying*?" It was an unlikely image, to say the least. He glanced at Willows for confirmation.

Willows said, "Bobby kissed her."

"*Kissed* her?"

Parker said, "On the forehead, Inspector. Chastely."

Bradley retrieved his fork. He balanced it between his fingers, like a teeter-totter. The fork tilted down. The tines chimed musically against the plate, and then were still.

"Chastely, huh?" Bradley tugged at his ear, pulling memories from years gone by. A slow pimp with the unlikely name of LaMer Ocean had turned up in a drainage ditch outside Blaine, Washington. The pimp's head had yielded two copper-jacketed .38-calibre bullets. The second round had impacted on the first, destroying them both. As evidence, they were useless. Bradley had found out about the pimp's fate shortly after his abandoned Lexus, complete with Washington State licence plates, had turned up in a False Creek parking lot. Neighbours had reported that, for the past few weeks, the pimp had been sharing a condo rented by a hooker named Sandy Newton.

Bradley should have made the connection earlier. He *was* slowing down. LaMer had died a long time ago. Eight, nine years? Had Bobby been working vice at the time of LaMer Ocean's death? The fork hung in perfect balance, but only for a moment.

Bradley decided he wasn't interested in Bobby's whereabouts on the night of LaMer Ocean's brutal, execution-style murder.

Not yet, anyway. He glanced up. Willows and Parker were both staring fixedly at him. He said, "What?"

"Nothing," said Parker a little too quickly.

Bradley decided it was the fork. Somehow, it had bent itself into an imperfect oval. How had that happened? No wonder Jack and Claire were looking at him so oddly. Yuri Geller, look out!

Parker and Willows were in the elevator, on their way up to the third floor, when Parker's beeper sounded off. She checked the number. Christy Kirkpatrick. She phoned the pathologist from her desk.

"Christy, what can I do for you?"

"*Au contraire*," said Kirkpatrick. "Remember Sammy Wu?"

"Vaguely. He scheduled?"

"Top priority. I'll get around to him some time next month, if he's lucky. The reason I called, we pulled him by accident. I'm scheduled to autopsy a gorgeous female model who jumped out a window ten minutes after eating a chocolate sundae. But when I pull back the sheet, I'm looking down at Sammy."

"That must have been a major disappointment."

"You better believe it. Anyway, Sammy's mouth's wide open, the overhead light's shining down on him, and I can't help noticing there's something stuck between his teeth . . ."

Kirkpatrick trailed off.

Parker waited, and waited.

Finally she said, "Christy?"

"Yes?"

"What'd you find?"

"I think you better drop by, take a look."

"Why's that?" said Parker.

"What I found, it's physical evidence. You better bring one of those little plastic bags with you."

"Will do," said Parker.

"Half an hour."

"Fine."

"I'll clear a table for you," said Kirkpatrick blandly, and disconnected.

They found the pathologist at his desk, lunching on an egg-salad sandwich. He waved them into the cramped office, drank quickly from a bottle of Snapple as he stood up. A paper napkin fluttered from his lap towards the floor. He snatched it out of mid-air and used it to wipe his mouth. He checked his watch against the wall clock. "You're right on time."

"We used the siren," said Parker.

"Not that it was needed," said Willows.

Kirkpatrick eyed him warily. Jack wasn't noted for a light-hearted approach to life, much less death. He tossed the balled-up napkin in his wastebasket. Two points.

"Follow me, detectives." Kirkpatrick snatched his smock and nifty elasticized cap off the coatrack as he went out.

Sammy Wu lay on a stainless-steel table, under a pale blue sheet. Kirkpatrick wriggled his hands into a pair of disposable latex gloves. He pulled the sheet down past Sammy Wu's collarbone. Sammy's eyes were shut but his mouth gaped open. He lacked the necessary bulk, but might otherwise have been a deceased opera singer.

Bradley tilted Sammy's head slightly to the side. He adjusted the overhead light.

"Right there? See it."

A spark of silver glinted between two molars. Willows predicted tinfoil. He guessed that Sammy had tried to swallow a small quantity of heroin. If there was a tinfoil packet in his stomach, Kirkpatrick would certainly unearth it during the autopsy. He wondered what all the fuss was about.

Kirkpatrick had a pair of stainless-steel tweezers. He said, "Watch." He flicked at the bit of silver with the tweezers. Willows saw that the thing, whatever it was, was far too flexible and shiny to be tinfoil. Kirkpatrick shifted his grip, closed the tweezers on the tiny scrap of material, and tugged gently but firmly.

The shiny fragment resisted his efforts. He pulled harder. The material came away in the tweezers' jaws. Kirkpatrick held it under the light. His hand was absolutely still.

Parker said, "What is it?"

"Beats me. Mylar? Some kind of fabric." Kirkpatrick led them back into his office, got a magnifying glass from his desk. He turned on his desk light and swivelled it around. He studied the scrap of Mylar-like material, and then turned the tweezers so he could look at the flip side. He said, "It's woven, for strength. There's at least two layers . . ." He handed the magnifying glass to Parker, who studied the scrap of material for a moment and then passed the glass on to Willows.

Kirkpatrick said, "It's such a small piece . . ." He finished the Snapple, and tossed the empty bottle in his wastebasket.

"Very tiny," agreed Parker.

Kirkpatrick picked the Snapple cap off his desk and began clicking it in and out.

Snap-snap. Snap-snap.

Willows was, in the blink of an eye, incredibly irritated.

Kirkpatrick said, "What kind of evidence you find at the scene of crime?"

"Virtually none," said Willows.

Parker explained the circumstances – that the apartment had been professionally cleaned just before the corpse was discovered.

"What about the bedroom, where she found the body? Soldier on, did she?"

Parker laughed. "No, she dialled nine-eleven."

"But I understand you found no evidence in the bedroom, either."

"Where'd you hear that?" said Parker.

"From Tony LoBrio. Is it true?"

"True enough," said Willows.

Kirkpatrick said, "Look, I've been thinking about this. Is it possible your perp was wearing coveralls, maybe an outfit similar to what the IDENT team wears, to avoid contaminating the crime scene?"

"It's possible."

Parker held out an open, clear plastic evidence bag, size small. Kirkpatrick dipped the tweezers into the bag, shook loose the piece of material. Parker sealed the bag.

Kirkpatrick tapped the bag with the tweezers. He said, "I'm just guessing, but this could be a piece of a lab suit."

"A lab suit?"

Kirkpatrick nodded. "Have you seen that Intel ad, the guys dancing around in those shiny outfits? They look almost like astronauts. They're covered head to foot in these shiny suits, wearing face shields, or goggles . . . You don't know the one I'm talking about?"

Willows said, "No, I don't think so." He glanced at Parker, who was clearly equally mystified.

Outside, there was a high wind. Clouds raced towards the horizon. Sunlight flickered across the sidewalk, and the towering glass faces of the skyscrapers.

Parker stopped dead in her tracks.

She said, "Bugs."

Willows unlocked the unmarked Fairlane's passenger-side door. He tossed the keys high into the air, turned gracefully, and caught the keys behind his back.

He said, "Bugs? As in, covert audio surveillance?"

"No, as in bugs. Really huge bugs."

Willows leaned against the car. There was no ceiling to look up at, so he looked away, down the street.

Finally he said, "I need another clue."

"Shiny," said Parker. "Bugs, huge and shiny."

Willows nodded thoughtfully. There it was. Now he had it. A two-storey walkup. A filthy apartment. Huge, shiny bugs. Chocolate-chip cookies. Tea laced with a generous shot of brandy.

He said, "Let's go see how Marjorie is doing."

"Good idea," said Parker.

Marjorie was doing very well, thank you. There was no need to knock; she'd heard footsteps on the stairs, and had her eye to the peephole as Willows and Parker made their way down the hall towards her.

"Well! My two favourite detectives! What a lovely surprise! Dear me, how terribly exciting. Come in, come in . . ."

The tidy little apartment had been stripped of everything but the furniture. The walls were dotted with nail holes where Marjorie's family pictures had hung. Presumably everything had gone into the cardboard boxes lined up against the far wall.

"Moving?" said Parker.

"Oh my yes, at the end of the month! I'm so excited!" Marjorie's blue eyes twinkled mischievously. "Is that why you came to visit, because you'd heard I was leaving, and you didn't want to lose touch?"

"Not exactly," said Parker.

"I wish I could offer you something to eat. But everything's packed, or at least nearly everything. I know it's a little early. Would you like a nice cup of tea?"

"No thanks," said Parker kindly.

"It's so stupid of me to be in such a rush, but I wanted to be sure everything was ready, so there wouldn't be any delays. Jack?"

Willows had been napping his way through the monologue. He made an effort to look attentive.

"Would you like a cup of tea? I've just made a pot, so it's nice and hot . . ."

"Thanks anyway."

"You're so very welcome. You wouldn't believe how much I'm so looking forward to getting out of this dreary little place. When I realized that Mr. Rules' apartment was *vacant*, I could hardly believe my luck!"

Parker said, "Excuse me? You're moving down the hall?"

"Well, wouldn't you? It's a corner unit. Windows on two sides. It'll be so much brighter, even in the winter. Oh, I know, it's a terrible mess. But I've never been afraid to roll up my sleeves and go to work. A bit of scrubbing, a new carpet from that roll-end place, spackle, a few cans of paint."

Marjorie drifted towards the door, and Willows realized she wanted them out of there, so she could go back to her packing.

She said, "Come back in a couple of weeks. I guarantee that you won't even recognize the place!"

Parker said, "Marjorie, we'd like to ask you a few questions."

"About what?"

Marjorie had changed course. Now she was drifting towards the teapot, which was standing on the kitchen counter next to a large bottle of brandy.

"About what you saw the night Lester Rules was murdered," said Parker.

"I didn't see anything, dear." Marjorie poured herself a half-cup of orange pekoe. She reached for the bottle. "Didn't I already tell you that?"

Parker said, "No drinking, please."

Marjorie stared at her, aghast.

"What a thing to say! In my own apartment! It's not as if I'm trying to drown my sorrows, or anything like that. This is strictly for medicinal purposes, young lady."

"I appreciate that. But we don't want you to become inebriated, no matter what the circumstances."

"Inebriated? You mean, drunk?"

"Tiddly," said Willows, smiling genially.

"Oh, I see." Marjorie made a snap decision not to turn nasty. She said, "That's different."

"The night we first talked to you," said Willows, "you told us his apartment was infested with cockroaches."

"Did I?"

"You said you'd had problems, but that you took great care to keep your apartment spotlessly clean. You said that, from time to time, you used insecticides."

"Well, yes. I don't remember saying any of that, but it's certainly possible."

Parker said, "You told us you saw a really huge bug outside Lester's doorway, the afternoon he was murdered."

"I did?"

"Yes, you did," said Parker firmly.

"Did I say what kind of bug it was?"

"Shiny. Huge, and shiny."

"Shiny?"

Parker said, "I'd like you to take a look at something."

She took the evidence bag from her purse and held it up to the light so Marjorie had a good view of the fragment of brightly gleaming material.

Marjorie's hand flew to her mouth. "Dear me! Now I remember! I thought I was imagining things. Sometimes I do that, if I haven't been feeling well, and I've had a lot of tea."

"You weren't imagining things," said Parker. "Tell us what you saw."

"You have to understand that I was looking through the peep-hole in the door, so everything was distorted. Like looking at the world through a goldfish bowl."

Parker nodded encouragingly.

"A man, it had to be a man, he was so *huge*, was standing by the door. Leaning against it, as if listening, to find out if there was anyone inside. He was wearing a silver suit. It was very shiny, like an enormous fish. A trout, or a salmon. But he was too fat."

Willows was making notes. Marjorie paused, to allow him time to catch up.

"Then he turned and looked right at my door, and I saw, I didn't really believe it at the time, but I saw that his face was covered with silver, and he was wearing a pair of goggles. Like swim goggles, but larger."

"Do you remember the colour of the goggles?" said Parker.

"Green. They were dark green. I don't know why, but he turned and looked right at me, as if he knew I was looking at him. I was so frightened! It sounds silly, I know, but there was something about him that was pure evil."

Marjorie sipped from her cup of unlaced tea. "Now that I've had time to think about it, I'm sure that's what made me think he was a bug."

"I don't understand," said Parker.

"He was missing something," said Marjorie. "I don't know how I knew, but I did. I sensed it, I suppose. Sensed that something was lacking in him."

She glanced anxiously at Willows.

"I thought he was a bug because I knew, somehow, that he wasn't quite human."

Relenting, they both had a nice hot cup of tea, before they left. Willows took his with a pinch of brandy.

Marjorie, on her second cup, said, "I'm *safe*, aren't I?"

"Safe as houses," said Willows.

The rescheduled meeting with the Bank of Montreal loans officer, Mary Sanderson, suddenly nagged at Parker. She glanced at Willows, and saw he hadn't made the connection, and found herself resenting his irresponsible lack of concern.

23

"What is it?"

"Pasta. With little tiny wee itty-bitty shrimp."

"Shrimp?"

"Little ones. They're out of a tin. From China, probably. What isn't. But don't tell Wayne, because he thinks they were fresh. Open wide."

Lewis's mouth sagged open. April filled it with cut-up pasta, shrimp, a pale, creamy sauce.

"Chew."

Lewis chewed.

"Good. Now swallow."

Lewis swallowed.

"Capistrano!"

Lewis tilted his head so he could look at her.

"It's what my mom used to say, when I was a little kid, and she was trying to get me to eat. Capistrano! Every time I swallowed a mouthful. It always made me laugh, because of the way she said it. Making a big deal, y'know. Capistrano! Try it."

"Capistrano!" said Lewis.

"Good, now let's do it together. Capistrano!" April dissolved into a fit of childish giggles. When she'd got herself under control, two or three seconds later, she said, "I don't know what it means. It's Spanish or Mexican, I guess."

She emptied the bowl of shrimp pasta into Lewis forkful by forkful, with infinite patience and goodwill. Lewis lay on the bed, in a voluminous pair of Harley-Davidson pyjamas cast off by Wayne when he'd realized he had been bilked – the jammies weren't the genuine article, licensed by Harley-Davidson, but a cheap Asian knockoff.

Wayne loved to talk bikes. He disdainfully referred to Japanese motorcycles as "Riceburners." He'd boasted that he'd never in all his motoring life raised his left hand in greeting when encountering a Japanese bike on life's highways. Honda, Suzuki, Yamaha and Kawasaki, they were all one and the same to Wayne. Inferior products, because they weren't fashioned of American iron.

The fact that many of these motorcycles were built in the United States meant nothing to him. Wayne had developed an attitude. Since it was such a comfortable fit, why would he ever change?

"April?"

"Yeah, what?" But she knew what was coming. Lewis's tone of voice had been weedy and wheedling. The boy was turning into a high-maintenance item. Left-over pasta-and-shrimp was the last thing he was interested in; but he'd cleaned his plate like a good boy, and now he wanted dessert.

Lewis wanted to eat the needle.

He was pale and shivering, his face glistening with sweat. He had that special junkie-knot in his belly, that junkie-knot in his heart.

Lewis was a junkie.

He needed to fix.

April was amazed. Lewis was an ideal patient, in the sense that he had made such rapid progress. Junk had robbed him of all desire, except the desire for more dope, another fix.

From personal experience, April had come to believe that people turned into junkies for as many reasons as there were needles in a needle exchange, but that the primary reason was because they'd been cursed with an addictive personality.

Lewis smoked like a chimney, drank like a fish. If he hadn't found junk, he'd probably have died of lung cancer, or liver failure. Horrible deaths, unlike a simple overdose.

She was doing him a favour, really.

But still . . .

He lay there on the bed, looking adorable. She told herself he wasn't actually all that cute, that she'd been seduced by the combination of his angelic face and the hard-ass biker jammies. But she didn't believe it, not even for a minute.

She was falling for Lewis.

Had already fallen for him, to tell the pathetic truth.

She leaned over the bed and kissed him lightly on the mouth, and whispered into his ear that she'd be back in a minute.

"I'm sick, April. I need to fix."

"I know you do, baby. Try to be patient, okay? I'm going to take care of you, don't worry."

"Where are you going?"

"To the kitchen, to do some cooking. Close your eyes. Try to relax. I'll be right back."

Due to their casual attitude towards bladder control, the dalmatians had been restricted to the kitchen. The lights were agonizingly bright; April noticed right away that the dogs were missing. But in any case she had no time for the dogs.

She had to cook up.

She was busy, busy, busy.

As it happened, the dalmatians were in the backyard. Wayne had taken them outside because he was in need of congenial company, and April, as usual, was otherwise engaged.

Conchita and Esmeralda, spying the neighbour's horses, had become extremely agitated. Wayne was in no mood for frolic. Using short lengths of rawhide, he'd tied the dogs together, rear legs to rear legs. If the beasts wanted to go anywhere, they had to move in perfect synchronicity, in what were essentially identical but opposite directions.

Wayne stood in close proximity to the barbecue, which was venting roiling black clouds of acrid smoke shot through with spiralling tongues of bright orange flame. The wind was in a shifty mood; he had to stay alert, if he hoped to avoid serving his lungs a lethally toxic dose of sooty chemicals.

Wayne was destroying evidence, torching the expensive silver coveralls that Sammy Wu had chosen to make his last meal. Wayne had hoped the coveralls could be repaired. He'd showed them to April, who, during her career as a lap-dancer, had often created her own ornate, wildly inventive costumes.

April had taken a quick look at the damage and said, "Yeah, I can fix that. Easy. All I need is a needle and some white or silver thread."

But then she'd smoothed out the material and laid down the piece Wayne had yanked out of Sammy's mouth, and changed her tune. There was no need to explain why. A small piece of material, a square about one-eighth the size of a fingernail, was missing.

Wayne had stomped all over the house, looking for it. He tore his van apart, hunting for that little square of shiny cloth.

Wherever it was, it was gone.

Frustrated, he had fired up his FXSTC Softail Custom and blasted around the city, running familiar twisties at such high speeds that the Harley's lowside footpeg often trailed a twenty-foot streamer of sparks.

High-speed antics on a powerful motorcycle is the very definition of risky business, especially in the city of Vancouver, where most drivers are apparently unaware that modern automobiles are equipped with turn signals and a functioning brake pedal.

Wayne's unavowed intention was to have a whole lot of fun, enjoy himself until he ran out of adrenalin or got caught up in the middle of a tangle of exquisitely chromed motorcycle parts lit up by a huge, high-octane fireball.

He was saved by an empty gas tank. The Harley, like most motorcycles, had a reserve tank. But insufficient fuel translated into a depressively unimpressive fireball.

The prospect of crashing spectacularly, only to suffer multiple fractures, extensive third-degree burns, and years of agony in an intensive-care facility, was not the least bit enticing.

On the other hand, no fuel at all meant he'd have to get out and push. The Harley weighed six hundred and thirteen pounds. Hey, so what! Wayne had dropped down into fourth gear and cranked it, slipped over to the wrong side of the double yellows and avoided a head-on collision with a cube van by a unit of time too small to measure. His handlebar had ticked the other vehicle's side mirror, blowing it to pieces.

Wayne had no idea what he'd hit. Something a lot bigger than a motorcycle. The impact had sent him off-line, and created a near-lethal front-end wobble. He churned up a couple of hundred feet of boulevard, and missed a concrete telephone pole by a whisker, before he was finally able to bring his machine under control.

He had motored home at not much over the speed limit. In the pit of his red-lined heart, he knew full well that, if the Harley hadn't been so strongly built, he'd have traded his life for a harp.

Or, more likely, a pitchfork.

Wayne poked at the barbecue's smouldering flames with a short length of branch stripped from the weeping willow. He kept hoping that April would come wandering out of the house with a six-pack, casually join him, maybe ask him how he was doing. Chit-chat with him, be his woman.

He turned and looked behind him. No April. There was no movement in the house.

Where was she? What was she up to? On the other side of the electrified fence, the horses shifted nervously.

By the time he'd barbecued the Mylar suit to death, Wayne smelled so bad the dogs had moved as far upwind as they could get. Cowering shamelessly behind the weeping willow, they studiously avoided eye contact when Wayne called to them, and patted his smoke-blackened thigh.

To hell with them. He stripped down to his underpants as he

beelined towards the house, and a hot shower, letting his filthy clothes fall where they may.

April found him in the tub. All of Wayne's anatomy that she could see was his head, bulging stomach, and knees. She didn't mean to be critical, but he'd sure gained a lot of weight, during the past few weeks. He'd turned out to be one of those men who tried to eat away his tension. The things you never thought to ask! To April, gaining weight didn't seem like a sensible way of dealing with stress.

But then, she knew absolutely zero about physics. Maybe Wayne had figured out that the burden of his tension would somehow be diluted if he increased his body mass.

He said, "Somethin' I can do for you?"

"Not really."

Wayne shifted position, getting the crimp out of his neck. A froth of soap bubbles clung to his beard. He was semi-glaring at her, the way he did when something was bothering him, but he wasn't sure what it was.

She said, "Want a beer?"

"You *see* any beer?"

Where was this going? April had no idea.

She said, "No, I don't."

"You sure? Take a good look around, sweetie."

April peered in as many directions as she could think of. She said, "Okay, I admit it – I don't see any beer."

"Why not?"

"I don't know. I guess because there isn't any."

"Think about it. If I wanted a beer, wouldn't I be drinking one?"

April shrugged.

Wayne said, "You can shampoo my hair, if you want to."

Oh frabjus fucking day. April got down on her knees, squeezed the bottle of herbal shampoo as if it were Wayne's throat. She told him to duck his head, and he did. She massaged the shampoo into his scalp, worked up a good lather. He had an incredibly gnarly head; his massive skull was as lumpy as a cobblestone road.

"Rinse."

Wayne leaned over. His protruding belly was an obstacle, but he managed to submerge his head as far as his ears. April sluiced the water around. She pulled him back, squeezed a fat yellow worm of shampoo onto his head, and went back to work.

"I'm clean," Wayne protested.

"No you aren't."

She twirled his soapy hair into elaborate twists, so his head looked a little like a lemon-meringue pie. "There we go, rinse, and you're all done."

Wayne said, "*Now* you can bring me a beer."

24

Antique crime-kingpin Jake Cappalletti lived just outside the UEL, the University Endowment Lands. His small mansion had been built in 1912, renovated by Jake when he'd bought it, way back in '67. The hardwood floors, oak with gum trim, had been covered with expensive pure-wool wall-to-wall carpets. The drafty leaded-glass windows had been replaced by aesthetically pleasing and much warmer double-glazed, aluminum-framed plate glass. Jake was so old he often couldn't remember how old he was. But he liked to think of himself as a modern, happenin'-type dude.

The grounds, just over an acre of prime-view real estate, were surrounded by a towering evergreen hedge. Cleverly hidden in the dense shrubbery was Jake's second line of defence – a twelve-foot-high chainlink fence, topped with "Screamin' Eagle" motion detectors, and coils of lethal razorwire. Security cameras surveyed the grounds. Jake's hulking minions patrolled the perimeter at frequent-but-entirely-random intervals. The thugs were under strict orders to take no wounded.

At the front of the house, there was an electronically controlled gate, and a manned gatehouse with a steel-clad door and bullet-proof glass windows.

Willows rode the unmarked Ford right up to the gate, so the heavy front bumper pushed the gate slightly off line. He rested his elbows on the horn, and peered impatiently through the windshield.

A slick-haired punk named Rico Cordoba sauntered casually out of the gatehouse. Rico wore a sharkskin suit the colour of polished aluminum, a black silk shirt, and a skinny white leather tie. The sky was heavily overcast, but Rico was never without his Serengetti sunglasses. His nails were professionally manicured, his shoes polished so ruthlessly that the leather had the reflective qualities of a cheap mirror. Rico was a detail man. His toenails were as well-tended as his fingernails. Twice a week, he drove downtown and paid twenty dollars to have his nose hair clipped. His *eyebrows* were gelled.

He cursed Willows with a death-stare, winked saucily at Parker, and went back into the gatehouse and pressed a green button. The gate swung open. Rico tried to wave the cops through, but too late; Willows had already gunned it up the crushed limestone driveway.

Inside the house, Jake's trusted right-hand man, Marty, said, "Here they come."

"Wunnerful," said Jake. He snapped his fingers. "Gimme muh wha-wha glaff."

Marty went over to the fireplace and took the water glass down off the mantel. He averted his gaze but held the glass rock-steady as Jake fished around for his teeth.

"Yeah, t'anks."

The glass was empty, Jake's mouth was full. It wasn't just his natural-born teeth that had abandoned him. So had his good health. He was hard-wired to a portable oxygen tank. Not a small tank either, but something that would have looked at home strapped to the flank of a Saturn rocket. Flexible plastic tubes ran from the tank's equalizer into Jake's hirsute nostrils. His favourite chair, a souvenir from a long-ago trip to his native Italy, had recently been motorized and equipped with a set of wheels. An elevator would be installed as soon as Marty had dealt with the snails down at city hall.

Marty, like his father before him, had been working for the old man for as long as he could remember. No, much longer. Once, and one time only, he'd tried to shed Jake. Take the high road to his own low future. He hadn't been able to pull it off. He was bound to Jake as if by a sticky spiderweb of blood.

Downstairs, the cops were pounding on the door.

"Dere some kinda cop 'ting against usin' da buzza?" complained Jake bitterly in his stones-rattled-in-tin-bucket voice.

The antique gangster's ears clung to his head like outsize clumps of pizza dough cut to the shape of a butterfly's wings. Ugly they might be, but man oh man, were they ever functional. Jake's hearing was so sharp he could detect a dropped pin in a mattress factory. His mind, in Marty's unhumble opinion, was sharper than a brand-new switchblade. For sure, age hadn't mellowed him. His ruthlessness quotient was way up there in the stratosphere. If there was a Mensa equivalent for viciousness, Jake would have weighed in at the head of the class.

Large feet thumped ponderously on the stairs. Marty recognized Klaus's loping, thunderous tread. Klaus, aka "Claws" aka "Sandy," was another in a short, but not short enough, line of East German recruits that Jake regretted signing. The contracts were all the same. One year, plus option. A variety of performance bonuses based strictly on the number and seriousness of crimes successfully accomplished.

The bonuses usually were freshly laundered cash, but sometimes Jake handed out all-inclusive weekend trips to Vegas, or triple-A baseball or Grizzlies basketball tickets. The past winter, the local hockey team, the Canucks, had performed so badly that recipients of gift tickets correctly assumed they'd been given the equivalent of a black spot.

The cow bell cunningly located above the front door jangled a cheerful warning, as the door was opened.

Muted voices drifted up from below, and then Klaus bellowed, "Jake! Der polizei be mit us!"

"Send 'em up!" hollered Jake.

Marty drifted over to the top of the stairs. In the foyer stood homicide dicks Jack Willows and his dishy partner, Claire. What a classy babe. In his bedroom wall safe, in the personal scrapbook he kept, even though the incriminating contents could lock him up for several lifetimes, Marty kept a dozen photographs of Parker that he'd clipped from local newspapers, over the years. He craned his neck so he could see her left hand, whether she was wearing a ring.

A couple of Jake's recent acquisitions, identical twins named Dave and Danny, were milling around down there, crowding his view while they tried to figure out if it was appropriate to frisk a policeman. The twins were slim and pale. They sported identical military-style haircuts, wore identical black plastic-framed prescription glasses, the same off-the-rack double-breasted black suits. The D-ringers even shared the same taste in music and food: salsa and Greek. They also worshipped the same film stars: Catherine Deneuve and Marlon Brando.

The twins were professional killers with impeccable reps, but they were a pain in the ass, because from the day they'd hired on, they'd bickered more or less non-stop about their possessions, and who owned what.

Worse, both twins wore several flashy quarter-carat diamond-stud earrings, one for each murder they had committed.

Dave owned three diamonds. He was everlastingly envious of the fact that Danny owned four.

Marty saw to his considerable relief that Parker still wasn't wearing a wedding or even an engagement ring. Lately, he'd heard rumours that she was going out with Willows. A married man!

Marty was mildly scandalized – about as scandalized as he'd have been scalded, had he fallen into a vat of lukewarm water. The pathetic truth was that he was jealous.

From time to time he wished he was a chartered accountant, or maybe a swim instructor. His gripe with the life of a gangster had nothing to do with the size of his retainer, or the macabre threats and infrequent-but-messy spurts of violence that were an unavoidable aspect of the profession.

What bugged him was that, despite his flashy clothes and good looks and smooth charm, not to mention his money clip full of hundred-dollar bills, he had a really hard time meeting women.

Not broads, or molls. What he wanted was a life partner. An attractive, sexy, wholly realized, totally mature, hard-thinking woman.

Some precious jewel who didn't chew gum *all* the time. Some-one who didn't find it absolutely necessary to backcomb her hair, splash on a quart of Chanel, and change into a push-up bra and five-inch stiletto heels, before she drove to the Safeway for a jug of milk and a couple loaves of sliced white.

Willows and Parker were on the stairs, had almost reached the landing. She was close enough to reach out and touch. He realized he was staring. Jack was aware of him, his undue interest.

Marty lowered his eyes and glided laterally towards his usual position by Jake's right elbow.

Jake greeted the cops with a casual wave. His hand was so liver-spotted he might have been the recipient of a skin transplant from a dalmatian.

He said, "Don' ya love it when Marty does dat Michael Jackson moonwalk 'ting?"

"Very nice," said Parker.

She had a lovely smile. Man, her smile was brighter than the night lights at Yankee Stadium.

Marty blushed. His acute embarrassment transmogrified into an unfocused, burning rage. His face felt hotter than a four-alarm fire. He was so overheated that his gold caps were in danger of melting. He spun on his heel and tramped out of the room.

Jake yelled, "Hey, where ya goin'! Don't leeme alone wit' dese bloodhounds!"

His rheumy eyes catalogued the highlights of Parker's body. Losing interest, he poked a finger in his ear, screwed it clockwise and then counterclockwise, and reluctantly withdrew it. Wax. He said, "As ya get olda, ya spoim count drops and ya production a wax quadruples. Is life ironic, or wha?"

He turned on Willows. "Ya got any kids, Jack?"

Willows nodded reluctantly. His private life was none of Jake's business. He felt threatened by the slightest interest Jake might show in him, and Jake knew it.

"Still in school, are dey? Waste a fuckin' time. Get 'em out onna street, where de can loin somethin' useful, a trade a whateva." With an effort, he sat up a little straighter in his chair. "Should de find demselves unemployed dis summa, send 'em ovah. Dey can tend da gahden, mow da grass a' whateva. Fifty bucks a hour sound about right?"

Jake's collapsed cheeks twitched spasmodically; Willows realized the ancient killer was chuckling at his own surly wit.

Parker said, "Jake, we've got some names. Photographs, if you'd care to look at them."

"Photos a wha?"

Parker enumerated the roll call of the dead, junkies and dealers. The fatality rate had not declined, in the days since the addicts had started falling. The fallen numbered more than two dozen.

Jake said, "Yeah, Lestah Rules. I knew him. Used ta be a jockey, one a dem li'l midget-type lightweight guys ride da ponies. I admit I made a few bucks offa him, placin' bets. He got inna da pain killahs, pretty soon graduated ta coke, den smack."

Jake stroked his nose.

"So he's dead, huh? Too bad." His smile segued with startling swiftness into an unholy scowl. He reached up and grabbed his incisors between his thumb and index finger, and yanked hard, jerking his entire set of teeth sideways in his mouth. "I 'member dis one time he was ridin', his pony stumbled, an' fell. Den it picks itself up offa da track an' runs full tilt boogie, headlong inta da rail. Knocked itself stoopid. It staggas around inna circle, does a nosedive inna toif. Lestah stayed inna saddle trew da whole 'ting. Aftah dat, we always called him 'Velcro.'"

Parker said, "Did Lester work for you, Jake?"

"Nah. Who tol' ya dat?"

"What about Tom Klein?"

"Da guy woiks inna theata, directin' a whateva?"

"No, that's Tom Kerr. Klein's a junkie."

"Never hoid a him."

"What about Melvin Ladner?" said Parker.

"He drive a race car?"

"They're all junkies, Jake. Most of them are dealers."

"You guys suggestin' I'm mixed up inna filthy drug scam?"

"Not at all," said Parker. "What about Warren Fishburg?"

Jake thought about it for a long time. When Marty came back into the room, he was so engrossed in his memories that he didn't look up.

Marty tapped him lightly on the shoulder.

Jake flinched, glanced up, blinking in fear.

Marty said, "It's that time, Jake."

"Fo' da pills?"

Marty nodded.

"Yeah, okay. Feed me, Marty."

The premier henchman's cupped left hand held a cornucopia of pills. Most were shaped like torpedoes, in subtle two-tone hues. Some were like buttons, and these were usually painted in the ever-popular primary colours. More than a few were tiny cannonballs, and these were black as the devil's heart. One pill that caught Parker's attention was a puffy orange triangle with electric-blue points. Marty fed the pills one after another into Jake's gaping, saliva-bright mouth. Now and then he offered him a glass of Italian red, to wash the pills down. Jake slurped and gulped, spilling far more than he drank.

Marty didn't seem to mind playing the role of nurse. His glossy eyes brimmed with heartfelt compassion. He was relentlessly attentive, and constantly murmured trite-but-encouraging phrases as he filled his boss with meds.

Dave and Danny slid silently into the room, and took up their usual positions by the fireplace.

Their earrings glittered in the light.

Jake said, "Scram, da bot' a ya."

The brothers beat it.

Willows reeled off a few more names.

Jake's eyes snapped open. "Run dat last one past me again."

"Madeleine Kara."

"Yeah, dat one. Rings a bell. Ya got a snap?"

Parker handed him a morgue photo.

Jake flinched. "Jeez. Talk about da ravages a time. Ya get da licence plate a da freight train what run ovah her face?"

Marty said, "Jake . . ."

"Ya right, I shouldn' speak ill a da dead." The photo fluttered into his lap. "I knew her twenny years ago. When she was hookin'."

"She was hooking until the day she died," said Parker.

"Ya kiddin' me? I'd ratha have sex wit' a couple a cold bricks! Anyways, I ain't seen her inna long, long time."

The names, most of them, apparently meant less than nothing to Jake. It was unclear whether this was because the murdered dealers played an insignificant role in his organization, or because he was a master at concealing his emotions, or because his memory was failing.

What was clear was that Jake was obsessed with his rapidly faltering health. He told the detectives that cigars had done him in. Cuban cigars. They'd turned his lungs into a couple of tar pits.

"I get aroun'. I know damn well itsa fashionable 'ting to hang out inna bars and lounges, smokin' cigars and lookin' cool. I hoid from Marty, who never lied to me in all his life, dat dere's women smokin' dem lethal, stinky 'tings. Women! What in hell's da woild comin' to?" Jake fixed an accusatory eye on Parker. "Ya indulge in da evil weed?"

"No," said Parker.

"I hope ta God ya tellin' me da gospel trut', truly I do."

Jake twitched minutely when Willows told him about the Polaroids left at several of the crime scenes.

"I don' 'member nothin' about dat on da TV," he said suspiciously, nibbling on his pendulous lower lip.

"We haven't released that information to the public," said Parker.

Jake knew something, she was sure.

She said, "Whisper a name, Jake. All we need is a name."

"I got nuthin' fo' ya. Whaddya harrassin' me? Do I gotta call a bunch a lawyas? Leeme alone, why doncha. I'm a helpless ol' man, and I'm tired, I wanna go ta bed an' watch dat 90210 show, 'wit da babes." He waved a limp hand. "Marty, get 'em outta here."

Jake's eyes eased shut. His snoring was overly loud and totally bogus.

Marty said, "I'll walk you to your car."

Parker's smile was dazzling. Marty was sweating. He hoped like hell that she wouldn't give him a hug and ask him to confess to a felony.

25

A glittering wraith drifted across the room. Lewis raised his head an inch or two. He must have been dreaming. Or hallucinating. A smear of pain emanated from the crook of his left arm. He let his weary head fall back on the pillow, and rolled over on his side. He'd lost patience when April was shooting him up, and had grabbed at the hypo, thrust the needle too forcefully into his arm. The pain had been agonizing, but he'd hardly cared . . .

"*Pssst.*"

Lewis reluctantly opened his eyes. The thing was back, looming over him, dancing festively away. It was wearing some kind of gold suit, like an astronaut's idea of formal wear. Its eyes were hidden behind dark goggles.

Now it was coming back at him, bouncing around, limbs flailing like a brutally misaligned puppet.

The bed creaked as the shiny, rumpled creature sat down. It wriggled and squirmed, making itself comfortable. Lewis found to his great relief that he was more confused than terrified.

He reached out and touched the shiny, silky-smooth material. It felt tougher than it looked.

The thing had something in its hand – a disposable lighter, a slim tube of burnished metal. Lewis couldn't help noticing that the creature's skin was so loose and wrinkled it looked as if it was about to shed. The snaky hiss of escaping gas tickled his ears. A lighter sparked, and a pointy, thin blue flame leapt towards him. He jerked back.

Wayne held the blue flame up to his face, illuminating the dark green goggles, his twinkling eyes.

"Hi there, Lewis."

Lewis said, "Hello, Wayne."

"Thirsty?" Wayne dipped his hand into a voluminous pocket, came up with a couple of cans of beer. He popped the tabs and offered a can to Lewis.

"Thanks."

"You're so very welcome," said Wayne. He turned the propane torch so it was pointed directly at Lewis's eye. "How's Mr. Pupil? Expanding? Contracting? You still high, Lewis?"

It was definitely Wayne.

He was wearing a shiny suit, goggles, latex gloves.

He wasn't some terrifying, extraterrestrial, *X-Files* thing that was about to wriggle out of its skin. Lewis smiled, and then, to his consternation, began laughing uncontrollably.

"What's so damn funny?" Wayne's voice was sharp. He extended his arm, and the blue jet of flame swept across Lewis's chest, scorching the *faux* Harley jammies and making Lewis fall back as if he'd been struck with an anvil.

"Hot enough for you?" Wayne's shrill cackle was reminiscent of disgruntled poultry. He said, "April sure is fond of you."

Lewis lay quietly. He looked as if he were trying to figure out what direction the next blow was going to come from. That suited Wayne just fine. He liked to keep people off balance, groping for something to hold onto, rather than having the leisure time to figure out how they were going to land *their* next punch.

Wayne said, "No offence, but I don't get it. What does she see in a loser like you? I mean, you got no job, you got no car . . ."

Lewis opened his mouth as if to speak.

"What?" said Wayne.

"I've got a truck."

"Yeah?"

"A van. An Econoline."

"Ford Econoline?"

Lewis nodded.

"There should be a song about Ford Econolines," said Wayne. "Them things been around forever." He unzipped his liquid-gold jumpsuit and fished around inside until he found his Marlboros. He lit one from the torch, but didn't offer the pack to Lewis. "What colour is it?"

"Brown."

"Nice colour," said Wayne, not putting much into it. He'd noticed a drab brown Econoline parked in front of an empty lot about three blocks away. No doubt the truck was Lewis's ride. Wayne smiled, and stroked his beard. Three blocks was just about exactly as far as he'd have guessed April was willing to walk, under any circumstances. Had she left the keys in the ignition, or thrown them away, or hidden them somewhere half-clever? He'd look before he asked. April was smart, but she wasn't much good at planning for the future. He remembered asking her about RRSPs and getting a blank look, the same kind of look a rock cod might give a waiter in a Chinese restaurant, as it was being carried into the kitchen.

Basically, a look that was dull far beyond merely uncomprehending.

He said, "Would you like to go for a ride in your Econoline, Wayne?"

"Where?"

"Where'd you meet April?"

Lewis struggled to remember. "The Eaton's parking lot."

"Metrotown?"

"No, downtown Vancouver."

"Man. I wouldn't shop there. That white tile wall on Granville Street? Looks like the world's biggest urinal." Wayne turned down the torch's flame, to conserve fuel. He said, "I'd take you home, eventually. But there's a guy I got to drop in on, along the way. I'll introduce you. He's a dealer of quality narcotics. If you find you can't kick the habit, you'll probably want to keep in touch with him." Wayne patted Lewis's knee. "Think you're gonna be able to kick, Lewis?"

"No problem." Not that he necessarily wanted to.

Wayne stubbed out his cigarette, stood his torch flame-up on the table beside the bed, and unzipped his jumpsuit from collar to crotch. He loosened the cuffs and nylon cord tie-downs at his ankles, and wriggled out of the suit. *Now* he looked like some fabulous mythical creature trying to shed its skin. He balled up the suit and tossed it at Lewis.

"Go ahead, try it on."

"Do I have to?"

"Yeah, Lewis. You have to."

"Can I leave my pyjamas on, or should I take them off?"

"Take 'em off."

Lewis modestly kept himself covered by the sheets as he levered himself out of the pyjama bottoms. Wayne didn't seem interested in his body, but he vividly remembered being asked if he was *normal*. What did Wayne mean, asking him a weird question like that? It made his skin crawl, just thinking about it. Of course he was normal. He was almost positive he was normal. Other than being kind of lazy, and a thief. His present situation excepted, of course.

He zipped up.

"Get outta bed. Walk around. Faster. You dance, Lewis? Show me how you dance."

Lewis danced around the room. The windows were covered with heavy black-out curtains. With the torch turned down so low, it was hard to see where he was going. He bumped into a piece of furniture, and staggered sideways, his arms flailing.

"Yeah," said Wayne. "Like that." He snapped his fingers, rolled his shoulders, tapped his feet. "Just exactly like that." He leaned forward, snapped on the bedside lamp. "Boogie on over here,

Lewis." Wayne did a two-hand point. "Just look at you! You could be one of them *Tap Dog* dudes, man!" He patted the bed. "Sit. I got something I wanna show you."

Breathing heavily, Lewis plunked himself down on the bed. Wayne offered him a handful of photographs, Polaroids he had carefully selected from his gallery of stars.

The photos were, without exception, shots of men and women lying on linoleum or carpeted floors. The photos had all been taken from a height of about three feet. Lewis studied them closely, each in turn. He'd thought he might be expected to recognize somebody, and he was relieved that he couldn't. There was something these people all shared, a certain lack of sparkle, that hinted at a high level of lifelessness.

Maybe, in fact, they were all dead. He shuddered.

"Something wrong?"

"I'm fine," said Lewis. "Why are you . . ." His voice faded, dwindled like a trail in the woods that petered out so gradually, so imperceptibly, that you were never sure exactly when you had arrived at nowhere.

"Why am I showing you these pictures?"

Lewis nodded, not at all sure he wanted to know the answer.

"I don't know," said Wayne. "I probably shouldn't. I guess I want you to understand the situation."

Lewis stared blankly at him.

"The current situation," Wayne explained.

"Where's April?"

"Can't help you there, Lewis." Wayne's blunt finger tapped the topmost overlapping photo.

"Know who that is?"

"No."

"No?"

"No, I don't."

"Warren Fishburg. This's Madeleine Kara, and that one there, that's Sandy Newton. Cute, ain't she? If you like blondes. You got a thing for blondes, Lewis?" Wayne shuffled the cards. "Neil

Winwood. Lester Rules." Wayne showed him several more pictures. "This last one, that's Sammy Wu. Check the expression on
Sammy's face." Wayne playfully nudged Lewis in the ribs. "Is that
a million-dollar smile, or what? I bet his dentist is proud as hell."

"Is he dead?" Lewis wanted to swallow his tongue. What a
foolish, foolish question.

"Yeah, he's dead. He was okay when the picture was taken. Well,
not exactly okay. But he was alive. Sort of. I mean, he was never
what you'd call a flamin' ball of fire."

Wayne flipped the Polaroid belly-up. There was a date typed
on the back.

"That's the day he died. I stand corrected – that's the day he
was murdered."

Murdered.

Wayne lined up the edges of the photos so they made a tidy,
quarter-inch-thick stack.

"They're all junkies, all dead. Overdosed victims of an uncar-
ing society, is one way you might put it." He fanned the pictures.
There was a sameness to them. Sallow, underfed faces. Stringy hair,
hollow cheeks. Burn marks. All those doomed eyes, so many of
them, stared incuriously up at Lewis.

Lewis wanted to be sick. His empty stomach rolled over. He
hadn't eaten for a long time. Hard to say how long, the way the
hours and days were slipping past. There was nothing in his belly
but bile.

Wayne said, "They look like junkies to you?

"Yes."

They did, too. He was sure of it, though he had no idea why. It
was like a sparrow stumbling across a flock of sparrows. Recogni-
tion was instantaneous, and that was all that mattered.

"What're you thinkin', Lewis?"

"I was just wondering how birds recognize each other."

"Huh?"

Lewis struggled to find the word. *Species.* He said, "I was just
wondering how birds of the same species recognize each other."

Wayne produced several more Polaroids.

"What d'ya think of these?"

The second set of pictures had been taken from varying angles, but each at a distance sufficient to squeeze the whole of the victim's naked body into the frames.

Lewis couldn't help himself. He had to ask. It seemed, somehow, in important ways he needn't understand, sacrilege not to bother. "Are they dead?"

"Almost, but not quite." Wayne chuckled. "They're feeling no pain, I can tell you that much."

"Are they the same people you showed me before?"

"Yeah." Wayne ticked them off. Madeleine Kara, Sandy Newton. "Not so much of a blonde any more, is she?" Warren Fishburg. Maggie Collins. Tom Klein. Neil Winwood. Lester Rules, Russ Green and Toby Clark, Sammy Wu.

The victims lay on their backs, ankles together, ribs and hip bones protruding, arms folded on their chests. Here a syringe, there a syringe.

Wayne said, "Yeah, they look like junkies. Sure they do. Why shouldn't they? But if you dressed them in expensive clothes, *then* who would they look like? Society dames? Captains of industry? The idle rich?"

Wayne stared at the photo of Sammy Wu. Was that a happy smile, or had his mouth been twisted by a semi-realized irony? Either way, you'd have to be out of your mind to confuse him with a captain of anything, except maybe the *Titanic*. He certainly was idle, though.

Well, no, he wasn't.

Wayne knew what was happening to Sammy Wu, and to dark-haired Madeleine Kara, and the almost-but-not-quite-still-delectable Sandy Newton, and chunky, pockmarked Warren Fishburg, and Neil Winwood, with his bandit moustache, and to double-happy Lester Rules, and all the rest of them. In the chill of the morgue, the pace of decomposition was slowed to an imperceptible crawl. Pull out a stainless-steel drawer, lift the sheet and take a quick look at what was underneath, you'd think the corpse was perfectly preserved. But inside, where it counted, the slow and silent, inevitable process of collapse and decomposition had been under way since the moment the victim had drawn his – or her – last ragged breath.

In terms of the pathologist's convenience, the deceased had been stabilized. But even though they were relatively secure in the environment of the morgue, their flesh continued to melt. When the morgue was done with them, when they'd been eviscerated to death, *sushi'd* to the max, the city would give them a pauper's funeral. In the warm earth of spring, the bodies would disintegrate at an accelerated pace. Soon there would be nothing left but tattered hanks of hair, heaps of pearly bones . . .

Lewis had hardly touched his beer. He didn't seem to notice when Wayne took it away from him.

Lewis was slowly coming down, inching towards being miserable, in dire need of his next fix. Wayne told him to take off the jumpsuit. While Lewis snuggled into his jammies, Wayne folded the suit and put it away in a cardboard box, with the photographs. The Polaroids that were now covered with dozens of overlapping fingerprints, all of them Lewis's.

By the time Wayne was ready to leave the room, Lewis was back in bed, buried up to his nose under the covers. He told Wayne he was cold. Wayne wasn't terribly interested in unsolicited bitching. He snatched up his propane torch, turned the burner on high and held it close to his hairy, demented face. A foot-long spear of pale blue flame was reflected, in vastly reduced miniatures, in Wayne's burning eyes.

Lewis scuttled under the sheets.

Lewis's body ached. He couldn't stop shivering. The bedroom was dark, and a warm spring rain pattered musically on the sheets. He risked a quick look.

April lay beside him. Her face was wet. She was crying, but all he could think about was his desperate need, his endless craving, for heroin.

Outside, in the yard, the dalmatians barked and horses whinnied and frogs croaked, and Wayne, enveloped in a cloud of Raid, cackled like an enormous, totally crazed chicken.

26

Willows idled the city's unmarked Ford down the crushed lime-stone driveway leading from Jake's front door to the street. He was a little surprised to see Marty, breathing heavily, loitering in the gatehouse. He nodded tersely as he drove by, but received nothing in return. Marty never even saw him. The punk only had eyes for Claire. The gate closed slowly but not quite majestically behind them. Willows made a hard right, slowed for the intersection. The view of the inner harbour and downtown core was postcard-gloomy. The freighters had their sterns to the Stanley Park seawall, which meant the tide was turning.

Willows was steaming. As they'd walked from the house to their car, they'd passed the open doors of Jake's twelve-car garage. The twins had exited the house via an unseen door and were on their way over to the garage for a stint of remedial dusting and polishing. The chrome noses of Jake's collection of purebreds glinted brightly. Willows was no automobile buff, but he was able to identify a prewar Jaguar, a burly Humvee, a Toyota LandCruiser, a Dodge Viper, and Jake's birthday gift to the twins: a matched pair of brand-new banana-yellow Volkswagen Beetles.

One stall was empty. Jake's favourite set of wheels, a Rolls-Royce Silver Shadow, squatted on the driveway in front of the garage. The Rolls was being lovingly washed by Jake's most recent acquisition, a massive, bald-headed, bright-eyed employee named Harvey "The Rabbit" Corville.

Harvey wore a studded black leather jacket, black jeans, heavy black leather boots with silver toe caps. The hairless dome of his skull shone so brightly it might have been waxed. Harvey was working hard, and with good reason. If Jake approved of the way Harvey washed the vehicles, he'd eventually be allowed to groom Jake's trio of dobermans, and his precious rottweiler, Butch. If and when Harvey cleared the not-insignificant hurdle of properly caring for Jake's canines, he would be introduced to the exotic world of threats and muggings. After that, the sky was the limit. In anywhere from five to ten years, if he behaved himself, he'd be trusted with the heavy responsibility of killing people. Not ordinary citizens, but criminals such as himself. Only Marty was so deeply trusted that he was allowed to bump off the good guys. And so far, if Harvey had it right, Marty hadn't taken advantage.

Harvey didn't understand how Marty could have so much self-control. Speaking strictly for himself, there were at least two or three times a day when he'd have whacked somebody, if he had immunity. For example that clerk at . . .

He finally realized it was *his* cellphone that was ringing. He dropped the sponge, wiped his soapy hands on his pants, unzipped his jacket and snatched the phone from an inside pocket.

"Hello?"

Jake said, "Where ya been, Harvey?"

"Right here, Jake."

"Yeah, yeah, but I can't *see* ya, dimwit! Ya been washin' da Rolls?"

Harvey nodded.

Jake said, "Da cops still dere?"

Harvey nodded again, more forcefully.

"Harvey!" Jake screeched.

"Yes, Jake."

"Are da cops still dere, yeah a no?"

"Yes, Jake." Christ, was the old man deaf?

"Give da phone to da woman."

Harvey nodded. His boots crunched on limestone as he sprinted towards Willows and Parker. The detectives heard him coming, and turned to face him.

Harvey offered the phone to Parker. "Jake would like to speak with you."

"About what?"

Harvey made the mistake of asking. The kingpin's overheated reply turned Harvey's unbejewelled ear the colour of an autumn leaf. He thrust the phone into Parker's hand.

Jake said, "Claire, what we was talkin' about, Marty's gonna sniff around a li'l, see what he can loin."

"Thanks, Jake."

"Will ya promise me somethin'?"

Parker waited, but not for long.

Jake's voice was a furtive, conspiratorial whisper she was just barely able to hear above the hiss and wheeze of Harvey's hyper-ventilating. "Come to my funeral, will ya?"

Was Jake serious? He'd never been anything but serious. Parker said, "Is that an open invitation, or . . ."

"I got no premonition when I'm gonna kick, if that's what yer askin'. But, Jeez, did ya take a look at me? I'm a fuckin' geezer. Most a these stoopids I got workin' fer me could be my grandkids, I should be so unlucky to have any." For Jake, it was a long speech, and it ended with as little warning as it had begun.

"Jake, you still there?"

"Fo' da time being."

Parker said, "Well, let me put it this way. I'd love to come to your funeral. But only if Jack's invited too."

"Goes wit'out sayin'," said Jake gruffly.

Was the old man weeping? Parker found herself listening intently to a dial tone. She tried to return the cellphone to Harvey. He refused to accept it.

"Jake said to give you the phone," he explained.

"Fine," said Parker. She started to turn away, and then stopped herself. "Harvey?"

He nodded.

"If Marty asks you if you'd like to go for a scenic drive in the country, just say no."

"Why?" said Harvey bluntly.

Parker told him.

He was still laughing, uproariously, when Willows made the hard right turn at the bottom of the driveway.

Parker said, "What d'you think, Jack?"

"About Harvey? I think he's going to end up feeding crustaceans at the bottom of Howe Sound."

"No, I mean about Jake."

"Jake isn't going to do us any favours. Why should he? We could pin six murders on him in the next ten minutes, Jake'd be out on bail five minutes later, dead of natural causes years before his trial was even scheduled."

They were closing in on Fourth Avenue. Willows lifted a hand from the wheel, and briskly snapped his fingers. The light turned green.

Parker feigned amazement. "How do you *do* that?"

"It's all in the timing."

"Where have I heard that before?" said Parker. The seatbelt was an encumbrance, but she managed to lean close enough to Willows to rest her hand on his thigh. They drove in companionable silence for a few minutes, and then she said, "Obviously the dead addicts are intended to send a message to the survivors. Buy elsewhere. Jake's got to be hurting."

"Hurting like hell," agreed Willows.

"The killer turned up the heat when he bumped off Melvin Ladner, cranked it up to the boiling point when he moved up the distribution ladder and killed Sammy Wu. The question is – does Jake have any idea who's trying to wipe him out?"

"If he did," said Willows, "he'd have reacted by now, and we'd know about it. Jake isn't the kind of guy who worries about hiding the bodies. Besides, he'd want plenty of publicity. Everybody in the business knows he's been hit. He'd want those same people to know he'd hit back."

Parker was in complete agreement with Willows' analysis of the situation. As soon as Jake found out who was bumping off his network of dealers, Marty and the Mirror Twins and a dozen other thugs would hit the streets running.

At MacDonald, Willows made a left, and ducked down to Cornwall. Traffic was light. In five minutes they were on the approach to the Burrard Street Bridge. The electric readout above the Molson's Brewery was obscured by a cloud of steam. Willows was unable to make out the temperature, but even so, he knew that it was a lot warmer than it should have been. In Vancouver, the cataclysmic warming of the globe seemed to be proceeding ahead of schedule. In another year or two, the variety of deciduous trees that graced the city's boulevards would be replaced by row upon row of towering palms.

Parker had been thinking. As they turned onto the bridge she said, "Didn't the Quick 'n' Easy Escorts receptionist ask if you were interested in two women?"

Willows sensed a trap. He said, "Yeah, but she thought she was talking to Sammy."

"That's not the point, Jack."

Willows concentrated on his driving.

Parker said, "Why did she think Sammy might want two women?"

"Because he'd used two in the past."

"The *recent* past," said Parker.

The third-floor squadroom was unoccupied but for Eddy Orwell. The beefiest of the homicide detectives was hunched over his desk. His posture indicated that he was hard at work, but, as Willows and Parker drew near, they saw he was immersed in a crossword puzzle. Orwell buttonholed Parker as she walked past his desk.

"Hey, Claire. How you doing?"

"Good, Eddy. Where's Oikawa?"

"You don't want to know. Give me a hand with this, will you?" He turned the folded newspaper so Parker could read it more easily. "Two across."

Parker read the clue. *Author of Animal Farm.* She smiled. "I wish I could help you, Eddy."

Orwell's deeply embedded paranoia, an unhappy consequence of his marriage, rose swiftly to the surface. "But what? You can't? Or you won't?"

"Got to get to work, Eddy." Willows had taken off his jacket and was reaching for his phone. Parker sat down at her desk. She scanned through the Sammy Wu file as Willows dialled the prostitute's private number. He leaned back in his chair, suddenly sat erect. "Holly, this is detective Jack Willows. I want to ask you a few questions about your visits with Sammy Wu . . ." His expression hardened. He said, "Listen to me, Holly . . ." He jerked the phone away from his ear, and slammed it down.

"Holly otherwise engaged?" said Parker sweetly.

Willows referred to his notebook. He picked up the phone and dialled.

"Quick 'n' Easy Escort Service, Debbie speaking."

"Debbie, this is Detective Jack Willows."

"What can we do for you, Detective?"

Willows said, "Holly wasn't always alone when she visited Sammy Wu, was she?"

There was a brief pause. He could almost, but not quite, hear Debbie's cogs slowly spinning.

Finally she said, "Jack, I'm not sure I should discuss that with you. Can I put you on hold for a minute?"

"Sure."

Willows found himself listening to recorded music. Madonna. Who else?

A heavy, aggressively masculine voice came on the line.

"Detective Willows, Edward Griffin. I'm a partner in the

company. Debbie tells me you're interested in Mr. Wu's dating preferences?"

"Right."

"Holly was always his favourite. If he was in the mood for a twosome, he'd ask for a friend of Holly's, a woman named Barbara. Unfortunately, Barbara – Barb – is no longer working for us."

It was a waste of time, but Willows had to ask. "Do you happen to know where we can reach her?"

"I'm afraid not."

Willows said, "If you hear from her, would you please get in touch with me as soon as possible?"

"Yes, of course. I believe Deb has your number?"

"I believe she does," said Willows. He politely thanked Edward Griffin for his time, and gently disconnected.

On her way past Orwell, who was still working on the crossword puzzle, Parker said, "Orwell."

"Yeah?"

"Yeah," said Parker.

The corporate headquarters of Quick 'n' Easy Escorts was located on the top floor of a three-storey walkup on Davie, just off Granville. It wasn't a great neighbourhood, and it didn't look as if it was in much of a hurry to improve itself. But it was centrally located, close to several moderately priced hotels. Parker thought that must be a consideration, given the nature of Quick 'n' Easy's business.

The receptionist, Debbie, was reading a tattered copy of the August 1996 issue of *Shape* magazine. The lead article was titled "Bikini Butt, 6 new moves for your best behind." She glanced up, more surprised than annoyed, as Willows and Parker brushed past her down-at-the-heels desk. Debbie was a perfectly accessorized redhead. She had big lips and big eye shadow, and she wore a really big sweater. Her glossy black fingernails were very big, and so was her attitude, when she finally realized what was going on.

"Hey, you can't go in there!"

Willows pushed his way into Griffin's office, with Parker close behind. She was careful not to slam the door.

Edward Griffin's desk was larger than Debbie's, and in much better condition. This may have been to compensate for the fact that Edward Griffin was smaller than Debbie, and in even worse shape. Griffin vaguely resembled Danny DeVito's considerably older, shorter, and less wise brother. He turned off his electric razor and carefully put it away in a desk drawer. Then, taking it one step at a time, he turned so he squarely faced the detectives, and offered them the most insincere smile that either of them had ever seen.

"You must be Jack. And you must be Claire."

Willows said, "But you can't be Edward, because he sounded so much bigger than you'll ever be."

Griffin shrugged. "I'm not supposed to meet people. That's not part of my job. It's the *girls* who meet people." He reached across his desk and picked up the phone, punched a button.

"Debbie, get me Barb." Clasping his hand over the receiver, he made eye contact with Willows and said, "Can I interest you in a Braun portable razor? New in the box, 20 per cent off retail?"

"Can I interest you in a cell?" countered Willows. "It's used, but still has plenty of years left in it."

"Barb? Edward. You in a cab? Get your ass over here, baby. I don't care about that. Don't keep me waiting, 'kay?"

Griffin hung up. He said, "She's in a cab, on her way over. Be here in a couple minutes." Griffin's tired eyes shifted from Parker to Willows and back to Parker. "Want a drink? No? You sure?" He slid open the desk drawer, held up his razor. "You mind?"

He was still shaving, working on his upper lip, when Barbara slipped into the office.

Willows wasn't sure what he'd expected. Someone like Holly, he supposed. Someone who looked like a hooker, not a tired, middle-aged nun. If Barbara was wearing makeup, she had applied it too subtly for him to detect.

She turned on Griffin. "Turn that fucking thing off, Edward!"

Edward Griffin promptly switched off his Braun.

Barbara leaned against her boss's desk. She dug a pack of filter cigarettes and a disposable plastic lighter out of her purse, lit up, and exhaled a cloud of smoke into Griffin's face.

"Cut that out, dammit!"

Barbara flicked ash onto Griffin's desk. To Parker, she said, "I got to get out of here. What d'you want to know?"

"You knew Sammy Wu?"

"Yeah, sure. But I didn't know anything about him. Except for his sexual preferences. I mean, we never talked about personal stuff. It wasn't that kind of relationship."

"What kind of relationship was it?" said Parker.

"Strictly business."

"When you visited him, was there ever anyone else there?"

"You mean, aside from Holly?"

Parker nodded.

"Just once, the last time I was there."

"When was that?"

"Two weeks ago today."

"Do you remember the man's name?"

"Mr. Smith," said Barbara with no trace of irony.

"Did you get the impression Mr. Smith was a friend of Sammy's?"

"Must've been, because Sammy paid his freight." Barbara frowned. "On the other hand, Sammy didn't have any friends. He wasn't that kind of guy. So I guess it was business with him, too."

Parker said, "Can you describe Mr. Smith?"

"Not really."

"Why not?"

"Well, you might find this kind of hard to believe, but I never really looked at the guy. He was big and had a full beard. That's all I can tell you. Truth is, I never look at any of them. I just let my brain go out of focus, know what I mean? They're paying for the use of my body, not my mind. So I'm there, but I'm not there . . ."

Parker nodded, getting it. She was aware that Willows was staring at her, scrutinizing her. Parker had been engaged, back in her twenties. Suffered a long-term relationship that went nowhere for years, before she finally wised up, and cut and run. She supposed she was going to have to let Jack in on her little secret, explain, and reassure.

She took his hand, and let him see the love for him that was in her eyes, her very soul.

Barbara saw it, too. She looked away.

27

He was alone, again. Sometime during the evening, April had slipped away. Lewis rolled over on his back and stared up at the ceiling. As usual, he had no idea what time it was or even what day it was. He tried to imagine where April might have gone. He pictured her in the mall parking lot, and then in the backyard, and then in the kitchen. The rest of the world, all of it, was a blank. His body tingled. He walked his fingertips lightly across his face, and wasn't at all sure he recognized the topography. He accepted that he had no idea where April was or what she might be up to or when she might return to him.

He rolled over on his belly, and clutched at either side of the mattress as if he were afraid it might fly away and not take him with it. He might have dozed off again, and, if he did, he was reawakened by the television. He rolled over on his side so he could face the screen. There was a tape playing in the VCR.

Some kind of crudely animated cartoon . . . Lush green fields filled the screen. Tall grass bent in the swirling blue wind.

Hump-backed cartoon grizzly bears waded the shallows of a picturesque stream. The bears kept slapping at the water, shoving their large heads under the surface as if they meant to commit suicide. One of them came up with a large cartoon fish. An improbably huge fish. The fish wriggled and squirmed, and then went limp. The camera moved in for a close-up. Large black crosses had been drawn across the fish's bulging eyes, signifying death.

The bear's teeth were yellow, and curved inward. They didn't look particularly sharp, but they sure were powerful.

The fish's rainbow body was streaked with blood.

The camera panned to reveal distant, stereotypically picturesque snow-capped mountains.

A cartoon bald eagle hovered above a turquoise lake nestled into a steep valley.

Rows of bent and twisted cartoon fruit trees, their branches heavy with fruit, dotted a sun-bleached meadow.

Spliced onto the end of the animated footage was a shot of a black Jeep launching itself over a rise. The Jeep came crashing down on scrub brush in a cloud of dust.

Brakes squealed.

Wayne smiled at the camera. He got out of the Jeep and reached behind him for a rifle. He leaned against the Jeep and sighted over the hood at an unseen target, and squeezed the trigger.

The sound of the gunshot was so loud it hurt Lewis's ears.

Wayne's bullet smacked into an actual living specimen of a grizzly bear, as the creature waded across a river with a salmon dangling from its mouth. In anguish, the bear thrashed the water to foam. Wayne shot it again. The bear stopped struggling. It drifted slowly downriver for a hundred feet or so, until its body was caught in a backwater.

Wayne's bushy head filled the screen. The rifle was slung across his back. He unslung the weapon and drew a bead on the camera, and fired. Lewis flinched. The bed trembled.

Flesh-and-blood Wayne reached out and patted Lewis on the hip. He offered him a Marlboro. They sat there in the semi-darkness, smoking.

Wayne said, "I don't care if I do get cancer. I don't care if I have to spend the last half of my life in a wheelchair, hard-wired to a tankful of oxygen. I don't care if I get Alzheimer's, either. Know why?"

Lewis shook his head.

"Know why?" persisted Wayne.

"No," said Lewis.

"Because it'll have been worth it. Man, there's nothing like a cigarette. A cigarette, and a nice cold beer."

Numbers frantically climbed all over themselves as the VCR's counter wound rapidly back towards quadruple zeros.

Wayne said, "After a long ride on my bike, that's when I enjoy a smoke the most. It's hard to explain, I mean, if you ain't been there, you ain't done that. But I feel so relaxed, kind of sleepy sometimes. It's a real pleasure to stretch out on the sofa, light up, and just lie there, nice and peaceful, and think about the ride."

To Lewis, it sounded as if Wayne enjoyed motorcycling the same way most people, *normal* people, enjoyed sex. He almost said so. But then he remembered April confidentially telling him that Wayne had never been sexually interested in her. So he kept his mouth shut, and kept on living.

The VCR clicked noisily as the tape finished rewinding. Wayne dipped his hand into his shirt pocket. He pointed the remote at the VCR, and pushed a button.

Lush green cartoon fields, tall grass bending in a swirling blue wind.

Wayne hit the remote's pause button.

"You hunt?"

Lewis said no.

"Big mistake. There's no place like the woods. You can learn so much out there, in such a short time." Wayne pulled on his Marlboro, flicked ash at the floor. Exhaling, he said, "You grab some guy off the street, drop him off in the middle of a forest with a pack of matches, a knife and a firearm, he'll learn more about himself in twenty-four hours than he'd have otherwise figured out in a lifetime."

Judging from the way Wayne was staring at him, it looked as if he expected a reply. Lewis tried to think of something appropriate.

He was wired, not thinking clearly or really interested in thinking clearly. At last he said, "How's that?"

"A man finds himself alone in the woods, he's got no one to depend on but himself. Ain't no 7-Eleven he can wander into, pick up a candy bar and a Slurpee. Whether he lives or dies is entirely up to him."

Wayne reached out and plucked Lewis's dwindled cigarette from his mouth and dropped it and his own cigarette butt on the floor, stamped the life out of both of them.

"Kill or be killed, that's the deal." He lit another cigarette, taking his time about it, making a production of it. "Seems like you been with us a long time, Lewis. It's like, well, it's almost like you're a member of the family. Dalmatian number three." Wayne slapped his beefy thigh. He chuckled throatily. "Hey, just kidding." He turned and pointed the remote at the VCR.

The cartoon grizzly fished in the shallows of a wilderness river.

The cartoon eagle played with the winds.

The black Jeep hurtled over a rise, skidded to a stop in a cloud of dust that slowly drifted away to reveal Wayne's hairy, grinning face.

TV Wayne grabbed the rifle, aimed and fired.

Real Wayne hit the remote's rewind button. Then stop, then forward.

TV Wayne grabbed the rifle, aimed and fired.

Real Wayne hit the pause button. He said, "Think back to when I got home, that day you moved in with us. Remember? That sly bitch April had changed the locks. I started bellowing and kicking at the door . . . Had to knock it flat as a pancake for the simple pleasure of making your acquaintance, Lewis. There any chance at all you still remember that?"

Lewis said, "I think so."

"So tell me, can you recall what you were thinking, in the moment my boots turned that door to kindling?"

Lewis furrowed his brow.

He said, "It seems like a long time ago."

"I bet it does. Time can get real tricky, when you're a dope fiend."

Lewis said, "I was frightened. I was afraid."

"Sure you were. Hell, why wouldn't you be? You're in some guy's house, fooling around with his girlfriend . . ." Wayne saw Lewis was about to protest, and warned him off with a raised fist. "You'd have to have titanium balls, not to be a little worried. But the thing is, who were you frightened for? Yourself, or April?"

The question was a real toughie. Despite his narcotic-befuddled state of mind, Lewis had sufficient smarts to realize that sometimes the right answer was the wrong answer. He tackled the tricky, peripheral-vision-straining chore of studying Wayne while pretending not to look at him. But what if the question contained more than one hairpin curve? Lewis considered this possibility at length. Meanwhile, Wayne seemed content to smoke his cigarette.

What if the question doubled back on itself twice, and cancelled itself out? The more Lewis thought about it, the more confused he became.

"Time's up," said Wayne. He scowled. "I got to tell you, the fact of you sitting there mulling it over at your leisure pisses me off something fierce."

"April," said Lewis.

"What about her?"

"When you were kicking down the door, I feared for April."

"Like hell you did, you goddamn liar."

"No, it's the truth."

"You'd just met her. Fuck me tender, she near killed you with pepper spray, kicked you in the balls and . . ." Wayne was a long way past confounded. He said, "Jesus H. Christ, she *kidnapped* you!"

"Did not."

"Excuse me?" Wayne's face looked as if it was trying to break down into its component parts. He tried a sardonic chuckle but came nowhere near pulling it off. "You're denying she bagged you? You're saying, what, you tagged along voluntarily?"

"She's a beautiful woman. I fell for her. She told me she was crazy about me. It was one of those love-at-first-sight deals." Lewis hungered for a Marlboro. He scooted down the bed until he was close enough to Wayne to reach out and sneak the pack from his shirt pocket. Wayne offered his lighter. Lewis lit up, inhaled deeply. Wayne didn't ask for his lighter back, so Lewis kept it.

He said, "Don't get mad at her, okay? It isn't her fault, any more than it's *my* fault. I mean, it isn't anybody's fault, it's just one of those things."

Wayne said, "I don't pretend to understand the deep recesses of the human heart. But I can tell you this much – I'm damn happy you said you love her. Know why?"

"No, why?"

"Rod McGuire. Ever heard of him?"

Lewis actually considered the possibility, even though he'd never met anybody with that name. Or even a similar name. Like . . . what? Well, how about *Tod Squire*?

Wayne said, "Hey! Wake up! Rod McGuire. D'you know him?"

"No, I don't think so . . ."

"Rod's a dealer," said Lewis. "You ever give pause to think for even ten seconds about where April got all the drugs she's been pumping into your miserable freeloading veins?"

"I guess not."

"You're a no-good fucking leech!" said Wayne contemptuously.

Lewis hung his head.

Wayne said, "April owes Rod about three thousand dollars. Some of it, but not much, was spent on projects other than yourself. But the point is, she needs our help, and we're going to give it freely. Aren't we?"

"If you say so."

"I *do* say so. I say so repeatedly. Gimme back my fucking lighter. Thank you. You know anything about computers?"

"Not really."

"Rod owns a computer, likes to play those crazy, violent games. *Death Chase*, crap like that. You and me, we're going to pretend we're computer repairmen, so we can gain access to his house. That's why you get to wear the nifty gold suit, Lewis. So you look like a bona fide computer technician. Once we're inside, we'll convince McGuire to leave April alone, just forget about her, write off the money she owes him as a bad debt."

Wayne smiled.

"How's that sound to you?"

"I'm not sure . . ." Lewis was confused. He said, "Is there something wrong with the guy's computer?"

"How should I know?" Wayne was exasperated. "The point is, we'll *tell* him there's something wrong with the damn thing. Or tell him the warranty expired, or some such bullshit. How the hell would he know otherwise? All he uses the damn thing for is to play a bunch of stupid, childish games."

Lewis still didn't get it. He was fairly sure his brain was only functioning at about 30 per cent, but even so, Wayne's scheme seemed particularly harebrained. You couldn't just knock on somebody's door and tell them their computer was broken and you'd come to fix it – especially in the middle of the night. A person would have to be a certified moron, to believe something that unlikely.

Wayne, too, was thinking it might be a good idea to work up a plan "B." The computer-repair pitch didn't sound quite so rock-solid, now that he'd said it out loud. Maybe April could come up with something. That girl's brain was as twisted as five miles of chicken wire. He said, "Don't fret the details, Lewis. All you got to remember is that we're going to do whatever it takes to convince Rod McGuire to leave April alone."

"Okay," said Lewis.

What choice did he have? None. Wayne outweighed him by about one hundred and fifty pounds, out-meaned him by a factor of about a thousand to one.

Wayne said, "Back in a minute."

Lewis spent the time wondering where April was. How could he have any idea? Maybe she was with the dalmatians. Or, maybe she was somewhere else.

Wayne was back, with a cardboard box. He dipped into the box, and, no surprise, came up with the shiny gold jumpsuit.

"Put it on."

"Do I have to?"

"Hell, no! You go right ahead and tuck yourself back under the covers and snooze away. Sweet dreams, if that's what turns your crank. Just don't come whining, all runny-nosed and ugly, to me or April, next time you crave some dope."

Wayne checked his watch.

"Which should be in about two hours' time, Lewis. So tell me, can you think that far ahead, or is it too big a challenge?"

The grizzlies, three of them, two adults and a cub, cavorted in the shallows of the wilderness river.

The eagle played with the winds.

The Jeep hurtled over a rise, skidded to a stop in a cloud of dust that slowly drifted away . . .

Wayne was staring at him, a brittle look in his eyes. Not saying a word. Waiting impatiently, breathing fast and hard.

Lewis mulled over his critically short list of options. He reached for the Mylar suit. As he wriggled into it, the shiny gold material rustled softly, like a roomful of conspiracies.

Behind him, TV Wayne was blasting away, having a wonderful time.

28

The unmarked Ford was parked, grill out, in the driveway of a cooperative citizen who lived a little under a block from Jake's mini-mansion. Willows was in the backseat, sleeping. Parker was slouched low behind the wheel. Her window was open a crack, to stop the car from steaming up. She had a clear view of the mouth of Jake's driveway, and the brightly lit windows on the home's second floor. Because they had no other solid leads, she and Willows had decided to stake out the house and hope for the worst. The continuing assault on Jake's network of dealers had to be hurting him badly. Jake had never been the kind of guy who was content to sit around licking his wounds, and hoping for better days.

Sooner or later, Jake was going to figure out who was trying to run him out of town. When that happened, the old man would strike hard, with everything he had.

Inside the house, Marty lay on the sofa, reading the paper. From time to time he routinely glanced over at Jake, checking to make sure his supply of oxygen was getting to him, that the old man was okay.

Jake sat there in his big, wheeled chair, stolid as a rock, watching the late-night news. He wore baggy black silk pyjamas with a white silk monogram, and white silk piping. A foot of unlit Cuban cigar hung from his mouth. He'd watched the national news, and then the local, and now he was watching the sports reports. He seemed equally fascinated by whatever happened to appear on the screen, including the commercials, many of which promoted products the old man couldn't possibly find any use for, or be interested in. But through it all, the entire hour, he never moved a muscle. Not that he had a whole lot of muscle to move, unless you counted the muscle standing at limp attention to either side of him.

When the news ended he glanced left and right to make sure the twins were paying attention, then lifted his mottled hand, a wrinkled finger.

"Dave."

"Right here, Jake."

"Tell ya brudder, Danny, ta change da channel."

"Sure thing, Jake. Got a particular channel in mind?"

"Leno."

"Right, Jake." Dave cleared his throat. "Hey, Danny."

"Right here, Dave."

"Change the channel, Jake wants Leno."

"Got it."

The twins were given control of the TV's remote-control device on alternating evenings. Sometimes Jake deliberately screwed up the rotation just to watch them wriggle and squirm. A year ago, he wouldn't have been interested in such minutiae. Marty worried constantly about Jake's dwindling horizons.

When Leno finally ended, Jake yawned and stretched, and told Marty he wanted a word with Harvey.

Marty folded his paper and put on his shoes. The twins watched him tie the laces as if they had never seen him tie his laces before, or perhaps assumed he would vary his technique in a way that would prove educational.

Harvey's compact self-contained apartment was over the garage. Marty thumped heavily up the stairs, bringing his heels down hard. Harvey must have heard him, because he opened the door just as Marty reached the landing.

"Marty!"

Harvey seemed surprised. Had he been expecting someone else? Marty tried to work up a list of heavy-footed people he knew, other than Danny and Dave. Harvey had faded back into the apartment, leaving the door open behind him. Marty wandered inside.

Romantic stringed music played softly. The table in the kitchen-dining area was set for three. A bottle of domestic "champagne" stood fairly upright in a bucket of ice. A bouquet of flowers huddled in a blue glass vase. Harvey's stainless-steel cutlery glittered in the light provided by a trio of sturdy pink candles.

Marty said, "Expecting company?"

Harvey killed the stereo, snuffed the candles, cleared away the dishes and silverware, and shoved the ice bucket in a cupboard drawer. "Not really."

"My mistake," said Marty tactfully. If Harvey had a secret social life, that was just fine with him.

Harvey wore a sleeveless T-shirt, black alpine climbing shorts, a pair of beach sandals, and a queer little green felt hat with a jaunty red feather sticking out of the band. He said, "I hope so. Jake'd kill me in a minute, if he knew."

"You got that right," said Marty.

"Should I quit?"

"Quit what?"

Harvey frowned, just then realizing how ambiguous his question might appear to someone who didn't know what he was referring to.

Marty smiled. "Quit Jake? Seek employment elsewhere? It ain't gonna happen, Harvey. Jake's terms of employment were explained to you when you signed on. Didn't you read the contract? Short-term or long, working for Jake is a lifetime commitment." He said, "The reason I dropped by, Jake wants to see you."

"Now?"

"No, a couple minutes ago."

Harvey reluctantly started towards the door. He veered away towards his bedroom. "Gimme a minute to change, okay?"

"Good idea."

Harvey was back in a minute, dressed for a funeral. "Jake say what he wanted?"

Marty smiled. "Be brave, okay?"

Harvey nodded uncertainly. He was still adjusting the lapels of his charcoal double-breasted suit as they entered the main house. Starting up the stairs to the living room, he turned and anxiously said, "How do I look, Marty?"

"Slow."

Jake thought so, too. He put aside his spreadsheet and made a show of dubiously scrutinizing his watch, giving it a shake.

"Where ya bin?"

Marty said, "He was eating, Jake. Wanted to get dressed, make himself presentable. Brush his teeth . . ."

"Yeah? What kinda toot'paste ya use?"

"Crest," said Harvey.

"Da paste, or dat new kind dey got, da gel or whateva?"

"Paste," said Harvey, sweating. He'd almost said *da* paste.

"Wha' flavour?"

"Mint."

Jake nodded judiciously. He said, "I gotta job fo' ya."

Harvey listened with ear-shattering intensity as Jake told him exactly what he wanted.

When he was reasonably confident that Harvey understood what was expected of him, Jake turned to Marty. "Da new vehicle arrive?"

"Yeah."

"All da papawoik, da plates an' insure, alla dat crap got taken care of, dealt wit'?"

Marty nodded.

"Give him da keys."

Parker saw headlights sweep across the road, and then the gate swung open. A few moments later a small white car crawled out of the driveway. The car came to a complete stop. The turn signal flashed. The better part of a minute later, the car turned on to the street. Parker reached behind her and gave Willows a shake.

"Jack, wake up!"

Parker hit the switch that killed the Ford's running lights, and started the engine. Willows climbed into the front seat.

"Buckle up."

"What time is it?"

"Late," said Parker. She ducked down behind the wheel as the car drove slowly past. She gave it a half-block lead, and then started after it. At this time of night, traffic would still be fairly heavy. Tailing the car shouldn't be too difficult, once they were on the main roads.

Willows scrubbed his face with his hands. He popped open the glove compartment and got out the binoculars.

The white car signalled a left turn half a block in advance of the intersection. Parker checked the speedometer. They were cruising along at a steady forty kilometres an hour.

Willows lowered the binoculars. He punched the car's licence-plate number into the Ford's onboard computer.

Harvey signalled a right turn. They were on Fourth Avenue, following the same route that Willows and Parker had taken to 312 Main after they'd spoken to Jake. Willows suffered a weird case of the *déjà vu*s while he waited for the computer to get back to him.

Finally the data popped onto the screen.

Parker said, "What've we got?"

"A 'ninety-eight Neon. Harvey's the registered lessee."

"The guy washing the cars?"

"Harvey Corville," said Willows. "But I bet he prefers to be called "Harv.""

Harvey signalled a right at Fourth and Alma. The light was green, but he stopped anyway. Parker had to admire his consistency. He managed to chirp the Neon's tires as he started off. Parker wondered if he'd decided to put the Neon through its paces. No such luck. Harvey was seemingly content with life in the slow lane. She followed at a discreet distance as he cruised sedately up Alma to Broadway, where he waited for all visible traffic to disperse before making a slow left and then a quick right, into the parking lot of a mini-mall dominated by a 7-Eleven.

Was he going to rob the joint? Parker doubted it, but fervently hoped so. Harvey's ridiculously conservative driving had set her teeth on edge, and she was eager to blow off the accumulated tension.

She parked the Ford in the lee of a dumpster. Willows adjusted the binoculars' focus.

Inside the brightly lit store, Harvey spent close to twenty minutes squinting furtively at muscle magazines, before finally settling on a copy of *European Male*. He also bought a copy of *Forbes* magazine, as well as a bottle of Tums antacid pills, and a large Slurpee.

"What flavour?" said Parker.

"Green."

"Lime," said Parker.

Parker was reluctant to spend more time crawling along behind Harvey, but Willows insisted he was too tired to drive.

Harvey burned more tread off the Neon's tires as he exited the parking lot. It was immediately apparent that his driving had markedly deteriorated. At first, Parker thought he'd overdosed on sugar; but it wasn't the Slurpee that was at fault. Harvey had turned on the Neon's powerful dome light. His nose was buried in his brand-spanking-new copy of *European Male*.

Not that he drove any faster. During the return trip, the Neon rarely achieved a speed of thirty kilometres per hour. A lucky thing, too, given Harvey's penchant for drifting into oncoming traffic. Fortunately his snail-like pace gave other drivers plenty of time to adjust to the possibility of a head-on collision, and practise the avoidance tactics they'd learned watching Jackie Chan movies.

"Maybe he skimmed the manual and misinterpreted the phrase 'breaking-in period,'" said Parker after a particularly close near-miss.

Willows didn't respond. She glanced across at him and saw that he'd fallen asleep.

Harvey made it back to Jake's against all odds. The gates yawned open and then swung shut behind him. Harvey parked the Neon in front of the twelve-car garage, killed the engine, and sat in the darkened car for a good fifteen minutes, before he finally delivered Jake's copy of *Forbes*, and his bottle of Tums.

"What took ya so long?" Jake's jowls quivered as he spotted something, and his head darted forward like a snake's. "How come da crotch a ya pants is all wet?"

Harvey's chunky face turned a peculiar shade of crimson. He shuffled from foot to foot.

Jake glanced at Marty, who shrugged warily and went back to the sports pages.

Jake said, "Wha' da hell happened to ya, Harvey?"

"I spilled my Slurpee."

"How's dat again?"

"Jake, I'm so sorry, but I spilled my Slurpee."

"Ya wha'?"

"My lime Slurpee, Jake. I had it between my legs, and it spilled all over the seat. I was afraid the upholstery would be ruined, so I stopped to clean it up . . ."

Jake waved him off. What in hell was a Slurpee? He scrawled a mental note to query Marty. Jeez, but the world was spinning at a hell of a pace. He tried to keep up, but it was impossible. All those things on television. *Products*. But most of it, he had no idea what it was supposed to *do*. One thing for sure, he hated the beer ads. It exhausted him, watching all those kids running around like that, having such loud fun . . .

Harvey was standing there, awaiting further instructions. Ditto the glimmer twins, Dave and Danny.

He asked Marty to tell them all to go to bed, take a nap. They had a long night ahead of them. They should get some sleep while they had a chance.

His three hoods scampered out of the living room like so many hyperactive mice.

Marty sagged back onto the sofa. Jake marvelled at Marty's ability to read a newspaper, any newspaper, for hours on end, his interest never flagging, as he slowly turned the pages.

Jake said, "You gonna get some sleep?"

"A couple hours?" Marty smiled. "What's the point? I'm better off staying up."

Jake nodded. "Yeah, probably ya right." He stretched, his bones crackling, and adjusted the clear plastic tube that disappeared into his left nostril. "I'm gonna hit da sack. Wake me, 'tings go sour."

Marty nodded, and went back to his paper. He and Jake had pored over Marty's list of recently deceased dealers, and quickly worked out that whoever was killing them had a linear personality. The murderer was working his way up Jake's ladder step-by-step. Sammy Wu's death had been entirely predictable. Jake figured, and Marty agreed, that there was a maximum of five upper-echelon dealers whose lives were now in immediate jeopardy. Jake had sent teams of guardian thugs fanning out across the city to watch over all of them but one – a dealer named Rodney McGuire.

McGuire had been out of town for the past few days. Jake had tracked him down in Vegas, where McGuire was getting a quickie divorce from a quickie marriage. His return flight was scheduled to land at 1:00 a.m. Jake had arranged to have people meet him at the airport, once he got through Customs, an arduous task that usually involved a strip search and verbal beating. Typically, the Customs hooligans detained known-but-unconvicted criminals like McGuire for upwards of four or five hours. The twins would have McGuire's Fairview Slopes condo under wraps by 4:00 a.m., well before McGuire's anticipated time of arrival. If he got in early, the punk at the airport would call Marty.

Jake went to bed secure in the knowledge that everything was taken care of.

At twenty to four, Jake's front gate swung silently open. Willows reached behind him and gently shook Parker awake.

This time, Harvey was driving the monstrous Humvee. He had two passengers. As the chunky, low-slung vehicle passed beneath a streetlight, the dome light was briefly switched on. Willows and Parker caught a quick glimpse of flashing teeth, glinting diamonds, dully gleaming weapons, and a matched pair of small dark objects that just might have been the twins' matte-black souls.

Then the light was extinguished, and the Humvee dwindled into the darkness.

29

Wayne was in a hurry, but Lewis wasn't going anywhere until April administered a little pick-me-up, via a hypo.

But even then, doped to the eyeballs, so heavily drugged it was all he could do to stand upright, Lewis continued to balk. Deep inside him, something primeval, something that predated the invention of the alarm clock by several thousand years, was triggered by forces too complex and subtle to be measured.

Lewis intuitively knew that his time was running out. He was about to die, and every cell in his body was in mute revolt.

He gathered all his feeble strength and mumbled, "I'm not going anywhere . . ."

"Without April?" Wayne cunningly suggested.

Had Lewis been holding out until Wayne agreed to let April come along for the ride? He wasn't sure.

Wayne said, "I'll go get her."

He found April in the living room, bouncing a lacrosse ball off the brick fireplace, driving the dogs crazy. Her face lit up when Wayne stormed into the room.

She said, "You changed your mind, didn't you!" He noticed she'd changed into one of her favourite outfits, a tight black sleeveless sweater and a miniskirt made out of shiny black plastic.

"Nope."

April's smile collapsed.

Wayne said, "He won't go without you. Just flat-out refuses."
He shrugged massively. "I could kick his ass, but I don't want
him causing any trouble on the way over. I could stuff him in
the trunk, but I don't want him causing a fuss when we get there.
So the easiest thing is to let him have his way." He smiled. "Let's
call it his last request. That way it won't seem like we're giving in
to him."

April jumped to her feet and threw herself at Wayne, knocked
him backwards an inch or two as she wrapped herself around him
with all the enthusiasm of a wisteria gone berserk. She'd harassed
him all day long, pleading to be allowed to go along on Lewis's
last ride. Predictably, he'd proved impervious to her flirtatious
charm. Predictably, she'd turned her viper's tongue on him, bedev-
illed him with all the persistence of a swarm of enraged hornets.
Her stinging words raised painful welts all over his brain. But
Wayne had considerably more experience dealing with vinegar
than honey, and was able to ride out the storm.

April had spiralled into a deep sulk. Wayne knew she'd get over
it. Didn't she always? Maybe in a day or two he'd plunk her cute
little butt down on his Harley, take her for a fast ride up to Whistler.
There was no better way to unravel your problems than to crank
the throttle on a big V-twin, and scrape the pegs through fifty miles
of quick twisties.

Well, no better way that Wayne would ever know.

April had already parked the Jag near the intended victim's
apartment. Now she fetched the Econoline. She and Wayne walked
Lewis out of the house and down the driveway to it. April swung
open the back door. Lewis leaned slackly against the van. He'd
drifted off, or pretended to. Wayne helped him into the back of
the van. Lewis's head bounced off the rusty steel floor. He moaned
softly.

April didn't like that very much. "Be careful with him!"

"What for?"

"Just . . . I don't know! Show a little respect, that's all."

Wayne eased shut the Econoline's rear door, grossly exaggerating the delicacy of his movements.

"What're you doing, Wayne?"

"Trying not to disturb him." Wayne leaned his considerable bulk against the door. The latch clicked. He stepped away from the van. "Lewis is gonna be dead pretty soon, April. He ain't gonna see the sun come up, and you better get used to the idea, because I can't have you causing me any problems, not now. You want to stay home, fine. You want to come along, okay. But only if you're gonna be a good girl."

Wayne lit a Marlboro. The ugly truth was that April had earned the right to come along for the ride. When he'd told her about his "computer repairmen" scheme she'd laughed so hard she'd fallen off her chair. In about two minutes, she'd come up with a far better idea. A scheme that might actually work.

Wayne listened to the music of the frogs. Didn't those suckers ever sleep? He wondered if it was possible to hunt down a frog that had a better voice than any other frog in the whole world, and make a buck off him. Probably not. The sky was clear. He tried to find Cassiopeia. Was that it? Maybe.

April said, "I'll be good, Wayne."

"We got a lot riding on this, baby."

"I know we do."

Wayne stood there in the shadows, listening to the cacophonous music of the night. When he'd had enough of his Marlboro, he flicked the butt away into the weeds. "Okay, let's go."

Rodney McGuire's Fairview Slopes townhome was lit up like Steven Spielberg's idea of a space ship.

Wayne's latex-clad finger pressed the doorbell. He and Lewis were standing to either side of the peephole. April was caught in the middle. Lewis's gold Mylar coveralls, the bug tuxedo the police were going to find him in, glinted in the light.

The peephole darkened as someone inside the apartment put his eye to the lens.

April said, "Rod?"

"Who wants to know?"

"It's Holly. Do you remember me, Rod? We met at Sammy Wu's, a couple of weeks before he was killed. I was wondering if I could come in for a minute, maybe have a drink?"

Silence. Rod was apparently thinking it over.

April said, "I'm on my own time, Rod." She lowered her voice a notch. "I'm not working, if that's what you think."

Thud of withdrawn deadbolts. Rattle of chains. It was all music to Wayne's ears.

McGuire opened the door a crack. Wayne tackled the opportunity. The door, and McGuire, flew backwards. The door crashed against a wall, but the drug dealer, lacking hinges, was propelled down a short hallway and into the living room, where he stumbled over a heavy glass coffee table, lost his balance, and fell awkwardly.

Wayne was all over McGuire like a giant moth on a tiny light-bulb, shushing him with flapping hands that had McGuire's close-cropped head whipping back and forth as if he were watching a taped tennis match in fast-forward mode.

April shut the door. She guided Lewis to the sofa, and sat him down. Glancing around, she said, "Nice apartment."

A mammoth fifty-two-inch TV was wedged into a corner. Drab, vaguely threatening creatures drifted languidly across the spacious screen. The perspective was as might be expected, given that McGuire had been playing a Nintendo video game – the business end of a double-barrelled shotgun leading the unseen player into a weeping dungeon.

Something large huddled in a dark corner swept aside a nest of cobwebs and hurtled towards the screen. The shotgun had it covered. *Ka-boom! Ka-boom!* There was blood everywhere, but it was no more substantial than a pint bag full of pixels.

McGuire was about five-six, not much over one hundred and

twenty pounds. He wore a black two-piece sweat suit, a red head-band and matching wristbands, shiny new Adidas sneakers. He looked as if he'd had a hard life, until it had suddenly got a whole lot harder. He had a wizened, dried-out, kind of pinched look about him that reminded Wayne of a jockey he'd known.

Wayne's finger poked McGuire's black-clad chest. He said, "Been out doing a little breaking and entering?" He waved the barrel of his sawed-off pump shotgun under McGuire's nose. "Be truthful, Rodney. You lie, you die."

"No, I was just out for a jog."

"At this time of night?"

"I couldn't sleep. I been in Vegas, caught an early flight back, got in around ten, breezed through Customs. I been staying up all night, playing the tables. My internal clock's all messed up . . ."

"Why the dark clothes?"

"I like to see people before they see me."

Wayne nodded. He said, "I can relate to that. How far d'you run?"

"Down to the bridge, and back."

"What bridge?"

"Cambie." McGuire looked as if he was thinking about going for another run, any second now.

Wayne said, "Relax, I'm not going to shoot you."

McGuire nodded. He was pretty cool, considering. So far, he hadn't even glanced at Lewis. Wayne wondered about that. In his gold bug tuxedo, Lewis was kind of hard to overlook.

He decided McGuire must have figured out what was going on, or something close to it. But if that was the case, why wasn't he fighting for his life?

Wayne stood up. He said, "You alone?"

"Yeah, sure." But McGuire had hesitated for a tiny fraction of a second; just long enough for Wayne to know he was lying.

McGuire sat up, rubbing his bruised shins.

"The money's in a wall safe behind the picture." He was pointing at a framed black-and-white photograph of Marilyn Monroe trying to hold her dress in place despite a strong wind rising up from a grate in the sidewalk.

Wayne said, "Where'd they take that picture?"

McGuire shrugged, went back to rubbing his shins. "How should I know? It's just a picture, that's all."

Wayne yanked the picture off the wall. He gave Marilyn a big smack on the lips.

April said, "Wayne!" Shocked and appalled, though he didn't know why. He let the picture drop to the carpet, put his foot right through it as he turned to ask McGuire for the combination to the safe.

McGuire said, "If I tell you, are you gonna let me live?"

"Sure," said Wayne. A wasted lie, because when he pulled on the safe's chromed handle the door swung smoothly towards him. The thing hadn't even been locked. He peered inside. The safe was bigger than it looked. There was plenty of room for a bulky stainless-steel revolver, wads of cash, a couple of kilos of drugs. Wayne grabbed the gun, shoved it in the waistband of his pants.

He held up one of the plastic bags. "Heroin?"

"Cocaine," said McGuire. "You can leave any time. Don't feel you got to stick around and make small talk."

Wayne said, "Get up."

"It's okay, I'm comfortable."

"Up," said Wayne.

He caught McGuire on the rise, his left hook smacking him on the temple, a hard right cross hitting him flush on the forehead. McGuire dropped, his body so limp it was as if he'd been deboned.

April said, "You killed him, you moron!"

Wayne was instantly contrite. He dropped to his knees, felt for a pulse. McGuire had a strong heart. His forehead ballooned, and turned purple, compelling evidence that he was still alive.

April emptied the rest of the contents of the wall safe into a brown paper Safeway bag she found under the kitchen sink.

Wayne reconnoitred the rest of the apartment. In the bathroom, a full-size cardboard cutout of Marilyn Monroe in a red dress had been stapled to the back of the door.

Lushly romantic music played softly in the dimly lit guest bedroom. A decidedly womanly shape lay beneath the blankets. A mane of silvery-blonde hair was artistically, perhaps even seductively, spread out across the pillow.

Wayne cocked his fist and crept slowly up to the bed. The woman lay absolutely motionless. The room, except for the silvery tinkle of a harpsichord, was absolutely silent. Wayne tapped the woman lightly on the shoulder. She failed to respond. Was she ignoring him, hoping he'd go away? Or did she assume he was McGuire, and was playing a little game? Wayne gave her a shake. Her skin felt unnaturally smooth. Her body, he realized with a shock, was room temperature, at best. He was no pathologist, and had no ambitions in that area, but he knew damn well that, when a woman's temperature had plummeted to about thirty degrees below normal, she was certifiably deceased.

He eased back the blankets inch by inch, until finally the naked woman was fully exposed.

Correction, you were dead *unless* you'd never been alive. Wayne went over to the doorway and snapped on the ceiling light. You could say McGuire's girlfriend was pure dynamite, if only because he'd blown her up real good. Wayne picked her up. She was light as a feather and stiff as a board. He pinched a shapely buttock.

In fact, McGuire had blown her up a bit too good. She was grossly overinflated, probably to the tune of about thirty pounds per square inch. It was surprising, how many men spent serious money on their girlfriends but refused to invest a few bucks in a tire gauge.

Wayne tucked her under his arm. Hurriedly exiting the bedroom, he accidentally bounced her head violently off the doorjamb. He paused, listening intently for a telltale hiss of disapproval.

But it was okay. Thanks to her durable fabric, she had come through the mishap completely unscathed.

As advertised, she was quiet as a mouse.

April did a cute double-take as Wayne came back into the living room. She said, "Who's your new friend?"

Wayne positioned the woman on the sofa next to Lewis. Her legs were tubular, and were at about a 50-degree angle, almost identical to his Harley's V-twin. Her breasts were unlikely. McGuire, or her manufacturer, had glued a patch of silvery-blonde hair between her legs. Was it real, or some kind of synthetic? Wayne couldn't tell. Either way, McGuire was the sickest puppy in the pound. The woman stared incuriously up at the ceiling. She appeared to be more comatose than bored. Apparently, she was content to lie there and pout.

Wayne tilted his head. If he looked at her from a certain angle, she bore an uncanny resemblance to Marilyn Monroe.

Jeez.

He said, "Lewis, I'd like you to meet Marilyn."

Lewis nodded disinterestedly. Wayne helped them shake hands. He sat down next to Marilyn so she was trapped between him and Lewis. They were so close their hips were touching. He lit a cigarette. You couldn't fault her personality. In terms of maintenance, you'd probably hardly know she was there.

Spend a couple of bucks on a bicycle patch kit, you were all set.

April knelt on the carpet beside McGuire, yanking his limp body this way and that as she worked the black sweatshirt over his head. She said, "Give me a hand with this, will you?"

"In a minute."

Wayne hardly ever enjoyed himself, but he was enjoying himself now, sitting on the sofa with his hand on Marilyn's robust thigh, never giving a thought to what she might be thinking. What a relief it was, to be able to just sit there, companionably, and not have to worry about making small talk.

Wayne pushed himself off the sofa and waked over to the Nintendo game player and methodically stomped it to pieces. The TV screen was a blur of strangely hypnotic, post-apocalyptic colours. Wayne yanked on the Nintendo's umbilical cords. Now he was watching Channel 3. The TV's remote was lying on top of the set. He switched to Channel 55, Speedvision. Motorcycles raced around a convoluted track. A-okay! Wayne cranked up the sound until the thunder of the exhausts threatened to shake the paint off the walls.

April helped herself to McGuire's red headband. She pulled his sweats down around his ankles, and fiddled impatiently with his sneakers, which were double-laced. She glanced up at the TV. "Don't you ever get tired of that stuff?"

Wayne said, "Not really."

Marilyn, he noticed, never said a word. He walked back to the sofa, brushed a strand of hair away from a bright blue eye. Looking at her objectively, he had to admit that her nose was too small, and that she lacked cheekbones. Or any bones at all, actually.

Okay, so maybe her physiognomy wasn't exactly normal. All that mattered was that she was normal enough for him.

April got the second sneaker off, and then the sock.

Time for the hypo.

Time to snap some artful Polaroids.

Time to light the torch.

Time, pretty soon, for Lewis to mumble his fond farewells.

Wayne patted Marilyn's thigh. "Back in a sec, honey."

He went into the bathroom and flushed the butt of his Marlboro down the toilet. Turning, he caught himself staring at his reflected image in a full-length mirror. Man, he looked downright creepy. He stepped closer to the silvered glass and saw that it was thickly speckled with flecks of dried toothpaste. He went over to the sink and turned on the cold water tap and wet the end of a towel and wiped down the mirror. There, that was much better, now he looked just fine.

He adjusted the revolver sticking out of his pants so the barrel wasn't quite so intrusive. Lighting another cigarette, he went back into the living room.

April toyed with her syringe. She said, "You shouldn't have hit him so hard. Unconscious people aren't much fun, Wayne. How long's he going to be out, anyway?" Her tone was whiny and impatient.

Wayne ignored her. He plunked himself down next to Marilyn, casually draped an arm across her shoulder.

Her pout was almost a smile. He could see she'd missed him, while he was gone.

30

The computer told them what they already knew – that Jake owned the Humvee.

Parker made the calls necessary to mobilize the VPD's Emergency Response Team. Because there was very little traffic, tailing the truck wasn't going to be easy, even with Harvey at the wheel.

Parker broadcast the Humvee's tag number, colour, and location, and requested help from all available unmarked units. The response was predictably enthusiastic.

She left it to the dispatcher to sort out the mess.

Willows charted a parallel course as the Humvee turned south on Alma. He'd assumed that Harvey had been casing the 7-Eleven during his earlier visit, and that he and the twins, *sans* Jake's blessing, were going to liven up their evening with an armed robbery.

But why the heavy weapons? What *were* Jake's mobsters up to? Willows didn't have to spend much time mulling it over. This was about all those dead addicts. The glitter twins had been sent out to even the score. Willows shared his theory with Parker, who agreed that Jake had likely sent the glitter twins out on a mission of revenge.

Where were the ERT trucks?

Willows was more relieved than surprised when the Humvee turned left on Broadway. He pulled into a gas station, gave Harvey a two-block lead, and then drove back onto Broadway. He tailgated an out-of-service bus, following the Humvee as it cruised slowly east on Broadway.

Harvey made an unsignalled right turn on Arbutus, drove half a block and pulled an illegal U-turn.

Willows had no option but to continue straight down Broadway.

Now the Humvee was behind him, trailing by less than a block, its lights dead-centre in his rearview mirror.

Parker was in constant contact with the dispatcher. The number of marked units tailing them on a parallel course, three blocks distant on either side, had grown to more than a dozen.

Willows was driving at a steady ten kilometres an hour above the speed limit. The Humvee had been keeping pace. At Granville, Willows eased into the left-turn lane. The light was red, and there was nothing he could do about it. He watched the Humvee grow larger in the rearview mirror. If Harvey pulled up alongside the unmarked Ford, there was every chance he'd recognize the car and its occupants. Willows had made a crucial mistake. Anticipating the red light, he should have made a right on Granville, clearing the intersection before the Humvee overtook him.

The Humvee was half a block away now, and closing fast. Parker slouched down low in the seat and Willows made a pretence of enjoying the view of the city. He'd blown the pursuit. He felt like an idiot, and for good reason. It occurred to him, too late, to get out of the left-turn lane, reposition the Ford so there was at least a chance Harvey would pull up behind him.

The Humvee filled his rearview mirror.

He heard the drone of its tires on asphalt, and then the fast-paced blare of salsa music, as Harvey pulled past them and cruised through the red.

Parker was laughing hysterically. She and Willows both holstered their Glocks.

The light turned green. An unmarked vice-squad Chevrolet joined the hunt. The drug squad chipped in with a Mercedes that had recently been seized under the "profits of crime" law, from a convicted marijuana grower. The dispatcher informed Parker that the first and second units of the Emergency Response Team had rolled, were racing across the city, and would soon join the pursuit.

The ERT cowboys were hot to take the Humvee down *now*.

Willows emphatically disagreed. He wanted to tail Harvey all the way to his destination, believing the glitter twins planned to kill whoever had been knocking off Jake's network of dealers. Radio traffic was chaotic, and rapidly getting worse.

Willows had made the left off Granville and now he made a right on Eighth Avenue, and accelerated hard. He lit up his fireball, but didn't use his siren. These were short blocks. He slowed at the intersections of Hemlock, Birch, and Alder. His blood was up, flushed with adrenalin. His heart rate was in the high one-twenties, and climbing. His vision was pinpoint sharp. Colours were brilliant.

The conflicting multitude of sounds engendered by a high-speed, multi-vehicle collision came to him with such crystal-clear fidelity that it was as if he'd been curled up in the heart of the accident.

Parker said, "What was *that*!"

It would be some time before they were able to fill in the details. Harvey had forgotten all his driver training. He'd driven up to Twelfth Avenue, turned left, and made a spontaneous and highly illegal U-turn, causing a rusty Saab stuffed with overworked nurses to drive head-on into a speeding Bentley driven by an exhausted emergency-room surgeon. Harvey cut sharply across a Vancouver General Hospital staff parking lot, and used the Humvee's stump-pulling torque, four-wheel drive, and vastly superior ground clearance to exit the lot. His routine evasive tactics were devastatingly effective. The drug squad's effete Mercedes had been trapped in the cul-de-sac.

The vice squad's Chevy hadn't done much better. They'd followed at what they hoped was a discreet distance as Harvey barrelled down one alley after another, seemingly at random. He'd braked to an abrupt stop in mid-block, squared the Humvee up to a tall wooden fence topped off with tight coils of razorwire, and hit the gas.

The fence had been built with a view to discouraging two-hundred-pound burglars. The Humvee's dry weight was a little over two-and-one-half tons. The vehicle effortlessly churned the fence to splinters. An obstinate or slow or just plain stupid guard dog, an outsized rottweiler, had the bad luck to be chained to a post just inside the fence, in the span of dead ground behind the building. The snarling rottie stood its ground. The Humvee flattened it almost as effortlessly as it had knocked over the fence.

The twins' manic laughter could easily be heard over the sounds of destruction, salsa music, and the bitter howling of a dog that had just learned it wasn't king of the world.

Harvey pointed the vehicle towards the narrow space between two cinderblock buildings. The Humvee was inches wider than the gap between the buildings, so Harvey had to drive through with his offside wheels on the ground and the other wheels up on the wall of one of the buildings. The irritated vice-squad cops estimated the Humvee must have been tilted at a thirty-degree angle, minimum, as it passed between the two cinderblock walls. Dejected and dispirited, they hadn't even bothered to try to emulate him. Nor could they try an alternate route. The rottweiler, down but not out, had charged the Chevy and chomped down hard, puncturing a tire.

Meanwhile, marked patrol cars established a perimeter through which the Humvee could not pass undetected. Willows and Parker and three unmarked cars that had recently joined the hunt continued to search frantically for the vehicle.

The thing was fifteen feet long and seven feet wide, and weighed five thousand two hundred pounds.

Where in hell could it have gone?

31

The mirror twins, Dave and Danny, were in a sparkly, diamond-hunting mood. They tumbled out of the Humvee the instant the massive vehicle skidded to a stop.

Dave, still chortling, pointed his MAC-10 machine gun at Harvey and yelled, "You the man!"

"Gotta be a real popular ride at Disneyland, baby!" shouted Danny.

"He's more fun than them damn electric race cars!" yelled Dave.

"And that's no lie!" the twins cried out together.

Harvey was astounded. The twins were not normally loquacious. In all the time he'd known them – almost six months – he'd never before heard either twin string more than a few words together, much less attempt a compound sentence.

But there was something else bothering him. Both twins were, as usual, equally keen to get the job done. But Danny was suddenly almost as serious as a dentist in the middle of a self-diagnosed root canal, while Dave acted happier than a recently gathered bucketful of red-tide clams. In the past, the twins had always functioned in perfect unison, rather like a duo of synchronized swimmers, no matter how trivial or commonplace their actions.

Harvey would never forget his first meal with them. Watching them eat spaghetti and meatballs together, the complicated twist and flip of pasta around their forks, the rhythmic and perfectly sequential rise and fall of identical jaws, the flash of cutlery, the blade-angle as knives sliced into meatballs, the patting of lips with red-stained napkins, the shift of elbows, the hasty gulps of wine and perfectly timed, tablecloth-rippling burps and belches. It was a spectacle, for sure.

Harvey hadn't touched his own meal. He'd sat there, stunned, while the twins cleaned their plates at breakneck pace, racing to a photo finish that had no losers.

Man, they were as fully synchronized as a pair of *lungs*.

It was one of the strangest experiences of his life, but just another day in the life, as far as the twins were concerned.

He said, "Danny, you okay?"

"Yeah, fine," said Danny tersely.

Dave, on the other hand, said nothing. Oddly, the twins seemed unaware of the difference in their moods.

Harvey said, "I'll be right here, okay?"

"Keep the engine running."

Harvey nodded. He checked the gas gauge. The Humvee's tank was more full than empty. He wished he felt the same way about himself. He wondered if he should get on the phone to Marty, tell him the twins were acting weird. Acting weird in an unusual way. Acting weirder. No matter how he phrased it, his complaint seemed to lack substance. This worried him. The last thing he wanted to do was confirm Marty's opinion of him – that scrubbing Jake's fleet of vehicles was about all he was good for. His ambition, no matter what Marty thought of him, was to be a thug like Dave and Danny. Well, similar to Dave and Danny. Pack a weapon, all that.

Dave racked the slide on his MAC-10. The MAC was ugly as a bulldog, but the thing sprayed bullets at an amazing rate. It was ideal in close-quarter situations, if you weren't too concerned about taking prisoners.

Danny laid two fat, artistically wavering lines of cocaine across the Humvee's hood. He and his identical brother stood on opposite sides of the vehicle, facing each other. At a signal visible only to them, they leaned forward, and started snorting.

Dave finished first, by several seconds. He wiped his nose with the back of his hand, sneezed a couple of times, brushed a spray of white powder from the lapel of his suit, and started up the sidewalk to Rodney McGuire's condo.

Danny said, "Hey, wait a minute!"

"No way, man! Get crackin', or get left behind!"

"Fuck you!"

"No, fuck *you*!"

Inside the apartment, April was counting money. Rodney McGuire had stuffed his safe with one-hundred-dollar bills, fifty bills to the bound packet. The math was simple, or would have been, if April hadn't insisted on tearing apart the packets and counting the individual bills. She sat on the carpet next to McGuire, who was still unconscious and showed no signs of reviving. As she tore apart packet after packet, McGuire was slowly buried in money.

Wayne surreptitiously loaded a new film cartridge into his trusty Polaroid. April told him, if he tried to take her picture with that thing, he'd regret it for the rest of his extremely abbreviated life.

Point taken.

Wayne asked Lewis how he was doing. Lewis sat there on the sofa with his arms by his sides. His mouth hung open, but his eyes were slitted like a dozing cat's. Wayne hunkered down beside him. He took a tiny Mag-Lite from his pocket and shone the beam into Lewis's eye. Lewis turned his head away. His movements were as ponderous as those of a heavily narcotized elephant. He shut his mouth, but it immediately fell open again. A line of drool free-fell to his lap.

Wayne said, "I'm gonna take another look around, see what I can see."

April told him to please shut up, she was counting.

Wayne went back into the bathroom, to empty his bladder. He was a little uncomfortable, with Marilyn standing there looking at him, a big smile on her face. She was only a piece of painted cardboard, but she sure looked real. He stood with his back to her for a long time, before he was able to urinate, and when he was done he was careful to zip up before he turned around.

She was still watching him. Knowing what was on her pretty little mind, he went over to the double sink, ran the water until it was hot, and thoroughly washed his latex-gloved hands.

In the bedroom closet, he found a well-oiled bicycle pump, and eleven plain brown cardboard boxes, each of which contained a Marilyn identical to the model he'd already met. He carried the boxes over to the bed and sat down, opened one up, and read the accompanying instruction booklet.

The Marilyns were the deluxe, fully functional model. Wayne was delighted to learn they came with washable, fluffy soft pubic hair, a long-lasting synthetic wig, Qwik-Patch® kit, and a "Saucy Winking Device." He learned that Marilyn's body was made of the same durable miracle fabrics used in the company's line of virtually indestructible inflatable pool toys, and was guaranteed for thirty nights from time of purchase.

Wayne lit a Marlboro. He fetched the bicycle pump from the closet and returned to the bed.

Marilyn was wrapped in flimsy yellow tissue paper. He tore the paper aside and saw she was folded neatly as a brand-new shirt, face up. Her flat blue eyes stared up at him. How long had she been in that box? Where had she come from?

Wayne checked the instruction booklet. Taiwan. God, such a long journey!

If she could think, what would she be thinking?

The pump was equipped with a hollow needle with a blunt tip, suitable for inflating beach balls, etcetera.

Wayne unfolded Marilyn and laid her down on the bed. She had razor-sharp creases at her knees and crotch, just below her breasts, and midway up her shapely neck. Could he iron them out?

Unlikely, not to mention risky. He'd never forgive himself, if he melted her.

He perused the booklet's fine print. The topic of crease lines was not covered, or even mentioned.

The bike pump's needle was meant to be inserted into a reinforced hole hidden in Marilyn's belly button.

How clever.

Lubricate before insertion, solemnly advised the instructions, on page thirty-seven.

Wayne did as he'd been told. He laboured over Marilyn for a solid ten minutes, pumping rhythmically away, revelling in the sight of her body slowly acquiring that vitally important third dimension.

He had the needle in her, and he was bringing her to life. What a nice change from all his previous work. Was it too much to think that he was godlike, in a strange, admittedly frivolous and insignificant way?

Absolutely. But that in no way detracted from the thrill of creation.

He was a sculptor, working in plastics and compressed air.

Marilyn's hips swelled.

Her breasts plumped up nicely.

Her fingers assumed their natural shape one after the other, until even her opposable thumb seemed operational.

Wayne was a little disappointed to notice that the manufacturer had shaved a few bucks off his costs by neglecting to give her individual toes. Her feet, in fact, were merely painted on.

As were her eyes, but since they were so lifelike and twinkly, it didn't really matter.

Wayne recalled the curious boast about a "Saucy Winking Device." He examined her more closely, and found that her left eye was equipped with a folding eyelid. Push it down, *voilà*, Marilyn was winking at him. Winking saucily! He pushed the eyelid up and down several times, and then resumed pumping away at her.

He wanted to get the pressure, the critical measurement of pounds-per-square-inch, exactly right. He wanted his special Marilyn to be perfect. Under his gentle-yet-eager hands she blossomed, pretty as a time-lapsed rose. Soon enough, she was as flawless as a human-shaped balloon can be.

Judicious use of a tube of contact cement (provided) secured her pubic thatch. Ditto her wig.

Practice makes perfect. The second through eleventh Marilyns were assembled with amazing speed. Wayne couldn't stop smiling. The bedroom was full of them. They lay everywhere, pointed in all directions, faceup and facedown, immodest as immodest can be.

Wayne gently gathered up his flock and herded them, jostling and bumping convivially against each other, out of the bedroom and down the hallway towards the living room. The lead Marilyns behaved almost as if they had minds of their own, toppling over in slow motion, ricochetting off the walls, drifting lackadaisically away from the mob. Their behaviour was remarkably similar to that of deep-space astronauts. Counting the one in the living room, he had an even dozen. Enough for a baseball team, and more.

Danny and Dave took the steps up to the condo's cramped little porch one step at a time. Harvey had already cased the joint. He had a tool that resembled a miniature telescope, which he'd pressed tightly against Rodney McGuire's front door's spyhole. The device reversed the spyhole's magnification, giving Harvey a crystal-clear fish-eye view of the apartment's interior.

It hadn't taken Harvey long to catch an eyeful of Rodney, who lay flat on his back on the carpet, apparently unconscious. Or dead. A woman straddled Rodney. She had her back to the door but was plainly armed with a loaded syringe, which she carried at port arms. Then, all of a sudden, there were all these weird pneumatic women . . .

Danny turned to his sibling. "All set?"

"All set, bro."

Below them and to their right, the city glittered with all the bright promise of a handful of sequins.

"Nice view."

"If you like views."

Their identical heads swivelled to look down at the Humvee. Harvey, back in the van, had turned on the dome light and was reading a magazine.

"Ready?"

"Yeah, I'm ready."

Dave's hand came up to his ear. He counted off his three stud diamonds, even as Danny took a fraction of a second longer to tally up his four. Dave wondered if, by the time he reached fifty, he'd have killed so many people that he wouldn't have any room left on his ears. What would he do then?"

"Danny."

"Right here, Dave."

"What're we gonna do if we run out of space on our ears, we got no more room for diamonds? We gotta stop killing people? I mean, it's a tradition."

Danny frowned. It was a darn good question. He stood there by the door, facing slightly towards the street, and the killer view of the city. The solution came to him in a flash.

"The ears get crowded, what we do, we make one ruby the equal of five diamonds."

"Take out five diamonds, stick in one ruby."

"Or it could be a sapphire, or whatever."

"An emerald . . ."

Danny shook his head. "Nah, emeralds are too faggy."

"What?" Dave laughed, not believing what he was hearing. "Too *faggy*? Is that what you said, too *faggy*?"

"You got a problem with that?"

"Maybe."

"*Maybe*? What's *maybe*? Maybe's nothing. No thing. So what's it gonna be, a yes or a no?"

"It's gonna be a maybe, that's what it's gonna be. I reserve my right to reserve my decision. This is a free country, ain't it?"

"Where'd you get that idea?"

Dave shifted his MAC-10 to his left hand and reached out and gave his brother a hard push.

Danny pushed back.

Dave slapped his face.

Danny kicked his brother in the shin.

The twins were starting to get into it, the bickering segueing into vicious insults, the kicks and punches coming harder and faster as they pumped themselves up for the slaughter that surely, they hoped, lay on the other side of the condo's door. Dave smacked Danny on the jaw, and in turn received a twisting blow to the kidneys that doubled him over and left him gasping.

Harvey heard the pained grunts and the sound of the blows above the mutter of the Humvee's idling engine. He glanced up, unconcerned, and then went back to his centrefold.

Aliens were a big deal, lately. *X-Files. Area 51. Star Trek.* All those space movies, *Independence Day*, *Men in Black*. In Harvey's opinion, a serious alien-hunter need look no further than the glossy pages of the muscle magazines. Some of those guys . . . Not to mention the women! He didn't care how many push-ups they did, no way you could get that kind of definition and mass by gobbling steroids, or pumping a couple million tons of iron.

Harvey was convinced that those body-builders, some of them, just weren't human.

Wayne said, "Look who I just met . . ." His voice trailed away to a whisper too faint to be captured by the human ear. The Polaroid camera rested on Rodney McGuire's heaving chest. McGuire was conscious. His bulging eyes stared up at the white-painted ceiling as if he'd never seen a ceiling before, and believed it was some kind of optical delusion that was about to come crashing down on him.

April pushed the needle into McGuire's grossly swollen vein, and slowly depressed the plunger. McGuire's face was as white as the ceiling. April withdrew the plunger and the syringe's barrel filled with swirling blood. She depressed the plunger, forcing the blood back into McGuire's body, sluicing the last traces of heroin out of the barrel.

She withdrew the plunger again, excruciatingly slowly, her eyes flicking from Rodney's face to the barrel, as it was swamped with a tidal flow of blood.

Lewis sat quietly on the sofa, apparently blissfully unaware that his role in this little adventure was about to come to an abrupt end.

The twins, with seven previous murders between them, had a fairly polished act. In a matter of minutes, they had worked themselves into a homicidal rage.

"Fuck you, Dave! It's *my* turn to kick in the door!"

"Wrong again, you ugly, foul-mouthed piece of crap!"

But what if the door wasn't locked? Dave reached for the doorknob, but Danny was a tiny fraction of a second faster. Dave's hand closed on his brother's. Together, they rotated the knob in a clockwise direction.

The door swung open, and the coked-to-the-eyebrows mirror twins, warbling horrible Celtic war cries they had learned watching historical films starring Mel Gibson and Sean Connery, burst into the apartment.

Dave kicked the door shut.

Danny yelled, "Nobody move!"

Excellent advice, but the jostling herd of pneumatic Marilyns were having none of it.

32

The rottweiler's left foreleg had been dislocated. The unfortunate creature was in considerable pain. It howled ceaselessly into the night, its great head lifted towards unseen stars. The animal's cries of anguish were so pitiful they would have brought a tear to the eye of Imelda Marcos, had she witnessed the scene.

The drug-squad cops, dangling hints of promotion, convinced a couple of ambitious uniformed patrolmen to transport the rottie to the animal emergency clinic on Fourth Avenue. Easier said than done. The patrolmen, all lights and sirens, were en route to the emergency ward at St. Paul's, for tetanus shots.

Willows and Parker, in conjunction with a rapidly growing fleet of unmarked cars, continued, with an increasing sense of urgency, to patrol the Fairview Slopes neighbourhood.

Fairview's original inhabits, circa 1900, had a splendid view of the Vancouver Soap Company, Gas Works, a sawmill, and two fully functional slaughterhouses. At the time, the city hoped the area would become a high-class residential district. Alas, it was not to be. Fairview had developed into a blue-collar neighbourhood, and had, despite any growls of protest you might hear from its present inhabitants, pretty much stayed true to its roots.

During the boom years of the seventies and eighties, block upon block had been filled with cramped, architecturally uninspiring three-storey condominiums. Clever developers had begun construction at the top of the slopes and gradually worked their way down towards the flats. The lamentable but entirely predictable result was that each new building partially obliterated the costly views of the recently sold structure directly behind it.

Because the neighbourhood had been rebuilt so recently, in strict accordance with modern building codes and requirements, almost all the parking, thousands of units, was buried underground.

Maybe that explained why all those cops were having such a hard time locating the enormous two-point-five-ton Humvee, and its trio of gun-toting occupants.

Or maybe not.

33

The Force-10 blizzard of stimuli experienced by Danny and Dave as they bulled their way into Rodney McGuire's apartment was identical in every respect. The mirror twins had fantasized all through their lives about double-dating another set of "identicals." The gender of these dream dates was essentially irrelevant.

Suddenly finding themselves in an apartment stuffed to the rafters with no fewer than a dozen absolutely identical women, the twins can be forgiven if they briefly assumed they had been transported Heavenward without suffering any of the usual inconveniences.

When the twins burst into the apartment, Rodney McGuire was dying of an overdose of heroin.

April was busy with, alternatively, her Polaroid One-Step camera, and her Radio Shack propane torch.

Startled by the sudden intrusion, she swung around to see what was going on.

Unnoticed, the propane torch's pinprick-sharp, white-hot flame settled on the over-inflated vinyl buttock of McGuire's personal Marilyn.

She promptly exploded.

The twins reacted to the gunshot-like explosion and accompanying vinyl shrapnel instinctively, thoughtlessly, brutally, and with maximum efficiency.

Assuming the classic firing-line position, they opened up with their MAC-10s, spraying the apartment with 9mm rounds.

The front rank of Marilyns was decimated. Many of them were killed instantly. The sound of their dying, a heavy boom similar in tone to a .45-calibre semiauto, convinced the twins their fire was being returned.

April knew enough to keep the lowest of profiles. She lay flat as a lost coin on the cartridge-strewn carpet, and then hooked her legs around Rod McGuire's limp body and did her desperate best to roll him over on top of her.

McGuire offered no resistance. She felt the burden of every last ounce of his weight. If he'd ever been a gentleman, that time had passed. His arms flopped all over the place, limp and useless as the rest of him. His eyes stared blankly at the carpet. His mouth sagged open, and his tongue lapped at April's throat. His sour breath, slow as molasses, crept into her ear, and made her shiver.

Lewis sat on the sofa in his glamorous party suit, unscathed.

Wayne's view of the proceedings was largely blocked by the surging mass of Marilyns. In the initial flurry of bullets, in the scant seconds it took the twins to empty the magazines of their MAC-10s, Wayne was shot four times.

The first bullet struck him in the fleshy part of the thigh. The wound bled copiously but hardly hurt at all.

The second round grazed his left forearm, and the third was a clean hit, striking him midway between elbow and wrist. Luckily, the bullet missed the bone. Even so, the wound hurt like hell, and he almost lost his grip on his revolver.

The fourth bullet struck him in the head.

It was this last bullet that saved his life. Stunned and bloody, he fell to his knees, escaping the lethal hail of lead that followed. From behind the sofa, he emptied the gun in the general direction of his enemy.

For the second time in less than half a minute, the twins ejected their empty magazines, and reloaded.

All but two of the remaining Marilyns had been slaughtered.

The survivors had drifted away from the line of fire, and leaned gracefully, or were wedged, into a corner.

Wayne wiped a torrent of blood from his face. His probing fingers discovered a shallow furrow in his scalp, about three inches in length, exactly where he liked to part his hair.

It felt as if he'd been run over by a Dinky-Toy-sized, but fully operational, John Deere tractor.

The twins, from their positions in the living room, started shooting again.

Wayne yelled at April to stay low. He crawled into the bathroom, snatched towels off a rack as he dove headlong into the bathtub.

Bullets zipped through the drywall, shattered mirrors and the tub's sliding glass shower door, chipped tiles.

The cardboard Marilyn caught a bullet between the eyes. Had her smile faltered, or was Wayne hallucinating?

He turned on the taps, splashed blood from his eyes, and wrapped a towel tightly around his head. He tore a second towel into strips and bound his leg and then his wounded arm.

He'd left his shotgun in the bedroom.

He rolled out of the tub, and crawled gingerly across the glass-and-splinter-strewn floor towards the open door.

There was a brief lull in the shooting. He heard the distinctive, metallic clacking sound of ejected magazines, stood up, and bolted diagonally across the hallway and into the bedroom.

Dave and Danny simultaneously shouted, "Get him!"

Wayne kicked shut the bedroom door.

The damn bed was covered in plain brown cardboard boxes and loose balls of yellowed tissue paper, and instruction booklets. Where in hell was his damn shotgun?

Was April still alive? Had she thought to pack a pistol? He hoped so, but doubted it. Firearms were supposed to be his area of expertise.

Over the rustle of disturbed tissue paper, he heard two muttered voices that had exactly the same tone. It was a strange effect, almost as if he was hearing one voice and an oddly distorted echo that had a mind of its own.

Dave said, "We gotta get outta here."

"But we can't leave no survivors. Except McGuire, and maybe not even him."

"True."

"Better kick down that door, see what's inside."

"Lemme do it."

"No, me."

"My turn, because I'm older than you."

Danny gave Dave a hard shove, the stubby barrel of his MAC-10 scraping painfully across his sibling's bony chest.

"Don't gimme that 'older brother' crap! We were born simultaneous, and you know it."

"Fuck you!"

"Hey, fuck *you*!"

Enough idle chatter. Dave emptied his MAC into the bedroom door and adjoining wall.

Danny kicked in the bullet-riddled door.

Wayne's arm was killing him. His head was hosting an exhibition of jackhammers. He couldn't find the shotgun. He shouldn't have cut it down, made it so small. Maybe he'd left it in the living room . . . The twins opened fire, shredding the bedroom door and wall. In an instant, the air was full of splinters and plaster dust.

Wayne rolled off the bed, and landed on the shotgun. He flicked off the safety and aimed and fired. The muzzle blast scorched the sheets and set them fluttering. The load of steel shot passed under the bed, striking Danny in both legs. His left leg absorbed most of the shot; the mass of pellets struck him just above the ankle. Screaming, he fell facedown on the carpet.

Wayne gritted his teeth. His left arm was useless. He'd fired the shotgun as if it were a pistol, one-handed, and the thunderous recoil had sprained his wrist. Pumping a fresh round into the chamber was no easy task. The towel around his head was saturated, and the left side of his face was awash with blood, blurring his vision.

He braced himself, anticipating a fresh onslaught of pain, squinted under the bed and saw Danny's squirming body. Wayne fired – but not accurately.

Dave hadn't yet been hit, not even by a solitary pellet.

But he *felt* as if he'd been hit, and that was all that mattered.

Amputees speak of the anguish of phantom limbs, of suffering pain in a leg that no longer exists.

Dave had a not-quite-parallel experience. He and his identical twin brother were like railway tracks that had fallen prey to the inflexible rules of perspective, and actually did converge on the horizon, with cataclysmic results. Their two fates were as one. Dave was in agony, experiencing in every horrible detail the train-wreck torment suffered by his one-footed brother.

When Danny fell screaming to the carpet, Dave involuntarily fell right alongside him.

In the living room, April was suffocating. She had been hyperventilating, and now she could hardly draw breath. When the twins had burst into the apartment she had so feared for her life that she had rolled Rod McGuire's drugged body over on top of her as easily as a desperate father might grab a bumper and hoist up the family car that pinned his beloved daughter to the asphalt. But then onrushing panic had, in the narrow space between heartbeats, drained her of all her energy and strength. She found herself trapped by the scant weight of McGuire's body, and the crushing burden of her own terror.

She wasted a double lungful of air crying out to Wayne for help. He never heard her, over the deafening roar of the MAC-10s and the infrequent-but-telling blasts of his beloved shotgun.

April had been buried alive by her own weight in recently deceased drug dealer. She was being suffocated to death at a pace that was excruciatingly slow, but at the same time terrifyingly speedy, and her mind was fully occupied by a single frantic, burning question. Where in hell was Wayne?

Lewis was starting to climb down off his high. He struggled to analyse the situation. Was he experiencing a really terrible hallucination? The air stank of raw fear and scorched cordite. The carpet was littered with the remains of all those Marilyns. The two survivors, huddled into a corner not inches from a bullet-shattered lamp, stared blandly at him, their blue eyes denying the inviting warmth of their luscious scarlet smiles.

The sight of April feebly striving to rid herself of the limp grasp of Rod McGuire's chalk-white, stark-naked corpse was so improbably bizarre that Lewis's brain flatly refused to believe his eyes.

He tried to identify the source of the shrill screams coming from behind him. He had no Peterson's Field Guide, or any other research material to aid him, but there was no doubt in his mind that whatever species the creature was born of, it surely wasn't human.

In the bedroom, Wayne yanked hard on the shotgun's trigger. The tight-packed wad of shot struck Danny square in the chest. His irreplaceable life was blasted away in a welter of bone chips, shredded tissue, and high-flying blood. Dave's sympathetic piercing shriek of pain was so high-pitched it almost cracked the late Rodney McGuire's contact lenses.

The twins lay still, belly-up, one leg twisted awkwardly, smoking machine-gun clenched in an outflung right hand, a left arm bent in what might have been a half-assed salute to the Grim Reaper.

Both men were splattered head to foot with copious amounts of blood.

Wayne's leg was soaked in blood from mid-thigh to his ankle. He felt a little light-headed, but not much more so than usual. He laboured to crank another round into the shotgun's chamber.

Surveying the carnage, Wayne could be forgiven for believing he had killed both men – if indeed there were two of them, and he wasn't seeing double.

He made his way gingerly into the living room. It was slippery going. His shoes were bloody, the floor was littered with vinyl fragments of Marilyns.

Lewis continued to sit passively on the sofa. Dozens of 9mm MAC-10 rounds had narrowly missed him, ripping the sofa's expensive fabric to shreds and exposing the sub-strata of light-weight foam.

But Lewis was, almost miraculously, still unscathed.

Wayne didn't know how he felt about that, or what, if anything, he should do about it. He decided to figure it out later, when he'd worked out what had happened to April.

Where *was* April?

Wayne glanced around. Lewis was on the sofa.

McGuire lay on the floor by the coffee table, covered in scraps of vinyl and spent cartridges.

But where was April?

Under McGuire.

Wayne dropped to his knees. He used the shotgun to lever the dead weight of McGuire's corpse off his beloved April.

Was she alive? Or dead. She didn't seem to be breathing, and surely that was a commonly used yardstick. He tried to take her pulse, but he was shaking so hard he couldn't keep his finger on her wrist.

He considered mouth-to-mouth resuscitation. But the way she was lying there, so still, and pale, and kind of squashed-looking, as if she'd just been introduced to a steamroller, wasn't too appetizing.

Wayne lightly batted her cheek. His hand was bloody. Tiny red flecks spattered April's cheek. Wayne couldn't help noticing. It was as if she'd been instantly *freckle-ized*. He tried to wipe away the flecks and made things much worse. Now she looked as if she'd used a whole lot too much makeup. It reminded him of her lap-dancing days, and he was instantly depressed. His energy level plummeted.

He blew into April's face so hard her eyelashes fluttered. "April? April, honey? Are you okay, baby?"

For all the response he got, Wayne might as well have been

cross-examining his neighbour's palomino, as it lay stone dead in the driveway, waiting to be picked up by a crane-equipped flatbed truck direct from the glue factory.

In the bedroom, Dave lay on the blood-and-gore-soaked carpet, thinking as hard as he knew how. Was he alive, or was he dead? It should have been an easy question – but it wasn't. A close-range shotgun blast to the chest causes its own special brand of irredeemable havoc. Danny had been so promptly and gruesomely dispatched that the violence of his passing must surely have set a benchmark for all to follow. But how could Dave be alive if his twin was dead? Their umbilical cords, confounding the attendant delivery-room quacks, had shared the same placenta. During all the years of their lives – and they were only a few days short of their thirtieth birthday – the brothers had been no less inseparable than they'd been in their mother's womb.

Now Danny was dead, and Dave wasn't. Neither brother believed in God. The concept of life after death was as alien to them as, for example, a random act of kindness.

Dave felt as dislocated, mentally and physically, as if he had been sliced in twain, split right down the middle from skull to crotch, and his two halves flung away from each other, over opposite horizons.

How could he feel so rotten, but essentially alive, when Danny was so obviously . . . at peace?

Impossible.

Dave opened his mind to each and every last one of the infinite possibilities for good and evil that the world offered. He was prepared to slip away, into the void. If it was time to die, so be it.

He listened to the thumping of his heart, and was not alarmed when the cadence abruptly slowed, lost all rhythm and force, and then, ever so gradually, faded away into flat-line silence.

Okay, he was dead. No problem. He could adjust. Just watch him.

But then the robust pounding of his heart came back, sudden as a high-school marching band swinging 'round a small-town corner. Dave was stunned. He was covered in gore and full of life. Lightning crackled and shivered all around him. His eyes bulged. He felt nothing less than *reborn*. Man, he and Danny had never been religious. It was weird, the things you took for granted. From now on, it was going to be different. He wondered if he was too old to be an altar boy.

He sat up, stiff and crinkly in his carapace of congealing blood. He flexed his arms and legs, turned his head this way and that, opened and closed his hands. He ejected the empty magazine from his machine-gun, and reloaded.

He stood up.

He straightened his bloody tie, and shot his bloody cuffs. He strode casually but determinedly, and somewhat clumsily, out of the bedroom and down the short hallway towards the condo's living room.

A decapitated head of a Marilyn stared unblinkingly up at him with huge, improbably blue eyes.

Despite the fact that her deflated head was flat as a day-old pancake, she looked as if she was desperately trying to blow him a kiss.

Spooky.

A guy in a shiny gold suit sat quietly on the sofa. He looked very relaxed. Or perhaps unconscious. Or even dead.

Dave wiped his brother's blood from his eye, took a closer look at the guy slumped on the couch. He looked like a partially deflated Oscar.

Or an angel, waiting patiently for the dust to settle, before he did his picking and choosing.

Three people lay motionless in a complicated tangle on the floor on the far side of the coffee table. Was one of them naked? Dave stepped closer for a better look.

The two surviving Marilyns leaned into the corner. They shifted slightly, from one painted-on foot to the other.

Dave whirled and fired. A Marilyn exploded. The shockwave pushed the second Marilyn sideways, and saved her.

The deafening roar of the MAC-10 was April's cue to open her eyes. She and Wayne found themselves staring at each other from a distance of about three inches.

April said, "Wayne?"

Dave turned towards the plaintive whisper of her voice. He found himself staring into the shotgun's cold black eye. He decided, a fraction of a second too late, that he wasn't quite ready to die. He pulled the MAC-10's trigger and saw, with preternatural clarity, the bullets stitch a ragged series of holes diagonally across the living-room ceiling.

For a moment, he couldn't understand why he had shot so high. Then he realized that he was lying flat on his back. No wonder his aim had been so erratic.

The man with the shotgun wavered into his field of vision. The man stood over him. He was speaking to him, but his words were soft and blurry, indecipherable.

Maybe he was foreign.

Dave's eyes skittered to the shimmering, golden creature on the sofa. It was leaning towards him, staring expectantly at him.

Wayne, staring at Dave, said, "How come you ain't dead yet?"

It was a fair question, considering the damage already done. Too impatient to wait for an answer, Wayne unleashed another hellish load of buckshot into Dave's chest, punching the life right out of him.

In for a penny, in for a pound. Wayne turned the gun on Lewis, and unceremoniously pulled the trigger.

The internal firing pin clicked sharply as it was propelled into an empty chamber.

He fumbled in his pockets for more shells.

April was back on her feet, wheezing, tenderly hugging her bruised and aching body, her whispery voice urging Wayne to get himself under control, mumbling something about improvising a new scenario . . .

What the hell kind of talk was that?

Wayne shoved fat 12-gauge shells into the shotgun. He was sick and tired of April and her dimwit, half-assed plans to rule the fucking universe. It was time to start afresh, with a clean slate. Just look at his arm! Just look at his leg! He'd bet anything that he was gonna need a major transfusion. It'd be months before he'd recovered enough to saddle up and ride his Harley again.

The shotgun was fully loaded. April was pawing at him, whining like a defective starter motor. He brushed her off, and cranked a round into the chamber. Her and Lewis. He'd kill them both, if he had to.

Or maybe even if he didn't.

34

"*Ooh, oohoohoo, hoo, ooh, oohoohoo, ooh, oohoohoo, hoo . . .*"

Harvey eagerly cranked the volume all the way up when the disc jockey announced a Spice Girls tune. He neglected to turn the radio down again when the song finally ended. Why should he listen to the ugly sound of the twins playing with their guns when he had such a fine stereo at his disposal? He found a "golden oldies" station. Sitting hunched behind the wheel of the idling Humvee, he hummed along to a series of catchy little tunes from yesteryear. Idly, he wondered if it was true that everybody actually did play the fool.

Song lyrics sometimes were full of wisdom, but he decided that this particular ballad was full of crap.

Jake had lived a longer-than-average life without making any dumb romantic mistakes. Ditto, Marty.

Harvey had never fallen in love, except for a brief fling in the sixth grade, which surely didn't count, because Miss Jamieson had only taken him home that one time . . .

He flipped through his new issue of *Washboard Belly* magazine until he found the centrefold. Angling the glossy pages away from him to reduce glare from the dome light, he squinted down at the Monthly Man's incredible pectorals. How did a normal person obtain a stomach like that? Looking at him, you'd think the guy's

father must have been a slab of concrete. Harvey's brain struggled
to calculate the number of hours and gallons of sweat that the
Monthly Man must have dedicated to his stomach muscles.

His fingers probed his own flat belly. Scattered across the following pages were numerous overlapping photos of the Monthly
Man's fabulous stomach as he absorbed blows from bruised fists,
pool cues, and even aluminum baseball bats.

Harvey, concentrating hard on his magazine, rocked by the blast
from the Humvee's elaborate, custom-designed-and-installed
surround-sound speaker system, never heard the raging gun battle:
the heavy shotgun blasts, the burly sewing-machine stutter of the
machine-guns, the percussive, big-balloon pops of bursting
Marilyns or the shrill cries and pathetic whispers of the wounded.

Nor did he hear the unmarked Ford as it cruised slowly up
behind him without the benefit of lights, stopping only a finger's
width behind the Humvee's sturdy rear bumper.

Parker was on the radio, broadcasting the condo's address, as
Willows eased out of the Ford.

Parker dropped the mike and went after him.

Willows, crouched low, Glock in hand, made his way cautiously
along the Humvee's throbbing flank. His clothing was dark, but
the Humvee's driver was bound to spot him, if he happened to
glance in his side mirror.

But Harvey only had eyes for his magazine.

Parker slipped around the far side of the Humvee, taking up a
position directly in front of the vehicle. She lined up her Glock's
front sight on the third button of Harvey's shirt.

Willows tapped his ring against the windshield. Harvey looked
up, and Parker switched on her Mag-Lite.

Harvey was blinded by the beam.

Willows yanked open the Humvee's door. He reached past
Harvey, his hand grazing the magazine, making a soft, rustling
sound that was lost in the clatter of the music. He turned the ignition key towards him, killing the engine.

He dropped the key in his pocket.

Harvey's hands were clasped on top of his head.

The magazine lay in his lap.

He was thinking that he was going to go to jail, for sure, unless he thought of something really clever, really quick. What if he head-butted the Humvee's powerful horn? Would the twins come rushing outside, all fire and thunder, and kill the cops? Harvey thought about how sweet it would be to go home, take a nice hot shower, and curl up in bed with a glass of wine and a stack of muscle magazines.

He wondered if his subscriptions were transferrable without extra mailing costs to a federal institution.

He found himself being eased out of the car, tried not to look down the short barrel of the lady cop's pistol as her partner efficiently frisked him. The cop found his armpit .45 first, then the switchblade, and then his stainless-steel pliers. Harvey couldn't have cared less about any of that stuff. It all belonged to Jake anyway, and was as easily replaced as a bar of soap. It pissed him off something fierce, however, when the cop found his ankle gun – a chrome-plated .44-calibre Derringer with custom-made elephant-ivory grips. He'd bought the pistol from a professional loiterer he'd met outside a gun show in Austin, Texas, just a few months before he'd signed on with Jake. The seller had piqued Harvey's interest by confiding that the gun had been used in a love-triangle homicide, and that the previous owner was now residing in Bangkok. Harvey, believing every word, had paid top dollar for the gun.

The cop led him around to the rear of the Humvee and handcuffed him to the rear bumper.

"Who's inside?"

Up until now, both cops had been mute, so the question took Harvey by surprise. It was a tricky situation. How should he play it? Was it best to cooperate? Jake would call it ratting out. He'd get Marty to take care of Harvey's bail, and then he'd get Marty to take care of Harvey.

Harvey pictured himself lying facedown in a shallow grave in the middle of a pine forest. Birds twittering in the branches. Suns and moons passing overhead, while he slowly turned to dust.

The cop grabbed a handful of trapezius, gave him a shake. "I asked you a question. Who's inside?"

More cop cars, plenty of them, ghosted silently towards him. He was surrounded.

He said, "The light's pretty good out here. Could I please have my magazine?"

The cop didn't pull back his arm so much as a quarter of an inch, just lashed out and caught him flush on the forehead with a hard right. It was a heavy blow, and it caught him completely by surprise. The back of his head bounced off the Humvee's fender a split-second before the rest of him hit asphalt. He decided to rest awhile, and eased shut his eyes.

The street was cluttered with marked and unmarked vehicles. So far, against all odds, no one had come screaming to a stop with lights flashing and siren wailing. Tony LoBrio and Ken DelMonte bailed out of their ride before the car had stopped moving, but because there was so much congestion, they'd been forced to pull over half a block away.

Willows and Parker sprinted towards the condo. The front door was unlocked. Willows went in first, and curled right. Parker was half a step behind him, off to his left.

The sole surviving Marilyn drifted demurely along a bullet-riddled wall. Bits and pieces of the other Marilyns lay everywhere.

Lewis lay on his side on the sofa, sleeping soundly.

Dave lay where he had fallen.

Rodney McGuire's naked body lay facedown on the carpet.

April crouched over Dave, her back to the condo's open door. If she felt a draft, she paid it no mind.

April was busy, busy, busy. Her fingers were bloody to the second knuckle. She'd relieved Dave of two of his diamond ear-rings, via the simple expedient of tearing them from his flesh. The third earring was proving difficult. Looting corpses was such a horrid, such a horribly *slippery* business . . .

She became aware of the pair of shiny black brogues pointing towards her. Her eyes twitched. She followed the legs up to Willows' pistol, and then his badge.

She said, "Oh, fuck!" She stuffed the bloody diamonds in her mouth. The cop made no attempt to stop her. She tasted blood, worked up a mouthful of saliva, swallowed her booty down. The cop cuffed her hands behind her back. He started to tell her that she had a right to an attorney, that anything she said . . .

The condo was filling up with cops. There were swarms of them, plainclothes and uniform, ERT guys, a sergeant, grey-haired men with pips, everything but a trained seal on a bicycle.

April shouted, "Wayne!"

From the bedroom, Wayne yelled, "Yeah, what?" Luckily for April and Lewis, his blood lust had faded so quickly that, by the time he'd reloaded his precious shotgun, he no longer wanted to kill anything. He came limping and lumbering down the hall, the shotgun tucked under his arm, his head lowered, his eyes on his cupped handful of glitter. He said, "The earrings' posts are threaded. You oughtta know that. Screw 'em counter-clockwise, they come off real easy . . ."

He saw the roomful of cops, made a flash estimate of the firepower pointed at him. He slowly raised his hands. The shotgun thumped on the sodden carpet.

He was seriously outnumbered, but that wasn't what stopped him from making a play.

It was the hungry look in the cops' eyes. All of them, especially the women, looked as if they were just dying to kill him. When he raised his hands, their taut faces were flooded with disappointment.

He turned to April. Her lips were red. Her eyes were bright. Jeez. He wasn't much good at sarcasm, but thought he'd better take a shot at it while he had the chance.

"Is there a plan 'C,' honey-pie?"

April said bitterly, "That's right, Wayne. But you aren't going to find out about it until it's way too late."

A cop snatched up the shotgun. Parker told Wayne to turn around.

He said, "I like your hair."

She cuffed him, and read him his rights.

Wayne said, "The guy on the couch? He did it. Me? I'm just an innocent bystander."

"Me, too!" insisted April.

Singly and in pairs, gun-toting cops continued to burst into the apartment, marvel at the butchery, and trample all over the crime scene.

"Show him the goddamn pictures of all your previous victims!" Wayne yelled at Lewis. The towels wrapped tightly around Wayne's head, arm, and leg wounds were drenched in blood. His pants pockets bulged with shotgun shells. His trembling hand tightly clutched Danny's bloody diamond earrings. His unruly beard was spattered with vinyl and gore, and the fire in his eyes was fuelled by a passionately sincere craziness.

He did not make a credible witness.

Tony LoBrio was wearing a brand-new suede trenchcoat, so his partner, Ken DelMonte, got to pat Wayne down without an argument. The search yielded eleven shotgun shells, a Swiss Army knife, two thousand dollars in American currency, and an article, ripped from a popular biker magazine, that explained how to install a Yost Power Tube. Whatever the hell that was. DelMonte's questing fingers stumbled across an unopened Polaroid film cartridge. What a shame the country's legal system didn't allow a death sentence, because he sure as hell had all the evidence the prosecutor's office needed for a first-degree conviction.

April, indicating Rodney McGuire, said, "I think he broke one of my ribs. It hurts to breathe." A thin trickle of blood leaked from the corner of her mouth. She licked it away with her tongue, and sat down hard on the coffee table.

Scattered around Rodney McGuire's body were a dozen full-colour Polaroid snapshots depicting the last moments of his life.

Parker wondered who'd taken the pictures, the guy, or the living doll. Her money was on Wayne, though she couldn't say why.

Soon, the air vibrated with the shrill wail of sirens. Engines growled as cops were reassigned. Tires squealed as several of the cars that remained made way for a trio of speeding ambulances.

Crime-scene photographer Mel Dutton had been routinely listening to background chatter on his police scanner as he breakfasted in his warm and cosy West End apartment. When he learned that a pre-dawn shootout at a Fairview condo had resulted in at least three apparently drug-related deaths, he was galvanized. Dutton was an experienced pro. Instantly realizing that a detailed photographic record of the aftermath of a grisly multiple murder had the potential to be a killer coffee-table book, he grabbed his gear and sped to the scene with undue haste.

A few days earlier, Dutton had purchased a brand-new Mazda Miata.

Tragically unaccustomed to the little car's high-speed handling characteristics, he'd miscalculated the trajectory required to successfully negotiate the off-ramp of the Granville Street bridge. A roostertail of bright orange sparks chased the car along the ramp as, sliding along on its roof, it ricochetted from guardrail to guardrail like a gigantic pinball.

Exiting the off-ramp, the Miata hit the wall of an under-construction prefabricated concrete building.

The wall trembled and swayed, and collapsed onto the car. Dutton would have been killed instantly, crushed under many tons of concrete, if the Mazda hadn't been neatly framed by a huge window opening.

The destruction of Dutton's new car was witnessed by the crew of a private helicopter that happened to be flying over the area. The pilot dialled 911 on his cellphone, and an ambulance was dispatched within the minute.

Wayne had been cuffed, strapped to a stretcher, and loaded into one of the ambulances parked on the street in front of the late Rodney McGuire's condo. A paramedic had assured him they'd be on their way in a few seconds. He asked Wayne how he was doing.

Wayne said, "Fine."

His blood pressure was alarmingly low. They'd intubated him. A clear liquid dripped down a flexible plastic tube and into a vein in his wrist.

The ambulance's siren wailed uncertainly. The vehicle must have been extremely well insulated, because Wayne couldn't hear a thing. The ambulance moved forward a few feet, began to pick up speed, and then jerked to a stop.

The paramedic attending him had a short, heated discussion with the driver, who was engaged in a heated argument with someone on the street. Both men got out of the ambulance to continue the argument with their unseen adversary.

Wayne had always believed paramedics were supposed to be the kind of guys who never got worked up about anything. He was surprised at how loudly they were yelling at each other. It was easy to listen in on the argument. Apparently there'd been a spectacular car crash only a few blocks away. The driver was alive and conscious, but his vehicle had been crushed, and he was trapped inside.

Wayne thought he heard the phrase, "Jaws of Life."

His leg was numb. The ambulance guys had left his towel in place, but applied their own tourniquet. It felt way too tight. Bending his gunshot leg towards him as much as he could, he wriggled and squirmed against the restraining straps.

He got his fingers on the paramedic's tourniquet. Velcro. He gave it a yank.

There now, wasn't that better? Wayne wondered who had been speaking to him, and then realized he'd been speaking to himself. He smiled, and shut his eyes, and daydreamed of a narrow, endlessly twisty tree-lined road, and the rolling thunder of his beloved Harley's exhausts.

Cresting a hill, Wayne saw earthmoving equipment, a wide channel that had been cut through the asphalt. Why hadn't the work site been signed? Where was the damn flag girl, in her skintight jeans? He got the Harley straightened out and brought his foot down hard on the rear brake pedal. His right hand squeezed the handlebar-mounted front brake lever. The Harley's tires laid down a string-straight strip of burnt rubber four inches wide and thirty yards long.

He saw he wasn't going to stop in time. He leaned on the brake pedal and the rear wheel locked up. The bike's rear end tried to shake hands with the front wheel. Wayne had dumped a bike just after he'd started riding, and still remembered the pain.

The Harley was on its side, shrieking, high-speed metal skidding across pebbly asphalt.

The flag girl was sitting in the shade, drinking a Coke. She waved as he went by.

The trench was a lot deeper than he expected. Bottomless, by the look of it. How could a harmless daydream go so terribly wrong? Was the Harley covered by his extended warranty? Dimly, as he rode the bike deeper and deeper into the endlessly black chasm, Wayne wondered if he had died, and gone straight to hell.

35

April's ribs were cracked, not broken. Even so, the emergency-room intern, an overly hirsute man named Robert Schwartz, insisted on keeping her under close observation for at least twenty-four hours.

A sturdy uniformed cop sat in the gleaming corridor, just outside her door, drinking coffee and fending off nurses.

April declined Parker's offer of a court-appointed lawyer.

"I don't need a fucking lawyer. Look at me! I need a *cigarette*. So tell me, how's Wayne?"

Willows said, "Would you like to make a statement, April?"

"Wayne's dead, isn't he?" April concentrated on Parker. "He's my husband, believe it or not. We were married in Greece, of all places. Don't ask me the name of the town, because I can't pronounce it. Nobody can, not even the people who live there. Anyway, I've got a right to know how Wayne's doing, don't I?"

Parker said, "First we're going to talk about you, and *then* we're going to talk about Wayne."

April thought it over, shrugged. The thin hospital gown slipped off her shoulder but she didn't seem to notice.

She said, "But Lewis is okay, right?"

"Lewis is doing just fine," said Parker.

April chewed on her lip. She was pretty sure she could feel the diamond earrings speedily working their way through her intestinal tract. She'd been eating a lot of pills, for the pain. They must have slipped her something, some kind of drug, a laxative.

She said, "Wayne murdered them all."

"Who, exactly?" said Willows.

"The drug dealers. He had their pictures in his pocket, didn't he? You bet he did. He carried them with him everywhere he went. Like trophies. He was so fucking proud of himself."

"How'd he kill them?"

"He overdosed them, what d'you think?"

Parker said, "Can you remember any of their names?"

"Yeah, sure. Melvin Ladner, Russ Green, Ralphie Lightman, a guy named Warren . . ."

April named eight victims. Willows and Parker were unfamiliar with one of the names – a man named Norwood Adams.

Willows said, "This guy, Norwood. D'you happen to know where he lives?"

"No, of course not." Despite the drugs, April felt a little twinge of pain. She let it show. "But he's in the book. Off Victoria, below Sixteenth Avenue? Somewhere in there. Ask Wayne, he'll give you the address."

"Good idea, thanks." Willows smiled. "So the idea was, Wayne would keep bumping off people in Jake Cappalletti's organization until Jake came after him, and then he'd take Jake out. Is that what was supposed to happen, April?"

"Far as I know. Or maybe he was hoping Jake would offer him a partnership. Wayne wasn't the kind of guy who liked to share his innermost thoughts."

"But you and Wayne were partners. Weren't you?"

"No way. I did what I was told, that's all. Wayne would've killed me, if I'd messed with him."

Parker smiled. "You were an unwilling accomplice."

"Yeah. No, wait. I was unwilling, but I wasn't an accomplice. More like his slave."

Willows had been standing by the foot of April's bed. He went over to the window and looked out. April's room was on the sixth floor. He tried the window to see if it would open. It did, but not enough to let April slip through. Not that he considered her a potential suicide. April was an optimist, for now. By the time she got out of prison she'd be something else entirely: a pensioner.

Willows said, "Did Wayne tell you to kill Rodney McGuire, April?"

"What kind of question is that?"

"McGuire died of a drug overdose. The heroin was uncut, April. It was a heavy enough load to kill one of your neighbour's horses."

April was shocked. "How did you find out my neighbour owns horses?"

She was so transparent, that Willows almost felt sorry for her. He said, "Your fingerprints were all over the syringe that killed McGuire, April. Your prints were all over the camera, and the photographs. The way the evidence stacks up, your choices are extremely limited. Did you kill McGuire because Wayne told you to, or because you wanted to?"

"Maybe I should talk to a lawyer."

"Good idea, April."

"But you should know that Wayne made me do everything. I used to be a stripper. A lap-dancer. I made good money, I had a boyfriend, I was happy. Then Wayne came along, and screwed everything up."

Willows nodded sympathetically.

April said, "Wayne's huge. I weigh a hundred and eleven pounds; Wayne weighs three hundred and twelve."

"Why didn't you leave him?"

"He watched me all the time. Ask him. Or, better yet, ask Lewis. He'll tell you what it was like, living with Wayne."

Willows nodded. He didn't know why he was in such an agreeable mood, but he wasn't going to worry about it. Lewis was in another wing of the hospital. He was being weaned off heroin, and it was going to be a slow and ugly process. So far, Lewis had proved an unreliable witness. Willows doubted they'd have even identified him, had an alert cop not recognized his description from a recently filed missing-persons report. The report had been filed by an attractive young woman named Elizabeth Bell, who claimed to be Lewis's fiancée. Her story was that Lewis had disappeared while they were shopping in the Eaton's Mall. They'd been browsing in the Gap clothing store, and she'd decided to try on a skirt. Lewis had said he was thirsty, was going to get himself an Orange Julius and would be back in a few minutes.

Miss Bell had denied any knowledge of Lewis's recent activities. Showed photos of Wayne and April, she failed to recognize either of them. She insisted Lewis had not dabbled in illegal drugs of any kind, and certainly had not been a heroin addict.

The physical evidence backed her up. The medical opinion was that Lewis had been shooting up intensively, but for less than a week. He had no old scars, no indications whatsoever that he was anything but a short-term addict.

The majority of his mostly healed puncture wounds were in his right arm. Lewis was right-handed. He'd insisted that, to the best of his recollection, April had shot him up. Despite his misgivings, Willows tended to believe Lewis's story. The kid was an unreliable witness, but he was faultlessly cooperative. Unfortunately his most vivid memories were a lot of nonsense – lush green fields and vast, sandy deserts, tables piled high with dead frogs.

Lewis had stopped hallucinating, but all his memories were of his hallucinations.

At least, they seemed to be hallucinations. One of Lewis's memories had involved a couple of "spotted dogs." Dalmatians. He'd rambled on about steel pens, and endless barking, disembodied tails that wagged much too slowly, as they drifted through the air . . .

There'd been two dalmatians in the house, guarding a garage full of Harley-Davidson motorcycles, and boxes of spare parts, aftermarket bolt-ons.

They'd tried the pound and then the SPCA. A volunteer named Cynthia remembered Lewis. She'd thought he was a deaf mute. It took her a few minutes to find April on the computer. She'd paid cash for the dogs. Cynthia was absolutely certain that April and Lewis were alone during the hour or so they'd spent at the SPCA. They'd taken the dogs for a short walk, to make sure they were companionable, and that they all got along with one another. Cynthia accompanied them, to make sure everything was all right. Sometimes people tried to steal the dogs. She was sure she'd have noticed a bearded three-hundred-and-twelve-pound man, if there'd been one lurking in the weeds.

If Wayne kept April on such a tight leash, where was he when she and Lewis visited the SPCA?

It was just one of many awkward questions that April would be asked in court, before they gave her life in a maximum-security federal institution.

Willows said, "April?"

"I'm sorry, but I really don't think I should talk to you any more."

"Okay, fine. I just wondered, how old are you?"

April considered the question carefully, before deciding there was no harm in answering.

"I'm twenty-two."

A life sentence added up to twenty-five years, maximum. She'd be eligible for parole in fifteen years. Willows wondered if he'd be retired by then. Not if he and Parker had children. Christ. Maybe he should switch to the commercial crime squad, put in a few years, and then try to get a lucrative job in the private sector. An ex-homicide cop he knew, Ralph Kearns, had started his own business and was doing pretty well, driving a Jag . . .

Willows wanted to drop in on Lewis, just for a minute. Parker was too tired to argue. They found him sleeping peacefully. Parker lingered in the doorway, but Willows went over to the bed, and stared down at him as if he was searching for something, the definitive answer to an unasked question.

For the next week or so, Lewis would be subject to withdrawal symptoms that included fever, aches, tremors, chills, sweating, and chain-sneezing.

He'd suffer from bottomless apathy, self-loathing. He would struggle against a huge psychological craving for heroin. Lewis's circumstances were highly unusual, but the average cold-turkey addict experienced an overpowering desire for the drug that filled his every waking minute for as long as six months.

But Willows had high hopes for Lewis, because he was a special case. Elizabeth had insisted he was not an addictive personality. Willows hoped she was right. The fact that his girlfriend was sticking with him was a big plus for Lewis. What happened to Lewis, in terms of crime and punishment, was, theoretically, still very much up in the air. But Willows and Parker both saw him as pure victim. From their perspective, April and Wayne had worked hard to set Lewis up as a fall guy.

Willows doubted he'd be charged, much less do any jail time. Parker lingered in the hospital doorway. Lewis was already on methadone. He looked so tranquil, though his dreams might rage. He'd had no visitors. She wondered if he had any family, if anyone loved him or even cared about him, aside from Elizabeth Bell.

Parker was exhausted. Too little sleep, too much work. She wanted to go home, to fall into bed and sleep for a week. How much longer did Willows intend to stay?

Willows was thinking about his son, Sean, who had been wounded in an armed robbery about a year earlier, and was still recovering from his wounds. He guessed Lewis was not much older than Sean. The two men would never meet each other, but they had a great deal in common. They were both victims, plucked at random, subjected to violent forces beyond their control.

They were unlucky, because they had been brutalized. They were lucky, because they had survived. He knew nothing about Lewis. What sort of person was he? How had he travelled from the Orange Julius into April's clutches? Would Lewis's brush with death turn him into a better human being, or would he fail to shake his addiction? Willows stared down at Lewis's sleeping face.

He hoped Lewis got lucky, and made something of himself.

Willows turned and moved towards Parker. His face was drawn.

She slipped her arm through his. Together, they walked slowly down the corridor towards the bank of elevators.

She couldn't remember the last time she and Willows and Sean and Annie had shared a meal. She and Jack had neglected the children at a time in their lives when it was the last thing they needed. How was Annie getting along with her new boyfriend, the one Sean so thoroughly disapproved of? How was Sean coming along? Lately, because he didn't feel he was making any progress, he'd been skipping his physiotherapy appointments. The house was going to be a mess. Or Annie would be in a foul mood, because she'd been doing all the cleaning . . .

They still hadn't signed the mortgage papers.

There were a stack of overdue bills to be paid.

The garden was overgrown.

A mile-high pile of clothing, hers and Jack's, needed to take a trip to the dry cleaner's.

They stepped outside. A bitter, stinging rain slanted down from behind the hospital's roofline. She felt the cold and damp seeping into her bones.

Willows put his arm around her, sheltering her. "Want me to drive?"

Parker nodded, too tired to speak.

Epilogue

A thousand willing hands yanked Jake Cappalletti downtown for questioning. It had been an intensive but short visit. Jake declined to be interviewed. Palsied but stolid, he sat on his tongue until he was sprung by his team of burly, overdressed lawyers, who heatedly explained that they could not allow Jake to be interviewed due to his considerable age and rapidly deteriorating state of health.

"Anyways," barked Jake, "I don' know nothin'!"

In truth, Jake was too busy consolidating his hold on his fractured drug empire to waste time chatting with the cops. He had vacancies to fill, job interviews to conduct. Some guys deserved promotions. Others deserved considerably less.

Harvey, for example.

A pal of Harvey's who spent a lot of time wandering the halls of 312 Main had informed Jake that Harvey had been perusing a magazine when Jake Willows and Claire Parker jumped him.

"Perusin'!" screamed Jake, "What da hell kinda woid is dat?"

The pal said that Harvey had turned the Humvee's radio up so loud that he wasn't even aware that McGuire's condo had been the scene of sustained automatic-weapons fire.

Jake had hung up, done some serious thinking.

That night, he asked Marty to take him for a ride in the Rolls. They'd cruised slowly past the scene of the crime. The exterior walls of Rodney McGuire's condo had been perforated by dozens of bullets. The well-tended grounds were littered with wood chips and fragments of dirty pink plaster. Jake marvelled at the damage. It was not much short of a miracle that no one outside the condo had been shot.

Harvey's bail had yet to be determined, despite constant pressure from Jake's battery of hard-charging lawyers. Jake had a hunch the cops smelled a weak link, and were mercilessly grilling Harvey in the hope that he'd collapse, and implicate Jake in the bloody Fairview Slopes shootings.

No matter how high Harvey's bail, Jake meant to cough up every last penny. He was perplexed. How could Harvey have been so unaware of what was going on inside McGuire's condo?

As soon as the poor sap was released, Jake meant to find out.

KARAOKE RAP

A WILLOWS AND PARKER MYSTERY

Ozzie believes he's planned the perfect crime. Wealthy stock promoter Harold Wismer is having an affair with a woman named Melanie Martel. Ozzie and his buddy Dean will kidnap Harold as he leaves Melanie's apartment, and then demand a five-million-dollar ransom from Harold's loving wife, Joan. Harold is famous locally for his loud mouth, endless cigars, and banana-yellow suits. He can easily afford five million. The original Trampoline Man, he's suffered numerous multi-dollar losses playing the market, and always bounced back.

Unfortunately, Ozzie is unaware that ancient-but-still-sharp-toothed mobster Jake Cappalletti also has a lively pecuniary interest in Harold. Ozzie's young and quick. But Jake is old, and methodical.

Vancouver police detectives Jack Willows and Claire Parker are assigned the task of investigating Harold's sudden and violent disappearance. Willows balks. His son, Sean has been critically wounded in a convenience-store holdup, and Willows doesn't want to abandon that case. But he is soon convinced that the two crimes are related, and the furiously paced hunt is on.

"A smart, tight novel by a writer at the top of his form."
– *Globe and Mail*

"A world of delicious characterizations, fast, complex plots, and best and most important of all, writing as light and flaky as excellent pie crust."
– *London Free Press*

"Gough skilfully marries a tight plot with side-splittingly funny scenes and mordant turns of phrase."
– Montreal *Gazette*

0-7710-3403-2 • $26.99 cloth   0-7710-3448-2 • $8.99 paper

MEMORY LANE

A WILLOWS AND PARKER MYSTERY

Ross's one good memory of the slammer was his friendship with Garret, in for robbery and murder. Now that Garret is dead, and Ross is out of jail, Ross and Garret's old girlfriend, Shannon, have gotten together. Are the two falling in love, or is Shannon hoping Ross knows where Garret stashed the loot from his robbery long ago?

Meanwhile, Willows and Parker are investigating the murder of a city police officer, who, it turns out, had an interesting sex life. Once again Gough brilliantly weaves together two taut plots as Willows and Parker race against the clock to prevent another murder.

"Gough twists the threads skillfully, tying up our attention."
– Saskatoon *Star Phoenix*

"Gough's accomplishment, once again, is his marriage of a tight plot and solid characters with mordant turns of phrase."
– Montreal *Gazette*

"Gough keeps the action moving right to the end and more than enough plot twists keep readers guessing."
– Margaret Cannon, *Globe and Mail*

0-7710-3437-7 • $26.99 cloth   0-7710-3404-0 • $7.99 paper

— HEARTBREAKER —

A WILLOWS AND PARKER MYSTERY

Shelley has it made: he's arranged his life in a way that affords him maximum comfort for minimum effort. He moves from one upscale house-sitting job to another, supporting himself with petty theft and the occasional job as a night-club bouncer. But a day on the beach turns sour when Shelley makes two crucial mistakes: he breaks into a car belonging to off-duty police detectives Willows and Parker, and he picks up a gorgeous beach-bunny named Bo.

Shelley is astonished at how quickly Bo worms her way into the most intimate details of his life – and equally surprised to discover that he's falling in love with her. Bo seems fond of Shelley, too. But Bo's former "business associates" want her back, and are eager and willing to do anything it takes to get her.

Meanwhile Willows and Parker are investigating the murder of a sleazy real-estate agent at a luxury penthouse condo, and, as the events in this fast-paced mystery bring everyone together, the results are – literally – explosive.

"This is the eighth and best book in the excellent series featuring the
Vancouver police team of Claire Parker and Jack Willows.
As always, Gough turns in a stellar collection of characters."
– *Globe and Mail*

"Mordantly funny ... moves at top speed."
– *Sunday Oregonian*

0-7710-3438-5 • $26.99 cloth   0-7710-3447-4 • $7.99 paper

KILLERS

A WILLOWS AND PARKER MYSTERY

It is mid-winter when the body of Dr. Gerard Roth is found floating in the killer-whale pool in Vancouver's main aquarium. Although he is known to enjoy tempting fate by swimming amongst the more dangerous mammals in the aquarium's collection, there are signs that he met his death at human hands. Detectives Jack Willows and Claire Parker are called in to investigate.

Meanwhile, feckless, unemployed actor Chris Spacy believes he actually witnessed Roth's body being dumped in the pool, but he's not exactly sure his blurred memory wasn't a drug-induced hallucination. With blackmail on his mind, he goes after the likely killer – an action that provokes further bloodshed, and complicates an already-murky case for the two detectives.

> "Consistently entertaining ... another excellent hardboiled
> novel from the Vancouver master."
> – *Ottawa Citizen*

> "Laurence Gough is high on anyone's list of the best authors
> in ... crime writing, and if you want to know why,
> you don't have to look farther than *Killers*."
> – Margaret Cannon, *Globe and Mail*

0-7710-3439-3 • $26.99 cloth   0-7710-3441-5 • $7.99 paper

FALL DOWN EASY

A WILLOWS AND PARKER MYSTERY

Greg is a cocaine addict, professional heartbreaker, weapons freak, a master of disguise – and bank robber extraordinaire. His latest heist, however, goes terribly wrong: a vicious fight ensues and a man is killed. Greg flees with the man's briefcase only to discover that it contains not, as he had hoped, money, but mysterious computer print-outs.

Willows and Parker are handed the investigation, and discover that the dead man was a plainclothes Panamanian policeman, in British Columbia for unspecified reasons. Are drugs involved, they wonder. And what about the bank manager and his beautiful daughter? Did they have personal dealings with the Panamanian? Complicating all this is Greg, the elusive thief whose chameleon-like ability to transform face and figure leaves Willows and Parker grasping to build up any sort of profile.

NOMINATED FOR BEST CRIME NOVEL
BY THE CRIME WRITERS OF CANADA

"An excellent mystery thriller ... non-stop action
and plenty of well-hidden secrets."
– *Toronto Star*

"One of the best crime novels of the season
– in Canada and anywhere else."
– *Toronto Sun*

"Compulsively readable."
– *Quill & Quire*

0-7710-3444-X • $26.99 cloth   0-7710-3443-1 • $6.99 paper